"Penny for your thoughts."

JB's soft question startled her. Issy's gaze shot up to meet his. There was nothing but mild curiosity in his dark eyes.

"You'll be disappointed, trust me."

"Let me make up my own mind on that."

Damn it. She should have made something up. He wouldn't give up until she told him.

"It's hard to talk about. Personal stuff."

He didn't say anything for a moment. "We shared a lot of personal stuff in Antigua. Why is this any different?"

Her throat ached at his gentle tone and the understanding in his eyes. She had no choice. The time had come to tell him.

Dear Reader,

Welcome back to the world of the New Jersey Ice Cats! It's time for another dedicated and delicious hockey player to face off against a lovely but challenging woman who will turn his world upside down.

There are some characters who steal your heart the minute they appear in a series. Jean Baptiste "JB" Larocque captured mine when he skated onto the page as an arrogant rookie who caused trouble for Jake "Bad Boy" Badoletti in *A Perfect Distraction*. From what many of you have told me, and the number of requests I've received for JB's book, I'm pleased that he's one of your favorite characters, too.

I hadn't planned for JB to redeem himself or to have his own story, but he had other plans! Of course, he had to wait until he'd grown up enough to be ready for love. And for the right woman to appear in his life. For sure, he didn't expect that woman to be mousy, uptight Isabelle Brandine.

As for Issy, if anyone needed a little detour from the neatly laid-out path she'd created for her life, she did. And who better to provide that unintended detour than JB? All of which goes to show that sometimes the unplanned journey can yield the greatest pleasure and the person you least suspect is the one who makes your heart sing.

I love to hear from readers. Please contact me at anna@annasugden.com or via my website (annasugden.com). You can also find me on Facebook and Twitter.

Former marketing executive **Anna Sugden** loves reading romance novels and watching films with happy endings. She also loves watching hockey and football, where she prefers a happy ending for her teams. When she's not researching hockey players (for her books, of course), she makes craft projects and collects penguins, autographs and memorabilia, and great shoes. Anna lives in Cambridge, England, with her husband and two bossy black cats. Learn more about Anna, her books and her shoes at annasugden.com.

Books by Anna Sugden

HARLEQUIN SUPERROMANCE

A Perfect Distraction
A Perfect Trade
A Perfect Catch

Other titles by this author available in ebook format.

Dedication

For Laura and Julia, with love.

For Keith, love always xxxxx

Acknowledgments

Wanda Ottewell—who helped me become a better writer and without whom there wouldn't be an Ice Cats series.

Jill Marsal—the best agent!

My gals—Beth Andrews, Terri Garey, Kathleen Long, Janice Lynn and Tawny Weber. I couldn't do this without you.

CHAPTER ONE

THE HORN BLARED. Game over. Players vaulted over the boards. Helmets, gloves and sticks flew into the air and rained down onto the ice.

As the arena erupted, Jean-Baptiste "J.B." Larocque stood stock-still—his mind numb—unable to believe it.

The New Jersey Ice Cats had lost. Game seven of the Stanley Cup Finals. In overtime.

So damn close.

They'd put everything on the line but they'd fallen short by one goal. One lousy goal.

He'd had the puck and the game...the Cup... on his stick.

Only, he'd missed. He'd freaking *missed*.

Worse, in the shocked seconds after, Denver's defense had grabbed the puck, streaked up the ice and done what J.B. couldn't. Just like that, it was all over.

Sudden-death overtime had never lived up to its name so perfectly before.

The aches and pains J.B. had blocked for the past two months came flooding back full-force, making him stagger. Leaning on his stick, he fought to stay upright. As terrible as he felt, he wouldn't let the watching world see him crumble.

Around him, his dejected teammates leaned listlessly against the boards. His closest friends, Kenny Jelinek and Taylor "Mad Dog" Madden, sat slumped on the ice. Scotty Matthews looked ashen beneath his gray-streaked play-off beard. The captain had stayed on, hoping to win one more Cup. Instead of retiring on a high, he'd hang up his skates as second-best.

J.B.'s throat tightened. Last time the Cats had gone to the Finals, he'd been the conquering hero. That meant nothing now.

He had to get out of here.

A stick tapped his leg "Come on, bro."

Jake "Bad Boy" Badoletti nodded to where Scotty and the Cats' veteran goaltender, Ike Jelinek, were skating slowly to center ice to form the traditional handshake line. The rest of the team followed to congratulate the victorious Avalanche players.

Damn, that was the last thing J.B. felt like doing. But he had to man up and show his opponents the respect they'd earned.

"The sooner we get this done, the sooner we can get the hell out of here." Jake laid a hand on J.B.'s shoulder. "Unless you plan to stick around for the Cup presentation."

"Yeah, like I'm a glutton for punishment."

Each stroke of his skate on the pitted ice jarred his joints.

"Your goal got us to overtime."

"I should've finished the job."

"Truth is we should've put the game away in the second period. Those missed chances came back to bite us in the ass in the third."

J.B. took off his glove and shook the first hand. He continued down the line, alternating between "good job, man" and "good game." When he got to Tru Jelinek, J.B. hugged him briefly, congratulating his friend and former teammate.

"Thanks. I'm just sorry it means you guys had to lose." Empathy shone in Tru's eyes.

J.B. hitched a shoulder. "Yeah."

"I'll catch you guys before you all fly home tomorrow."

"For sure."

Never had J.B. been so relieved to get off the ice. Though he felt like crap, he tapped the hands of fans hanging over the glass by the tunnel. But he couldn't face the disappointment in their eyes, so he looked straight ahead.

The quiet in the locker room was unnerving. Guys stripped off their gear and showered without saying a word. Here and there, pockets of bright light shone as the media carried out their postgame interviews quietly. They understood how devastating this loss was to the players.

J.B. slumped onto the bench at his stall, knowing his turn would come. He took off his skates, then rested his arms on his thighs and stared at his hands, unable to stop replaying those last moments in his head. When the light shone on him, it was almost a welcome relief.

Until the dumb questions started. How did they freaking think he felt?

Fighting his growing irritation, he toed the party line. "It was a tough series. Both teams were evenly matched." Blah, blah, blah.

"Take us through that last play. What happened?"

Seriously? J.B. glared at the polished TV presenter, barely resisting the urge to shove the idiot's microphone where the sun didn't shine.

The jackass stared back at him intently, as if he'd asked the one question that would reveal something earth-shattering the public didn't know already.

"My. Shot. Went. Wide," J.B. said through gritted teeth.

"Do you feel responsible...?"

"Enough!" J.B. surged to his feet and pushed the mikes and cameras out of his face. "We lost. It sucks. If you'd ever strapped on a freaking pair of skates and played, you'd know exactly how it freaking feels and what freaking went wrong."

He stomped to the shower room, ripped off his gear and stood under the pounding water, eyes closed.

"You just blew your Mr. Charming image to hell," Kenny said beside him.

"Maybe the rest of us will finally get airtime," Mad Dog added from the other side.

J.B. opened his eyes and swore colorfully. "The jerk deserved it."

"Definitely." Mad Dog's blue eyes were shadowed from the loss. Probably also from the niggling pain in his lower back that he'd been playing through for the past few games. "Dude always asks the dumbest questions."

"That's why he got tossed from the Rangers' locker room last year." Kenny winced as he worked his jaw. A bruise was forming where he'd been caught by a high stick in the dying seconds. "Man, this blows chunks. I thought for sure the ice tilted our way when you got the equalizer."

"Yeah." J.B. leaned his head back against the tiles and let the water stream over his face. He swallowed to ease the tightness in his throat.

The three friends finished their showers in silence, each lost in his own miserable thoughts. By the time they walked back into the locker room, the media vultures had departed to cover the Cup celebrations.

While the players dressed, their equipment was packed away and loaded onto a cart for the journey home. The next time they saw their gear would be in a couple of days, when they cleared out their lockers at the Cats' arena. The final act of the season.

J.B. pulled on his suit jacket. First he had to get through tonight. Because they were playing in Denver, it was still only 9:00 p.m.

"Ten minutes before the bus leaves," one of the trainers called out. "You miss it, you walk back to the hotel."

The good-natured heckling he got was subdued.

Mad Dog hefted his duffel bag over his shoulder. "What's the plan now?"

"Tru told me about this rock club downtown that's supposed to be real sweet." Kenny ran a comb through his wet hair. "Great food and hot babes. You with me?"

"Hell, yeah. What about you, Larocque?"

Part of him wanted to hole up in his hotel room with a bottle of Jack. The other part preferred to drown his sorrows in the company of a sexy woman rather than his long-time roommate, Rick "Ice Man" Kasanski.

"Count me in."

A few hours later he wondered if he'd made a mistake. His head throbbed from the loud music, his stomach roiled from the fiery nachos and tequila shots, and his entire body felt like it had gone the distance with a heavyweight boxer.

Kenny and Mad Dog were busy with a couple of hockey groupies in town for the game. Hailey, the blonde J.B. had been chatting with, wanted to dance, but he knew if he stepped into that mass of sweaty, gyrating bodies, he'd either pass out or puke. Or both. Kasanski was looking better by the minute.

"Sorry, Hailey. Another time. I'm beat. I'm gonna cut out of here."

"Stay a *little* longer. Please." She trailed a finger down his chest.

"I can't. I'm dead on my feet." He smiled wearily. "But I'll take a rain check. Next time I'm in Denver with a free night, I'll look you up."

J.B. turned to let his friends know he was bugging out.

That was his first mistake. His second was underestimating how unsteady his legs were.

Hailey tugged his arm. As J.B. pulled himself free, he felt his feet slide out from under him and went down hard, smacking the back of his head on the floor.

Unfortunately, as he fell, J.B. caught Hailey with his arm and knocked her backward.

All hell broke loose.

"Oh, my God. That jerk hit Hailey," a woman yelled.

"You drunk ass," shouted another.

J.B. tried to check if Hailey was all right but couldn't see her through the gathering crowd. "I didn't mean to hit her," he tried to explain but no one was listening.

A male voice joined the rising wave of female

outrage. "We'll show you how we treat bullies in this town."

"Bastard," someone else swore.

J.B. felt the kick but didn't see it coming. Curling his body to protect himself brought on a wave of nausea. He should get up, get out of there, but he was so woozy he could hardly move.

After that, everything was hazy. J.B. was vaguely aware of Kenny and Mad Dog pulling people off him, dragging him to his feet and out of the club, and shoving him into a cab. They managed to get him back to his room before the nachos and tequila made a violent reappearance in the bathroom.

At some point they must have put him to bed because, when he awoke the following morning, he was facedown on the bed, still fully clothed. His mouth tasted like he'd spent the night licking his hockey gloves.

"Coffee, ibuprofen, juice and dry toast," Kenny said.

J.B. groaned and gingerly rolled over.

"Do you want the good news or the bad?" Mad Dog's quiet words triggered memories of what had happened the night before.

J.B. swallowed the pills, then drained the juice before answering. "I'm in a crapload of trouble. History has pretty much repeated itself, only this time no one can bail me out."

Back in his rookie season J.B. had got into a

predicament in a nightclub that could have ended his career before it got going. Not only had his teammates rescued him, but Bad Boy had taken the blame in the media. It had been a rude wake-up call and J.B. had steered clear of situations that could go belly-up ever since.

Until last night.

"Yeah. And the story is all over social media," Kenny added helpfully.

Damn it! "Coach Macarty will love that. Not."

"He's taking it better than expected, but he doesn't want to see your face until this has died down."

"How am I supposed to avoid him? We're taking the same plane back to Jersey."

Mad Dog looked uncomfortable. "He's arranged for you to fly home separately so you can keep a low profile. I volunteered to go with you."

"Thanks, man."

"Coach is also delaying your end-of-season interview for a week," Kenny said. "He reckons he'll have cooled down by then."

Not only did J.B. feel like crap he also had the indignity of having to sneak out of Denver like a crook on the lam. Plus, he'd blown his reputation to hell—once again. "And the good news is?"

"Instead of going home," Mad Dog said. "I thought it'd be better to get out of the country altogether and hang out for a few days someplace where they don't follow hockey."

"Where's that? The Sahara Desert?"

"Funny." His friend slapped a piece of paper on the bedside cabinet. "Antigua. The Golden Sands Resort. All inclusive. Adults only. A two-bedroom, beachfront bungalow."

J.B. frowned. "Isn't that the place we're heading to in a couple of weeks for our vacation?"

"Ding, ding! Give the man a prize. I got hold of Tracy at Making Your Move and asked her to pull our reservation forward to tomorrow. Not today, because I don't want you spewing in my lap at thirty thousand feet. We fly at noon."

"But I'm supposed to go to my parents' place."

"You can head to the farm after you've got back from the Caribbean."

"We haven't got the right clothes with us."

"Jeez, chill. You can buy what you need when you get there."

"Okay. Great." Maybe he'd feel half-human by then.

Kenny shook his head. "A vacation on a tropical island. Even when you screw up, you land on your feet. Think of me. While you're sipping frothy drinks with umbrellas, I'll be working with hordes of kids at Ike's summer hockey camp."

"Them's the breaks." Mad Dog grinned.

Kenny flipped him the bird. "Just make sure Larocque stays out of trouble."

"It was a freaking accident," J.B. protested, massaging his aching temples.

"We know. But bad stuff always seems to happen to you, even if you don't go looking for it."

"I promise to be on my best behavior. I'm not interested in anything but chilling and deciding which 'frothy drink' to have next."

Besides, how much trouble could anyone get into at a fancy Caribbean resort?

"I CAN'T WEAR THIS." Isabelle Brandine held up the tiny but admittedly cute red polka-dot bikini she'd just pulled out of her suitcase. "It's so...small."

"It'll look great on you." Her best friend, Sapphire Houlihan, who was lounging on the other bed in their resort room, waved her hand. "It'll show off your fabulous figure."

"That's not what I'm worried about it showing, Sapphie." Issy dropped the bikini on the bed and continued unpacking.

"Tough, because your frumpy one-piece is in the trash back in New Jersey."

Issy stopped for a moment. "You threw away my swimsuit?"

Sapphie sipped the Antiguan rum punch they'd been given at check-in. "You've had it since college. Consider it a gift for coming on the trip with me."

Though she knew it wouldn't change anything, Issy made a token protest. "You already paid for my ticket and this gorgeous beachfront room. Besides, this is meant to be *your* thirtieth celebration. You should be getting presents, not me."

"This *is* for me." Sapphie shot her a wicked grin. "No hot guys would come near us if they saw you in that ancient thing. Now we'll be fighting them off."

"I'm not interested in a holiday fling."

"Why not? A few days of sun, sand, sea and no-strings sex, and you'll feel like a new woman." Her friend sighed happily. "I certainly will."

"You know that's not me." That sounded as frumpy as her trashed swimsuit. "I can have fun without having sex with a stranger."

"Of course you can."

Having grown up together, in the same small town, on the same wrong side of the tracks—not that there was a right side—they had no secrets. They'd been friends almost since birth; their heavy-drinking, heavy-partying parents were cousins. The two girls were even conceived at the same Labor Day blowout, though their birthdays were ten days apart.

Issy and Sapphie had spent their childhood being the responsible ones, looking after their younger siblings and trying desperately to make ends meet when their parents wouldn't or couldn't. When the two girls had left their small Southern town together at eighteen, they'd promised each other they'd never be like their parents.

Issy was determined to build the traditional

family life she'd always dreamed of. She had a
steady job at an exclusive private school for girls,
which meant she didn't have to worry about where
her next meal would come from or how to pay her
bills. She'd managed to save enough that she'd celebrated her own thirtieth birthday by buying herself a small apartment in a nice suburban town.
A solid roof over her head was worth all the extra
hours she'd worked to achieve tenure.

Someday she hoped to find a good, honest,
hardworking man. Together they'd raise their children in the kind of happy and stable environment
she'd been denied growing up.

Sapphie, on the other hand, was committed to
her work and the highly successful corporate consulting firm she'd built, and rejected permanency
of any kind in her personal life. Home for her
was a serviced apartment on each coast, as well
as one in Chicago. She had a similarly casual approach to men.

"Sex isn't *required.*" Sapphie shrugged. "I want
you to enjoy yourself while we're here."

"Then I'll take the sun, sand and sea, and leave
the rest to you."

Her friend made a face. "I got you the bikini's
matching sarong wrap."

"Thank you." Issy pulled a couple of short but
equally unfamiliar sundresses out of her case.
"Did you toss out all the outfits I packed?"

"Nope. The rest of your clothes are back at

my apartment. Though you may not want them after this." Sapphie finished her drink and swung her legs off the bed. "Are you going to waste the whole afternoon unpacking? I want to hit the beach and get this holiday started."

To heck with it—the world probably wouldn't come to an end if Issy didn't get everything put away right now. "Give me five minutes to change."

A short while later the two friends headed down to the beach. As they strolled along the path, Issy hitched the red polka-dot sarong firmly around her chest. Though the bikini wasn't as revealing as she'd thought, and it did flatter her figure, she was glad for the cover.

It didn't take long to slip into the laid-back, Antiguan tempo. The rhythmic tinkling of the resort's steel band by the pool bar seeped into her blood and gave her hips a subtle swing. The warm sea breeze, fragrant with lush tropical flowers, caressed her skin. The water was so clear and blue it looked fake. If she hadn't been here, her toes sinking into the soft white sand, she'd never have believed it was real.

They managed to find two beach loungers in the shade of some tall palm trees. Sapphie had put their cooler under the table, shimmied out of her flowery beach shorts and settled onto her chair before Issy had straightened her towel.

"Stop dithering, Issy."

She inhaled deeply then undid the wrap and

draped it over the back of the lounger. When no one fainted at the sight of her scantily-clad, too-curvy body, she applied sunscreen and lay on the towel. But she found it hard to relax.

"You're as stiff as a board." Sapphie sighed. "Don't worry—the chances of anyone from Farlingdale Academy being on this beach are slim to none."

"I'm not worried." Though the school had a strict morality clause, she doubted it applied to a tiny swimsuit. "It feels odd to be doing nothing."

"So read your book." Sapphie whistled softly under her breath. "Don't look now, but a couple of prime examples of manhood are walking this way."

Issy glanced up and caught her breath.

"Dibs on the one on the right and please don't let him be gay."

Both men were tall with finely honed bodies. Walking barefoot through the lapping water at the sea's edge, they wore mirrored shades, ball caps with a logo that featured a snow leopard's head and long, brightly colored swim shorts. Sapphie's choice was dark-haired and good-looking with a nice smile. Totally her friend's type.

But it was the somber man walking beside him who caught Issy's attention. So handsome, he was almost beautiful. His straight nose, high cheekbones and angular jaw were so perfectly formed they could have been carved by a sculptor, and his lips were full, without being feminine.

How would they feel pressed against hers?

Shocked by her thoughts, she lowered her gaze. But only as far as his shoulders and broad chest. Her fingers tingled with the urge to stroke the man's caramel-brown skin to see if it was as smooth as it looked. To trail over the ridges of that amazing six-pack.

He was clearly an athlete. Hardly the kind of dependable, responsible man she wanted in her future.

Issy snapped up her book and forced herself to focus on the text. She hoped Sapphie would put her heightened color down to the tropical temperatures and not...him.

Still, she couldn't resist sneaking another peek as he came closer. Grateful that her sunglasses hid the direction of her gaze, her heart kicked when his head turned toward her. A bead of perspiration trickled down between her breasts.

Oh, my! Issy couldn't help licking her dry lips.

When he turned away, she was unreasonably piqued at his easy dismissal. *Don't be silly*, she scolded herself. That man was so far out of her league, she'd need a space rocket to even get close.

Beside her, Sapphie smiled and wiggled her fingers at the men. Issy tried not to grind her teeth when the one on the right grinned and waved back.

"Doesn't act like he's gay," Sapphie said. "Hopefully we'll see them at the beach party this evening."

Issy gave a noncommittal reply. She pretended to be engrossed in her story, not watching the toned butt and great legs of a man who was clearly not interested in her.

"You know, there's something familiar about those two," Sapphie mused. "I swear I've seen them somewhere before."

"On TV?"

"I'm not sure. It'll bug me until I know."

Sapphie drove Issy crazy for the rest of the afternoon as she tried to figure out who the men were. It wasn't until they were dressing for the beach party that Sapphie snapped her fingers. "Of course. The ball-cap logo. I can't believe I didn't make the connection. It's not like I'm not a huge fan."

Issy cursed the slight tremble in her hand as she applied her lipstick. The man's identity made no difference to her. "Who are they?"

"Ice Cats." At Issy's blank look Sapphie added, "Hockey players. From our very own Jersey team. They were just in the Stanley Cup Finals. Unfortunately they lost."

"Oh." Not only in a different stratosphere from

a private-school English teacher, but her suspicions had been correct—an arrogant sports star.

Professional athletes with their irresponsible attitude to life and money reminded Issy of her family.

Back in college she'd struggled to maintain her grades as she'd worked two jobs. Meanwhile the jocks with their scholarships had partied and barely attended classes. Later, when she'd taught in a public school, she'd had to fight for every resource while money was frittered away on the athletics program.

"My guy's Taylor Madden," Sapphie said. "Yours is Jean-Baptiste Larocque."

Even his name was beautiful. "I told you, I'm not interested."

"Uh-huh." Sapphie looked over Issy's shoulder into the mirror. "And you weren't checking out his amazing body earlier?"

Issy blotted her lips then turned away—to get her clutch, not to avoid her friend. "I can appreciate good looks without having to sleep with the guy."

"Sure, but what a waste."

"I'm capable of entertaining myself. Let me know when you want to disappear with Taylor and I'll go back to the room." She held up her key card. "Make sure you have your own key, so you can let yourself back in."

"I won't abandon you." Sapphie frowned. "What kind of friend does that?"

"One who's getting the birthday present she really wants." Issy smiled. "It's fine. I'll be happy sitting on the balcony and reading. Things are heating up in my romantic thriller."

"They'd heat up in real life, too, if you'd give them a chance," Sapphie grumbled as they headed out the door.

"I'm content with the way things are."

"Boringly predictable."

"I've had enough excitement and unpredictability to last me a lifetime."

"A little spontaneity won't turn you into your parents or Rosa."

"I know."

Despite Issy's best efforts, her younger sister had followed in the family tradition and partied heavily, then ended up pregnant. The father, one of the town's football stars, had chosen a college scholarship over marriage, so Issy had taken care of both Rosabelle and her daughter, Tinkabelle, until she'd left home.

Once she'd graduated and had a job, Issy had offered to move them up near her, but Rosa had preferred to remain with their parents. She knew her sister hadn't chosen sides, as much as the easier path, but it had still hurt. And reinforced how different she and Rosa were.

The physical Brandine genes had missed her

completely—they were all tall and slim, auburn and green-eyed, while she was short, curvy and dark-haired with blue eyes—why not the other genes, too? "I promise to have fun while we're here. All right?"

"Okay." Sapphie linked arms with her. "So how's your limbo dancing? I hear there's a contest with big prizes at the party, including a gorgeous emerald necklace."

"What am I letting myself in for?" Issy shook her head and laughed, then let her friend lead her down the beach.

CHAPTER TWO

"You owe me, man, and I'm collecting."

J.B. responded by clapping Taylor on the shoulder as they walked toward the flaming torches stuck in the sand. "Want tips on how to chat up that hot blonde you were drooling over earlier?"

"Funny." Mad Dog punched him in the arm. "Good thing you make your living handling a puck, not doing stand-up."

J.B.'s grin faded. "Yeah, well my puck skills aren't so hot, either. We wouldn't be here now if they were. We'd be riding around town in an open-topped, double-decker bus, showing off Stanley."

"We agreed you wouldn't beat yourself up over that while we're on vacation."

"Sure."

Plenty of time for reflection and self-recrimination once he was alone. He owed Mad Dog, and repayment meant ensuring his friend had a great trip. Especially given Taylor was just as cut up about the loss, even if he tried not to show it.

He cracked his knuckles. "What do you need from the master?"

"Use your charm on the hot blonde's mousy friend. Keep her occupied so she won't mind when her roommate disappears with me."

Ordinarily, J.B. wouldn't have minded the request. Women were the perfect antitdote to a life filled with way too much testosterone. And the brunette in the red bikini wasn't exactly mousy, though her dark hair had been scraped back into a severe braid. She was pretty in a girl-next-door way and her curves were definitely in all the right places.

What had given him pause was the stiff way she'd held herself, her full lips pinched, while supposedly relaxing. "She seemed a little uptight."

He'd learned the hard way to steer clear of uptight women. They were impossible to please. They took things way too seriously and saw hidden meanings in innocent words or actions, which led to unfortunate misunderstandings. Like the woman in the Atlanta nightclub who'd nearly derailed his NHL career. Frustrated he wouldn't take advantage of her blatant offers—J.B. didn't mess with married women—she'd turned the tables and accused him of coming on to her. It was only thanks to Taylor, Jake and his other teammates that J.B. had come through the crazy situation relatively unscathed.

Still he'd chalked that up to experience. It had

taken a female stalker, then a woman who'd lied about him fathering her child, for J.B. to decide uptight women were trouble.

Taylor winced, understanding in his gray eyes. "Maybe she was jealous that I waved at her friend. Women fight over me all the time."

J.B. snorted with laughter. "In your dreams, bro."

"Who got the highest bid in the Ice Cats' charity bachelor auction?"

"Yeah, yeah. Shame the winning bidder was your mother's age."

"Gilda was a sexy, mature lady with a great body, a lot of experience and an insatiable appetite."

"Glad to hear she got her money's worth."

Mad Dog swore. "Will you help me out or not? We're only here for a few days and you'll never see her again."

J.B. hesitated as they reached the torches. The women were standing by one of the tables closest to the shoreline. Taylor's blonde looked stunning in an ice-blue sheath that dipped low and clung to her body before ending mid-thigh. But it was her friend that fired J.B.'s blood. She wore a strappy knee-length red dress. Her dark hair was loose, the slight curl at the ends dancing over her bare shoulders as she laughed.

"She's not looking mousy or uptight now," Mad Dog said. "Pay your dues, man."

J.B.'s reluctance vanished. He strode forward. "You got it."

When they reached the table Mad Dog asked, "May we join you, ladies?"

"Sure," the blonde replied enthusiastically.

J.B. noticed her friend didn't say anything but smiled. He figured she was the shy type.

"I'm J.B. and this is Taylor." He offered his hand to the brunette, who hesitated before taking it.

The blonde shook hands with Taylor. "I'm an Ice Cats fan. Season ticket holder, though work keeps me from getting to as many games as I'd like. I'm Sapphire, Sapphie for short, and this is…"

"Bella," the brunette said firmly.

"Good to meet you, Bella."

Mad Dog clapped a hand to his chest dramatically. "A beautiful woman who likes hockey, I'm in heaven!"

J.B. shook his head and looked at Bella, who rolled her blue eyes. The moment of shared humour was surprising and encouraging.

"You look like you're in need of frothy drinks with umbrellas," Taylor said.

Sapphie wrinkled her nose. "They're too sweet for me. But I wouldn't say no to a champagne refill."

Bella held up her glass. "Ginger ale would be lovely. Thank you."

"Your wish is my command," Taylor said.

"I'll come with you and help carry the glasses." Sapphie stuck her hand through his arm. "I'll try not to go all fangirl on you."

"I can handle whatever you throw at me."

The pair walked off toward the bar, laughing.

"There's nothing fragile about your friend's ego," Bella said drily.

"He's all talk. Under that boyish charm is a good guy."

"Sapphie can handle herself. And him, too."

Those uptight vibes were back. Perhaps Mad Dog was right about the jealousy thing.

J.B. stifled a sigh. It was going to be a long night.

Bella turned to him. "While they're gone, I wanted to say that we know how the evening will end for them and you mustn't feel obliged to stick with me."

Her earnest comment caught him off guard. "We've just met and you're already preparing to ditch me?"

She bit her full lower lip. "I'm sure you have things you'd rather do than entertain the spare-part best friend and I won't be upset if you do them."

He should be relieved; she'd given him the perfect out. Yet, inexplicably, he was slightly irritated that she was so keen to be rid of him. He smiled.

"Let's see how things play out. The night's still young and there's plenty of party left."

"All right." This time she gave him the puzzled look.

Good. He liked that he could throw her a little off balance. "How about we scout out the buffet table while we wait for our friends to return?"

"We might lose our places."

He leaned past her, flipped out four napkins and turned over four water glasses. "Now it's obvious someone's sitting here."

She glanced over her shoulder at Mad Dog and Sapphie, who were engrossed in each other, at the bar. "You're right. It looks like it might be a while before we get our drinks."

He cocked an elbow in invitation and she put her arm through his. His senses immediately snapped to attention at the touch of her soft skin. As they walked to the heavily laden buffet table, her fragrance—delicate, floral, but with an unexpected hint of spice—teased his nose. The contradiction intrigued him.

Hell, Bella was full of contradictions and they all intrigued him. She was as prickly as a porcupine, yet when she let her guard down, there were hints of a dry sense of humor. At times she seemed both innocent and uncertain; at others forthright and honest. Definitely able to give as good as she got, she stood up for herself but had an air of vulnerability that made him feel strangely protective.

As they filled their plates, she ribbed him that he was stockpiling enough food to feed a small army. He couldn't help noticing that she carefully arranged her food so none of the portions touched. When he teased her about only taking one spoonful of the dishes she wanted, she replied coolly that it was polite to leave some for others to enjoy. Yet she gave him a conspiratorial grin when she sneaked an extra helping of potato salad.

Back at the table J.B. was pleasantly surprised that she didn't pick at her food like a lot of the women he dated. But she was as prim and proper as if the Queen of England were seated beside her.

He mischievously speared a coconut-battered shrimp from her plate.

"Hey!" She jabbed him with her elbow. "You've got two mountainous plates. Leave mine alone."

"But I didn't get one of these." He bit the end. "Mmm. Delicious."

Bella surveyed his dinner. "Well, I didn't get one of these chocolate-dipped maraschino cherries, so turnabout is fair play."

J.B. plucked a cherry from his plate and held it to her lips.

Her gaze snapped up to meet his, indecision swirling in the blue depths. Then the tiniest spark of heat flickered. Her lips curved into a sultry half smile as, without releasing his gaze, she bit slowly, delicately, into the cherry.

Fire shot through him, tightening his groin. What the hell?

"Mmm. Delicious," she said huskily.

J.B. popped the rest of the cherry into his mouth. "Not bad."

"Looks like you guys started without us." Sapphie laughed as she and Taylor appeared behind them, holding glasses.

Bella blinked. "We were wondering when you'd be back with our drinks."

The edge was back in her voice, dousing the heat in J.B. as effectively as if she'd tipped her icy drink in his lap. He studied her, considering. He'd seen several sides to Bella this evening and he wasn't sure which was the real one.

Would it be foolhardy to take the risk of finding out?

"It's TIME TO lower the bar!"

As the DJ played "Get Down On It" and the crowd chanted and clapped, Issy wondered how she got into these situations. She stood on the sandy dance floor, beside the other three finalists of the limbo competition.

Unlike her fellow contestants, who were lapping up the spotlight, she felt awkward. Other than when she was with her class, Issy preferred to be in the background. So why was she out here, center stage?

Because of Sapphie.

Ever since her childhood friend had teased, cajoled, pushed and dared Issy beyond her comfort zone. Although Issy was older by ten days, Sapphie had been the first to walk, talk and get into trouble. She'd also been the first to learn how to work the washer at the Laundromat. And how to sneak money from her mother's purse so she could buy groceries.

Sapphie had also been the one to encourage Issy to follow her dreams. She'd bluntly pointed out that if Issy didn't leave the town and her family behind, she'd spend the rest of her life taking care of them instead of having a family of her own.

Plain and simple, Issy wouldn't be where she was today, so close to achieving everything she'd always wanted, without Sapphie.

So, although Issy didn't want the emerald necklace, her friend clearly did, and Issy would try her damnedest to get it for her. Which meant winning the limbo contest Sapphie and the two hockey players had already crashed out of.

"As this is the final, we're taking the bar down *two* notches," the emcee announced.

"How low can you go?" the crowd chanted.

Part of her wanted to fail so she could return to the relative anonymity of the sidelines. But another part refused to surrender without trying. She hated to just give up.

"First up is the lovely Bella. Step forward and *lim-bo*."

Issy walked over to the bar, which looked ridiculously low, and waited for the musical cue. The audience whooped and hollered.

"Go, Bella!" Sapphie's voice mingled with Taylor's deeper tones.

"You can do it," J.B. encouraged. "Take your time and relax."

How was she supposed to relax with him standing in front of her, his dark eyes watching every sway and shimmy? Making her feel sexy and a little naughty? Making her imagine a different, more private, dance with him?

Hot, hot, hot, blared the speakers.

Issy dropped her shoulders, arched her back and bent her knees. Slowly she inched forward.

When her chest brushed the wooden pole, she thought she'd blown it. Although the bar rattled on the stand, it stayed up. Even so, she didn't move again until she was sure. Then she held her breath as she carefully made it through.

Giddy with success, she straightened to boisterous cheers. Sapphie ran over, squealed and hugged her tight, then pulled Issy off to the side. J.B. lifted her in the air and spun her around.

As he stopped and began to lower her slowly, their gazes met. Suddenly she was intensely aware of the hardness of his body as hers slid down the length of him. Of the crisp scent of his aftershave mingled with the heady fragrance of clean male skin. His arms around her seared her through the thin cotton of her dress.

Plastered against him—breast to chest, thigh to thigh—she felt every plane and dip of his taut muscles. Her cheeks flamed as his arousal pressed against the cradle at the top of her legs.

She should move…break his hold…step back… something.

The message in his dark eyes—he didn't want to let her go—thrilled her.

She was venturing into dangerous, uncharted waters. For the first time in her life Issy wanted to dive straight in.

Excitement warred with her reason. As wonderful as that would probably—definitely—be, it would also be a mistake. There were bound to be consequences.

J.B. was like no one she'd ever met before. Her reaction to him was like nothing she'd ever experienced before.

And, he clearly wanted her, too.

Loud groans from the gathered crowd and the clatter of the limbo bar interrupted her thoughts, breaking the moment.

J.B. eased her away from him but anchored her to his side with his arm around her shoulder. His reluctance to let her go thrilled her. A few more minutes couldn't hurt. Besides, Sapphie and Taylor couldn't keep their hands off each other; they'd disappear once the contest was over. Then J.B. wouldn't have a reason to hang out with her anymore.

That was for the best. Really. In the meantime she'd enjoy the pleasure of the moment and the undivided attention of a gorgeous man.

More groans signaled the third contestant had failed. One more to go. If the last man succeeded, it would delay the end of the contest and extend her time with J.B. On the other hand, she'd have to step back out into the spotlight and do more limbo. A devil's choice.

Raucous cheers told her which path had been chosen for her.

"Down, down," the crowd chanted as the DJ made a show of lowering the bar another notch.

"You can take that guy. No problem," J.B. murmured in her ear.

The feather touch of his breath against the sensitive skin of her neck made her shiver deliciously.

As she gently disengaged herself, he pulled her back, then tilted her face up to his. "A kiss for luck."

Her knees went weak. Who knew that could really happen?

Good grief—it was the slightest brush of his firm, warm lips against hers. What would happen if he kissed her properly?

Issy managed what she hoped was a casual smile before heading over to stand beside the remaining contender.

"Bella and Kent, are you ready for 'winner takes all'?" the DJ roared.

Hell, no.

"Ladies first," Kent said with an exaggerated bow and a cocky grin.

"Age before beauty," she retorted to the delight of the crowd.

Where had that come from? She never made that kind of snappy comeback.

Clearly it had shocked Kent, too, because his gaze narrowed, assessing. He waved his arms to pump up the audience then strutted over to the limbo bar. The music started. With a flourish, Kent bent his knees and leaned back.

He almost made it. But his arrogance did him in at the last second. He raised his head to gloat before he was fully clear of the bar and knocked it to the ground. He acknowledged her victory with a rueful smile and another bow.

J.B.'s laughter made her grin. But she blushed when she read the dark, delicious and definitely dangerous promise in his eyes. Now she *had* to win.

It didn't help that Sapphie was in her line of sight, standing with Taylor behind her, his arms around her waist. Envy twinged.

"Go, Bella!" the crowd chanted.

Issy swallowed her nerves and positioned herself behind the bar.

Hot, hot, hot. Clearly her theme song tonight.

Whether it was the incentive or practice, this time she cleared the bar without trouble.

The crowd went wild, congratulating her and patting her on the back. Even Kent gave her a grudging "well done." Sapphie couldn't stop jumping up and down and hugging her.

Issy's heart thudded heavily as she waited for J.B. to make his way through the mass of people. What would he do?

She didn't get a chance to find out as the emcee called her over. Swallowing her disappointment, she joined the DJ on the stone promenade and accepted the necklace gratefully, thanking him and the resort.

Back on the sand she presented it to Sapphie. "Happy birthday."

"You're kidding?" Her friend's eyes welled with tears. "You've earned this."

"So have you, my dearest friend." Issy hugged her, then helped her put it on.

Taylor and J.B. dutifully admired the necklace, as around them the party kicked up another gear. The DJ raised the volume of the music and people started dancing.

J.B. gave her a one-armed hug. "Great job. You made it look easy."

Not exactly the celebration she'd been anticipating. What had happened to the promise she'd seen in his eyes? "Thanks. It was fun."

Behind her she heard Taylor say softly to Sapphie, "I can't wait to see you model this Marilyn-Monroe-style, only without the radio."

"I don't get it," Sapphie replied then laughed huskily. "But let's find somewhere private, so I can channel my inner Marilyn." She raised her voice. "Issy, I'll see you later. Okay?"

Suddenly, being alone and reading didn't appeal quite so much.

Damn it. Why couldn't she be as casual about a holiday fling as Sapphie?

Issy smiled brightly at her friend. "Have fun."

As the pair walked arm-in-arm down the beach, Issy turned back to J.B., who was watching her, his expression thoughtful. Issy wished she had more experience with men so she'd know how to read him. And know what to do next.

She blurted out the first thing that came to mind. "Let's get some champagne."

"I thought you didn't drink."

She wasn't a teetotaler, but her family's weakness had made her cautious. "I only drink on special occasions and I think this qualifies, don't you?"

"Okay. Let's get you some bubbly."

His ready acceptance lifted her spirits. They soared when he rested his hand in the small of her back as they walked to the bar.

Once he ordered their drinks he said, "Giving Sapphie the necklace was nice."

"She liked it more than I did." Issy shrugged.

"Still, that's a generous gift."

"An expensive necklace is nothing compared to what she's done for me."

"Sounds like a fascinating story." He handed her a champagne flute.

Issy didn't want to spoil the evening by talking about her past. She wanted to enjoy the moment. And, if she could pluck up the nerve, live a little dangerously.

She sipped her drink. The bubbles went straight into her blood, giving her the courage she wanted. "Another time, maybe. Right now, I want to dance."

"Then let's dance." He linked fingers with her as they walked through the palm trees toward the makeshift dance floor.

When they put their glasses on their table, J.B. said, "I hope I don't embarrass you. My moves won't match up to yours."

Issy laughed. "I'm afraid you've already seen the best of my moves." She lowered her voice conspiratorially. "Sapphie and I used to limbo when we were kids. Except it was usually under a barbed-wire fence and the prize was apples from the farmer's orchard."

He grinned. "I bet Kent wouldn't be happy to hear he was beaten by a ringer."

She leaned forward and pressed her finger against his lips. "Shh. It's a secret."

"Your secret's safe with me." He kissed her finger.

Just as before, her knees went weak.

Maybe it was those bubbles, but Issy'd had enough of being teased. Of fleeting little kisses that left her wanting more. Much more. Time for payback.

She traced his mouth with the tip of her finger, lingering over his full lower lip.

The fire she'd seen earlier in the depths of his dark eyes sprang back to life. He caught her finger between his teeth and licked the tip.

Need pulsed through her. Before she could second-guess herself, Issy stood on tiptoe and replaced her finger with her lips.

CHAPTER THREE

J.B. WAS IN trouble again.

That internal warning—the feeling in his gut when he was about to be blown out by an opposition D-man—was flashing. Still, he refused to back out of this woman's kiss.

He'd only known Bella for a couple hours and she'd already managed to keep him off balance with those damn frustrating, damn intriguing contradictions. She definitely had an uptight streak, but instead of putting him off, it enticed him to dig deeper. To see if he could loosen her up.

Even her kiss was a contradiction. He sensed her inexperience, yet the way her tongue teased his lower lip was anything but innocent. She tasted of champagne and chocolate-dipped cherries with a hint of Caribbean spice. Sweet yet intoxicating. Slightly wicked.

J.B. took her up on the invitation she so blatantly offered and deepened the kiss. When his tongue touched hers, she sighed softly. He could feel her smiling. That made him smile, too.

A bump against his shoulder brought him back to reality.

"Oops. Sorry. Carry on." A tipsy blonde waved a hand with hot-pink nails.

Bella stiffened in his arms and blushed as if suddenly realizing what they were doing.

"Perhaps we should take this somewhere a little more private," he suggested.

"Oh." She bit her lip.

Sensing she might bolt, J.B. gave her an easy out. "Or we could dance, like we planned."

Bella brightened and reached for her champagne. "Dancing sounds good."

J.B. grabbed his drink, drained the glass, then took hers and put both flutes on the table. "Sounds like they're playing our song."

She tilted her head, arching an eyebrow. "'Thriller' is our song?"

"For sure." He lifted his hands, fingers curled into claws, and waggled his eyebrows like an old movie villain.

Bella fluttered her hand against her chest. "Hey-yelp. I'm so scay-urred."

Her damsel-in-distress voice made him grin. "Come with me, my pretty, and I'll make sure you're safe."

As the DJ called out instructions, J.B. and Bella joined in and laughed their way through the zombie steps.

After "Thriller" came the "Macarena." J.B. rolled his eyes and tried to head back to the table. But when Bella started dancing in front of him—

suggestively swaying those hips, invitation in her eyes—once again, he couldn't resist.

"How come you know all the right moves?" he teased.

"One of the benefits of teaching preteen girls who like to work on dance routines during recess," she replied primly.

"Is it appropriate for me to be grateful to those girls?"

"Why not?" She grinned. "I am."

When the DJ played the next song, a group of older people whooped, then sat on the sand in a long chain. They started swaying from side to side, patting the sand in time to the music. Then they shimmied their shoulders forward and back. Soon a second line had formed.

"You can all do this one," the DJ called out. "It's a bit of 'Oops Upside Your Head.'"

J.B. and Bella looked at each other, confused by the strange dance.

"Come on, it looks like fun." She grabbed his hand and dragged him over to join the end of a line. She dropped to the sand, pulling him down with her. "Scootch up behind me."

Maybe this weird dance wasn't so bad, after all, he thought as she nestled between his legs. They knocked heads when he leaned forward while the rest of the line leaned back. She looked over her shoulder at him and they laughed together.

It didn't take long to realize that as pleasurable

as it was to have the curve of Bella's butt pressed against him, his body saw it as foreplay. The song was barely half-over and he was rock hard. There was no way Bella couldn't have noticed; when she shimmied backward she was practically lying in his lap.

Think cold. Ice. A big sheet of clean ice.

Another freaking shimmy. *Think colder.* Freezing his ass off doing chores on a winter morning on his parent's farm up in Canada.

That did the trick. His brothers might love being tied to the farm and that spit of a small town, but the mere thought chilled J.B. to the bone.

Bella jumped up the moment the song ended and headed back to their table. Her champagne had gone warm and flat, but J.B. snagged rum punches from a passing waiter.

"That's delicious," she said. "Very refreshing."

"Yeah, but don't have too many or you'll be dancing on the tables. The rum packs a punch, if you're not used to it."

Bella put down the glass with such force that the drink splashed onto her hand. She rubbed it off with a napkin as if it was acid, an accusation in her eyes.

Surely she didn't think he was trying to get her drunk?

"I don't think one glass will do you any harm," he said lightly.

Uptight Bella was back. "I should probably go back to the room, anyway. It's getting late."

J.B. debated trying to convince her that it was still early, but figured he'd cut his losses. "I'll walk you."

"There's no need. It's safe here."

"I know."

A hint of a smile curved her lips. "Honestly, you don't have to hang out with me any longer. Your duty's done."

"Maybe I'd like to." He took off his loafers. "Let's walk along the beach."

Bella nodded. Instead of reaching for his hand as she had earlier, she removed her sandals and held them by the heel straps. She started off at a decent clip, heading toward the accommodation block on the far side of the property. But, even barefoot, it was hard to walk fast along the soft, shifting sand, so she soon slowed. Beside her, J.B. matched her pace.

Though lamps cast a golden glow along the promenade, down by the water's edge their way was lit by the large, almost-full moon. The clear sky was filled with a mass of stars, the constellations showing up in brilliant relief.

The sounds of the party faded as they strolled farther along the beach. The silence between them wasn't tense, but it wasn't comfortable, either. J.B. wondered what he'd done to piss her off. Only one way to find out.

"Whatever I said to upset you, I apologize. It wasn't intentional. For sure, I don't want to ruin a great evening."

She didn't say anything for several moments before she sighed. "It wasn't your fault. I'm a little sensitive about people getting drunk."

He tried not to wince. "A bad experience?"

"You could say." Her short laugh had a raw edge to it. "My family has an unfortunate tendency to drink too much. As a result, I only have alcohol on rare occasions and then nothing strong."

J.B. sensed a wealth of pain behind that bald explanation. "Your parents are alcoholics?"

"My whole family drinks heavily. Though, to be fair, so does a lot of the community in the small town I come from in North Carolina," she clarified. "There aren't many jobs and even they pay poorly. But alcohol is cheap and helps everyone make it from week to week."

That explained a lot.

J.B.'s parents had never disappeared into a bottle, but plenty of their neighbors had. Then again, his parents had two sons who'd devoted their lives to keeping the farm afloat.

He pushed aside the familiar guilt twisting his gut because he'd hated that life and got out as soon as he could. It didn't matter that his earnings now enabled his family to have a financial cushion. He'd always be the black sheep.

J.B. cleared his suddenly tight throat. "The

farming community where I grew up has similar problems. A bad crop or a problem with the animals and life gets real tough."

Bella stopped and looked at him in surprise.

He hitched a shoulder. "You thought I grew up with a silver spoon in my mouth? Everyone was responsible for doing their part on the farm. And as a player, I've worked damn hard to earn every penny I have."

She gave him a chagrined smile. "I never really thought about where you came from or how you got to be where you are."

He tapped her chin with his finger. "See, you shouldn't judge a book by its cover."

"Really? And you don't live up to the image you present?"

This time, he did grimace. "Busted. I've made more than my share of mistakes because I drank too much. But that doesn't change the fact that I understand how difficult it is growing up with poverty on your doorstep."

"In our house, poverty was in the front room, making itself comfortable on the couch." Bella shook her head. "I'm sorry. This is hardly the topic for a Caribbean evening."

Even though he was curious to learn more about Bella, he backed off. "No problem. Now I know not to give you alcohol unless you specifically ask for it."

She wrinkled her nose. "You make me sound like a killjoy."

"Nah. You forget, my job requires me to be in prime physical condition. I have more than my share of drink-free nights during the season. Especially now that I'm older. My body takes longer to recover at twenty-five than it used to."

"Twenty-five?" she squeaked, her eyes widening.

"How old did you think I was?"

"I don't know. My age, I guess. But I'm *thirty*."

"Cool. I like older women. And you make a pretty hot cougar."

She rolled her eyes. "I'm hardly cougar material."

J.B. let his gaze wander slowly, deliberately, down her body. Over those curves, down the length of those gorgeous legs to her dainty feet and back up again. Then he stepped closer. And closer. Until he stood toe-to-toe with her.

Bella held her ground, though he sensed that one wrong move would have her scampering like a scared rabbit. She tilted her head up until their eyes met, then ran her tongue over her lower lip.

He leaned down, just a little, and mimicked her action with his tongue. Once. Twice.

Her eyelids fluttered closed. She dropped her sandals in the sand.

His loafers joined them. Then he took her mouth completely.

He didn't know how long they stood there locked in each other's arms, lost in each other's kisses, but the swirl of cool water around their ankles startled them. They jumped apart, laughing. Realizing the tide had caught their shoes, they retrieved them and headed up to the promenade, holding hands.

It didn't take long to reach the building where Bella's room was located. They continued up the stairs to the second floor.

Outside her door, she turned to him. "Would you like to come in for a nightcap?"

Her tentative question was yet another contradiction—her tone was an invitation, but he could read indecision in her eyes.

It would be so easy to give in. Hell, his aroused body was screaming at him to take advantage of what she was offering. If her kisses were this mind-blowing, there was no question the rest would be amazing. Yet she didn't seem the type who'd be happy with a holiday fling, and he didn't want anything more. Which meant the whole thing could blow up in his face big-time.

The memory of the crazy redhead who'd stalked him for a year almost made him shudder. He'd naively thought they were on the same page about the one-night stand.

"I'd love to." The regret in his voice was genuine. "But I don't think you're ready to go there tonight."

He was pleased that her disappointment mirrored his own.

"We both know if I cross that threshold, we won't be sipping drinks on the balcony." Gently stroking a wisp of hair from her cheek, he teased, "At least not until breakfast."

"There was me thinking I'd get it brought to me in bed."

J.B. laughed softly. Once again she'd surprised him. "I'll keep that in mind."

He ran a fingertip across her bottom lip, leaned down and gave her one quick, hard kiss, then pulled back with a heavy sigh. "Now go inside before I change my mind."

"Thank you." She smiled and turned to open her door. "I'll see you tomorrow?"

"Sure. How about breakfast at the beachside restaurant?"

"I'd like that." She fluttered her fingers at him. "Good night. Sleep well."

J.B. waited until the door closed behind her and then walked away. As he headed back along the beach to the bungalow, he noticed that the resort was quieter now. He passed several couples, arms wrapped around each other as they made their way to their rooms, and envied them.

He'd been right to leave Bella tonight, no question. But he couldn't help feeling that doing the right thing sucked.

THE SNICK OF a key card in the door woke Issy, pulling her out of a very steamy dream starring J. B. Larocque.

She kept her eyes closed for several seconds, trying to hang on to the amazing feelings coursing through her, moaning softly with frustration as they faded. That J.B. featured in her dream was hardly surprising. Although she'd spent the past couple of days on the beach with Sapphie, the evenings had been spent alone with J.B. after her friend and Taylor had disappeared. Both nights had ended with hot, thrilling kisses that even now aroused her.

The lock clicked again, followed by muttered curses. She should get up to help but she wanted desperately to go back to sleep and rekindle the dream that had become...interesting.

Sapphie finally managed to work the key card and crept in, holding her sandals.

"I wasn't expecting you back until morning." Issy sat up, leaning on one elbow.

"It is morning." Sapphie pointed her shoes at the floor-to-ceiling windows where the sun was peaking over the horizon. "And a beautiful one, too."

"True, but it's still early. Yesterday and the day before, you got back in time for us to make the last call for breakfast in the restaurant. Is everything okay?"

Her friend flopped onto the bed and yawned.

"It's great, but I must be aging. I need some sleep." She grinned. "Give hockey players their due— they are the fittest athletes. They have amazing stamina."

Issy fought the color that rose in her cheeks. She really didn't need further fuel for her fantasies. She'd seen enough of J.B.'s body to know that he was in prime physical condition. Her palms tingled at the memory of running her hands over the firm muscles in his arms and back. Her nipples tightened, as if they were still pressed to the solid wall of his chest.

"That's TMI." Issy hoped her friend would put the husky note in her voice down to her having just woken up.

Sapphie laughed. "That's exactly the kind of information you need. If you're going to break your sexual drought, you should do it with the best. J. B. Larocque is perfect. Far better than that other idiot you slept with."

The problem with best friends was that they knew all your secrets. Like the fact that Issy had only had sex once before, in college, and it had been an unmitigated disaster.

She'd fancied herself in love with the skinny, studious guy who'd sat in front of her in English. He'd been the complete opposite of the hulky, square-jawed jocks who attended reluctantly to fulfill their scholarship criteria. She'd been thrilled when he'd started paying attention to her.

Until the night the jerk had spiked her drink.

Her only consolation was that he'd barely got inside her before he'd come.

Luckily, there hadn't been an unwanted pregnancy. Still, the whole miserable experience had soured her on men. She'd buried herself in her courses and focused on getting top grades.

"I haven't made up my mind whether I'm going to—" Issy twirled her finger in the air "—you know."

Scorching-hot kisses were one thing. Going further was something else altogether. And not just because J.B. had probably slept with hundreds of gorgeous, confident women who were probably wonderful in bed.

"I figured you were dithering when there wasn't a Do Not Disturb sign on the door." Sapphie sighed heavily. "This is a great opportunity. You get an amazing night with a superstud like J.B., then you won't have to see him again. He won't want more than a fling, either, so it's a win-win."

Issy ignored the twinge beneath her breastbone. She didn't want, nor was she ready for, a relationship right now. Once she got her promotion to head of department, and her future was stable and secure, then she'd think about settling down. Besides, as nice as he was, and as much as he turned her on, J. B. Larocque would not be the right man for her to have a relationship with.

Still, one night was very tempting. "Sounds too good to be true."

"What could go wrong?" At Issy's raised eyebrow, Sapphie shook her head. "You're *not* Rosabelle. Or our parents. Besides, there's this wonderful invention called contraception."

"Funny. I've been on the pill since college."

"Then you're okay, because J.B. won't want a child to interfere with his career. Nothing bad will happen because neither of you will let it."

"I suppose so." Could she take the risk? Should she?

"You know you want to," Sapphie said gently. "It's now or never—we leave tomorrow. I don't want you to regret a missed opportunity."

Issy was thirty years old and had never enjoyed anything like that. How many more chances would come her way? Surely, if she was very careful...

"All right." Issy nodded. "I *do* want to and I will. Tonight."

"About time." Sapphie clapped delightedly.

Anticipation began to fizz through Issy's veins. "What if he doesn't want to?"

"Trust me, the man is desperate for you."

She smiled. "As long as he doesn't run away from me screaming."

"Puh-lease. He could've spent his vacation with any woman on the island. He's *chosen* to be with you."

"What if I'm not good enough? I'm not exactly experienced and he...is."

Sapphie's expression softened. "One of the benefits of his experience is that he'll understand you're not and he'll make sure it's great for you. He'll definitely make you forget what happened before."

"He'd have to be a magician."

Her friend winked. "From what I've heard, he has amazing hands and a..."

"Please don't mention his magic wand." Issy rolled her eyes.

They both laughed.

Sapphie yawned again. "Now, I really need some sleep. Especially if I'm going to help you prepare for your big night."

Issy wished she had her friend's confidence. "What you mean is you want to make sure you're ready for one more all-nighter with Taylor."

"That goes without saying. I plan to enjoy every moment."

Issy bit her lip. "It doesn't bother you that it's only a holiday fling?"

Sapphie shrugged. "It's what we both want. I'm sure I'll see him again—probably at a hockey game—but neither of us wants commitment. Would it be nice to hook up again? Of course. Will I be upset if it doesn't happen? Disappointed, but nothing more."

"And he feels the same?"

"Sure. We've both been up-front about it from the start. As long as these past few days have been as much fun for him as they've been for me, then it's all good." Sapphie closed her eyes. "See you in a few hours."

Her friend fell asleep in seconds. Issy, on the other hand, was wide awake. She slipped on the cotton robe the resort had provided and went to sit on the balcony. Pulling her legs up to her chest, she rested her chin on her knees and watched the resort slowly coming to life.

"How do you go about asking a man to sleep with you?" she wondered aloud.

She'd never thought of herself as one of those women who longed to be swept off her feet by a swashbuckling hero, but it would certainly make things less awkward if J.B. could do the honors.

Issy was no closer to figuring out how to even raise the subject with J.B. when Sapphie awoke and they headed to the beach for the day. Taylor and J.B. joined them after lunch and the four decamped to the pool bar, where they frolicked in the water and enjoyed cocktails. Issy was touched that J.B. made a point of ordering her the virgin version of whatever colorful concoction they were drinking.

She watched his behavior closely. Sapphie was right; he didn't look at anyone but Issy, even though there were several stunning women who tried to get his attention. Not only was J.B. solicitous, but he also touched her a lot. Her arm, her shoulder, tucking a curl behind her ear, playing footsie with her when they were seated on the bar stools. When she lay on the pool float, he rested his arms beside her and occasionally dropped a kiss on her lips.

Each touch, each kiss, heated her blood far more than the blazing temperatures. They also built her confidence so that she found herself impatient for the sun to go down.

"A TOAST TO the four most fabulous people in Antigua." Sapphie raised a champagne flute.

"Make that the Caribbean," J.B. added, clinking his glass against hers.

"You guys are too modest. It's the world." Taylor grinned.

"I'll drink to that." Issy took J.B.'s glass and sipped from it before returning it to him.

The look he sent her was so hot, her skin practically sizzled. When he made a point of placing his lips exactly where hers had been, Issy's insides turned liquid. The promise in his dark eyes suggested he might be the mind reader she'd hoped for.

Dessert couldn't come quickly enough.

Issy's nerves returned when Sapphie and Taylor left them to go dancing. The moment of truth was getting ever closer.

"How about a walk along the beach?" J.B. took

her hand, pressed his mouth to the pulse point at her wrist, then linked fingers with her.

She smiled. "Sounds perfect."

They took off their shoes, headed down to the water's edge and strolled through the water until they were away from the main part of the resort. While they walked, they talked—about her job and his, about his family and hers. They carefully avoided mentioning the future, not even what they'd be doing when they got home.

At the end of the property there was a long stretch of empty beach with no buildings or lights, only a few palm trees. The moon turned the sand silver, making the place look magical. J.B. and Issy sat beneath one of the trees—he leaned against the trunk, while she sat between his legs, as she had during that crazy dance on the night they'd met—and watched the twinkling lights of the vessels out at sea.

And kissed.

Long, slow, deep kisses. Hot, hard, urgent kisses.

Soon, it wasn't enough. J.B. jumped up and helped her to her feet. Arms wrapped tightly around each other, they didn't stop walking until they were outside her door.

This time, Issy didn't invite J.B. in for a nightcap. Now that the moment was actually here, she couldn't say the words. Her throat was too tight. Her mouth too dry. So she grabbed his hand and pulled him inside. Then she took the Do Not Dis-

turb notice and hung it on the handle before closing the door.

J.B. stood in front of her, his expression sol-
emn. "Are you sure?"

She closed her eyes briefly. *Last chance to back
out.*

The knowledge that he'd accept her decision,
even if it was no, gave her the courage she needed.
"Definitely."

"Thank God," he murmured before lowering
his head and taking her mouth.

CHAPTER FOUR

J.B. HAD PLANNED to take things slowly. Not that he'd taken anything for granted. He'd hoped, for sure. Tonight was their last chance, with Bella leaving tomorrow, but he'd known the odds of ending up in her bed were as evenly balanced as a shoot-out.

Although this was only a one-time thing, he understood it was a big deal for her, so he needed to make tonight special.

No pressure.

It had taken every ounce of self-control to let her set the pace while they'd kissed. Especially when the tip of her tongue had slipped between his lips and tentatively touched his. The combination of sweet innocence and passionate intent was killer.

Even once they were inside her room, he'd been determined not to rush.

And he didn't. Not when she eased his shirt out of his pants. Not when she undid his buttons, her knuckles brushing against his chest with each one.

Things got a little dicey when she pressed soft, moist kisses to his bare skin.

When she licked the ridges of his six-pack, his good intentions began to crumble. He closed his eyes and bit back a moan.

J.B. held strong until she reached his belt buckle. Then his intentions were blown to hell.

"My turn." His hoarse words sounded sharp in the silent room.

Bella's hands stilled. Her uncertain gaze shot up to meet his.

He stroked a finger along her cheekbone and down to her mouth. "We don't want this over before you've got started."

She didn't look reassured, so he traced her full bottom lip. "Trust me. Any more ready and I'll embarrass myself." He smiled.

Bella frowned. "But...?"

His finger across her lips silenced her. J.B. replaced his finger with his mouth, letting his hot, deep kiss take over the convincing.

Her resistance melted. He felt the nervous tension ease from her body, to be replaced quickly by desire.

When she tried to wrap her arms around his neck, J.B. caught her wrists and lowered them to her sides. "Uh-uh. Turnabout is fair play."

She bit her lip but didn't argue. Curiosity and need replaced the uncertainty in her eyes.

J.B. licked her lip, kissed both corners, before nibbling his way along her jaw. He dipped his tongue into the hollow behind her ear, then tugged her earlobe gently with his teeth. His smile broadened at the tremor that went through her.

Unhurried, he alternately kissed and nipped his way down the side of her neck and along her collarbone to her shoulder, relishing the way she sighed with pleasure. He licked along the edge of her strapless dress, across the swell of one breast, through the valley between and over the other, before returning to the center and the pink, flower-shaped top button of her dress.

He slipped the button out of its hole and pressed an open mouthed kiss to the fragrant skin he'd revealed. Bella's breath hitched, straining the fabric around the second yellow button.

Undo. Kiss. Hitch. Repeat.

The next button was orange, the one after green. It was like eating a bag of hard candies. Different colors, different flavors; each more mouthwatering than the one before.

Her dress fell partly open as he reached her waist, the fabric catching on the peaked nipples of her breasts. She wasn't wearing a bra. His erection surged as he freed both sides, laying her bare.

Beautiful. He wanted to taste and touch every delicious inch.

J.B. swept Bella into his arms and carried her to the bed. He laid her down, then sat beside her. He continued unbuttoning until the dress was completely undone, while he explored her with his mouth. As he trailed his tongue along the underside of each creamy breast, then circled each taut, dark cherry nipple, his fingers caressed the tanned skin of her belly. The muscles of her stomach tightened at his touch, but she didn't stop him.

He went lower still...to the top of her white, silky panties. Then under the lacy trim to the dark curls beneath. He deliberately avoided touching the most sensitive part of her, even though she raised her hips, slightly offering him access. He also didn't dip his fingers into her damp heat, despite her tiny mewl of frustration and his own need.

Hooking a finger into the elastic, he pulled the panties slowly down her legs before tossing them aside.

Her hands tugged his shirt open and stroked feverishly over the heated skin of his chest. When she tried to push his shirt over his shoulders, he pulled it off, throwing it behind him before returning to her side. "Where was I?"

Bella shook her head. "Not so fast. Pants, too. You're overdressed."

J.B. did as she instructed. He kept his boxer shorts on; the last barrier protecting his sanity. He also took several condoms out of his wallet and placed them on the bedside table.

"Thank you," she said softly. "I'm already protected, but I appreciate you being responsible, too."

"Better safe than sorry." He stretched out beside her, his head propped on one hand. "Okay?"

"Definitely." An appreciative smile played over her lips as her gaze skimmed the length of his body. But the uncertainty returned to her eyes when she spotted the unmistakable bulge in his shorts.

"I know you're desperate to get your hands on my magnificence, but you'll have to wait. It's still your turn."

She giggled. "Your 'magnificence'?"

He feigned offense. "I assure you it lives up to its billing."

"I'm sure," she soothed. "Can I call it Mag for short?"

And there was another intriguing contradiction. She was nervous, but she was making jokes. That was more of a turn-on than any seductive move.

"Lady, there is nothing *short* about it," he growled.

Her eyes widened. "So I see."

He rolled over onto his back and pulled her on top of him.

Other than a squeak of surprise, Bella didn't protest. Her smile turned worldly as she stretched her body along the length of his. Her breasts crushed against his chest, their stomachs flattened against each other, their legs tangled. And Mag fit perfectly into the V at the top of her thighs.

Their kisses became a duel—who could turn the other one on more—with hands, mouth and… everything else. In truth, it wasn't much of a contest. Bella had one hell of an advantage. Then again, she was ready for him, too. But she didn't make a move to commit them to the final stage. Almost as if she didn't know how.

He lifted his head. "I reckon you're all caught up, don't you?"

Her lips twisted wryly. "I'm not very experienced at this, but I think you're right."

"This…isn't your first time, is it?"

She wouldn't meet his gaze. "No. But it might as well be. The first time was in college. It was… awful."

Her softly spoken words set off alarm bells. "Do you want to talk about it?"

"Not really. I don't want to kill the mood."

Crap. He didn't like the sound of that. "Honey, nothing you say could do that." He placed her hand on his erection. "Mag can handle whatever you tell me."

"Impressive." She left her hand there. "Suffice it to say the guy I was with didn't worry too much about foreplay."

J.B. bit back his rage. Better he didn't know the details. It wasn't like he could hunt down the jerk and pound him to dust. It also didn't help Bella. "At least tell me he embarrassed himself by coming too quickly."

"Almost immediately." Her eyes twinkled with humor. "I rewarded him by throwing up all over him."

A surprised laugh escaped him. "Atta girl." He kissed the tip of her nose. "I'm glad you told me. I'll be careful. Anything you're not comfortable with, say so. Okay?"

She nodded firmly.

"Good. The only rule tonight is that you enjoy yourself."

"In that case, can we stop talking and get to the fun part?" Her gaze was clear; all signs of uncertainty gone.

"Hell, yes." He flipped her beneath him and proceeded to kiss and caress her to fever pitch.

It didn't take long. For either of them.

J.B. held off, even though he knew from the way she writhed beneath him that she was ready for him. Instead he slipped his finger inside her and used his thumb to rub her swollen bud.

Bella gasped, then moaned.

Only when he was certain that she hovered on the brink of orgasm did he put on the condom and ease into her. And nearly embarrass himself like that college ass.

She was tight, wet and so hot.

He gritted his teeth and held still as he waited for her to adjust to having him inside her. His body raged against his restraint, but he refused to give in. Only when she began to grind her hips against him did he give in to her wordless demand.

Slowly at first, then, with increasing speed, he

began to pump in and out. She met each thrust eagerly, urging him for more. Their rhythms synced, as it had when they'd danced.

Harder. Faster.

Sweat slicked their skin.

His body seemed to be on fire. He wanted to explode, but he couldn't. Not yet. His muscles quivered with the effort of maintaining control.

Just when he thought he couldn't hold on a moment longer, she came apart beneath him with a keening cry. As she pulsed around him, J.B. finally let go and claimed his own release.

Before he could collapse on top of her, he rolled and pulled her with him into his arms. Her head rested against his heaving chest as he rasped in oxygen.

"Wow." Bella's voice was unsteady but awestruck. "That was pretty amazing."

"Yeah." J.B. grinned wearily. "Any more amazing and you'd have killed me."

She giggled. "Mag certainly lived up to his promise."

"Thank you, ma'am."

They lay silently for a few minutes while their bodies cooled and their breathing steadied. Her fingers traced a meandering path across his chest and stomach. He twirled a lock of her hair around one finger. Despite the reasons for being in Antigua earlier than planned, he couldn't complain. Otherwise he'd have missed Bella. And this.

He was half-asleep when she said softly, "J.B.?"

"Hmm?"

"Do you think we'll be able to do that again before I leave?"

He laughed. That was his Bella—always keeping him off balance. "Give me half an hour and I'll see what I…and Mag…can do."

Issy didn't want to open her eyes.

From the bright light filtering through her closed lids, she knew it was morning but she didn't want to break the wonderful spell. Or leave the cocoon of J.B.'s arms.

She'd never spent the night with a man. Never woken up with a man in her bed. She probably wouldn't again for a long time. It was a moment to savor because all too soon reality would intrude. For now, though, she was content to snuggle closer to J.B. and enjoy it.

They fit together perfectly. He was curled around her, every inch of him pressed against her back and legs. His knees curved into the back of hers. His hand cradled her breast. His even breathing stirred the tiny hairs at the back of her neck. Definitely the best way to start the day.

Issy found it hard to believe how amazing the night before had been and how special J.B. had made her feel. Everything she'd read about in romance novels but never thought could happen in real life. Not for her. Certainly not with a guy like

J.B. A successful, professional athlete; a charming lady-killer.

His consideration and understanding had been as unexpected as the responses he'd managed to elicit from her. Although she didn't have much to compare him with, he'd more than lived up to anything she could have imagined. Who knew it really was possible to make love three times in one night?

Issy stifled a giggle. She felt deliciously wanton and a teensy bit proud. After all, she'd made sure that J.B. had enjoyed himself as much as she had.

He'd recovered surprisingly quickly after that first time. Then he'd carried her into the bathroom. Under the rainfall shower, he'd carefully washed her from head to toe. The memory of his skilled hands, slippery with soap, turning a simple task into an erotic adventure, sent heat flooding through her. She'd probably never be able to take a shower again, or smell cherry-blossom soap, without recalling her unbelievably intense climax.

Then J.B. had handed her the fragrant bar and encouraged her to do the same to him. Uncertain at first, but with increasing surety as his unbridled response to her touch made her heady with confidence, she'd lathered his incredible body. His smooth, caramel-colored skin, the ripped muscles of his back, his broad chest that tapered to a well-defined six-pack. His powerful legs, with thighs and calves so firm they could have been carved out of stone. His ridiculously sexy feet.

Once they were rinsed clean, the exploration had begun again, teasing and tasting with their hands and mouths, until they'd both been so turned on they could hardly stand.

A satisfied smile curved Issy's lips. Recovery for both of them hadn't been nearly as fast as the first time. Exhausted, they'd slept for a few hours.

The third time had been slower, softer. Although neither of them had voiced it out loud, they'd known time was running out. They'd moved to the balcony where, on cushions they'd taken from the room's sofa, they'd made achingly sweet love beneath the slowly lightening sky.

Tears pricked her eyes. If only…

A beeping sound alerted her to a text. Raising her head slightly, she saw it was from Sapphie.

We need to pack. Shuttle leaves at 12. You have one hour. Make the most of it!

And there it was—the reality she'd dreaded. Like the clock chiming midnight for Cinderella, the message signaled the end of Issy's night and with it the fairy-tale world she'd been living in. Even though she'd known it was only for one night, the thought that she probably wouldn't experience anything so wonderful again for a long time, if ever, was hard to take.

As the last remnants of her afterglow faded, so did Issy's confidence. She began to feel awkward and a little foolish. However she dressed it up and in spite of the exotic setting, she and J.B. had still only had a one-night stand. Was she really so different from her family?

Stop! She wouldn't beat herself up and she wouldn't allow herself regrets. The night, the experience, had been too special to be spoiled by recriminations.

Even so, suddenly she wasn't as comfortable sharing her bed with J.B. She shifted slightly, trying to ease away from him before he woke up. But he stirred behind her, pulling her tighter against him. He brushed a kiss against her neck, below her ear. His second kiss was a little lower. His third at the curve of her shoulder.

With each kiss, Issy's pulse jumped. How was it possible that he could still coax a response from her so easily? She'd have thought that he'd wrung every last bit out of her.

Clearly not.

"Hello, beautiful." His husky voice sent a delicious shiver though her.

"Good morning," she said with false brightness as she started to move away again.

He wouldn't let her. "Not so fast."

His erection pressed against her bottom.

She swallowed hard. "I see Mag is an early riser."

"Honey, with you around, he never sleeps."

The urge to wriggle against him, to reposition her body so he could easily slip inside, almost overwhelmed her. She reveled briefly in his hardness against her, but she couldn't shake the feeling that it would be a mistake. It certainly wouldn't change anything.

Issy pushed out of his embrace and sat up. "Our time's up. Sapphie will be coming back to the room shortly."

J.B. propped himself on one elbow. "Shortly, as in she's outside the door, or do we have a few minutes to welcome the new day properly?"

She could lie—tell him Sapphie was nearby—but she didn't want to. Not when she could create one last precious memory with him. Knowing she'd probably curse her weakness later, she gave in. "We have less than an hour."

"No problem." He reached over, snagged the last condom and rolled it on.

Their lovemaking had a desperate edge this time. They drove each other higher, faster, using what they'd learned through the night about their bodies, their needs and their desires until, as one, they shattered. Though the throbbing from their completion had faded, they clung together tightly, still intimately joined, for long minutes afterward.

A tear trickled down Issy's cheek. This really was the end.

"So…" J.B. cleared his throat as he gently dried the damp trail with his finger. "I know this was meant to have been one night, but maybe we could see each other again. It wouldn't be too hard, since we both live in Jersey. We could meet up for a drink or dinner. No pressure, no commitment."

Her heart leaped, but she quickly tamped it down.

Much as she hated to admit it, that simply wasn't possible. Spending any more time with J.B. raised too many red flags. Even though he'd changed her opinion of a professional athlete— from their conversations over the past few days and especially last night—she knew that they wanted completely different things from their lives. She couldn't risk ending up like her sister or derailing the course she'd set. Ultimately he could be nothing more than a pleasant—okay, a wonderful—but dangerous distraction.

Fighting the urge to agree, she shook her head. "I don't think that's a good idea. This has been incredible—the best night of my life—but we're from two very different worlds."

Frustration filled his dark eyes, mirroring the feeling that clawed at her. "We're only talking dinner."

Be strong. "We both know it wouldn't just be dinner."

"Okay, dinner with a really nice dessert. Would that be so bad?"

"Of course not." She caressed his cheek apologetically. "But if we do it once, what's to stop us doing it a second time? Then a third. Or more. How long will we let it go on before we know we have to call it quits? A month? Six?"

He started to speak but she stopped him.

"You know about my family, my background. Why I want stability and security. If I start a relationship, I want to be sure it's with someone who feels the same. Who's ready for and, more importantly, wants commitment."

The regret in his expression told her that he wanted to disagree but couldn't.

"It's okay. I know that's not what you want." Issy smiled sadly.

J.B. was silent for a few minutes. Finally he sighed. "You're right."

Even though she knew it was the correct decision, she couldn't help feeling disappointed that he didn't argue his corner a little harder. "If it's any consolation, I wish I wasn't."

"Yeah. Me, too." He pressed a quick, hard kiss to her lips, then eased away.

She missed his warmth instantly and wrapped her arms around herself.

"Damn it!" J.B. jumped up. "Freaking condom broke."

Issy's gut tightened. "You're kidding."

"That's one thing I don't ever joke about." He stalked to the bathroom.

No! She'd only stepped outside her carefully drawn lines once—*once*—it wasn't fair. This couldn't be happening. She buried her head in her hands.

The bed dipped as J.B. sat beside her and draped his arm around her shoulders. "Hey, it's not as bad as you're thinking."

His soothing voice had the opposite effect. "It's a disaster. I can't get pregnant."

"The chances of you getting caught this one time are really slim. You're on the pill, aren't you?"

She nodded.

"Then you're protected. The condom was only a backstop. Trust me—it'll be fine."

While her panicking brain fought to deny his reassurance, his logic seeped in and began to calm her. Her thundering heart slowed.

"Of course," she said finally, when she could trust herself not to sound hysterical. "I'm sorry. I lost it for a moment there."

"That makes two of us." His chuckle sounded relieved. "All's well that ends well."

He turned her more fully into his arms, leaned down and touched his forehead to hers.

They remained like that, silently, lost in their own thoughts, until the clatter of a trolley on the path outside jolted them out of their reveries.

"I should go." J.B. eased himself from their embrace and gathered his clothes.

Still feeling vulnerable after the scare, Issy wound the sheet around her. "Thank you. For... everything."

"Thank *you*." He shrugged into his shirt. "You are an incredible lady. Make sure you choose a guy who really deserves you."

A tall order after last night. "I'll do my best."

"I'll see you before you leave. I'll help you take your luggage to the shuttle."

She wanted that so much—to have a final hug, one more kiss—but it was hard enough to let him go. Delaying would only make it tougher. "I think we should say goodbye now. Make a clean break."

J.B. looked surprised. "Are you sure?"

No. "It's difficult enough here, in private. It'll be impossible in the crowded lobby." Her voice wobbled on the last word.

He rubbed his hand across the back of his neck. "Okay. Sure."

J.B. pressed one last, hard kiss to her mouth and then walked out the door.

By the time Sapphie returned to their room, Issy had regained some composure. Obviously not enough, judging by her friend's concerned look and tight hug. Issy was grateful that Sapphie didn't ask any questions while they packed, but chattered cheerfully about how much she'd enjoyed the holiday.

As they checked out, Issy tried not to watch for J.B. She told herself he wouldn't be there, yet she couldn't help one last glance as they boarded the shuttle bus.

Her heart skipped when she saw a familiar silhouette in the shadows of the lobby. He stood there until the bus turned the corner and she couldn't see him anymore.

"You'll be all right," Sapphie murmured, squeezing her hand.

Issy let out a heavy breath. Yes, she would.

The line to get through security stretched out in front of the airport. She and Sapphie joined the end and began the torturous process of inching toward the passport-control booth.

Once they were finally through security, she and Sapphie got sandwiches and soft drinks at one of the airport cafés. After all the fabulous resort food, the stale roll was hard to swallow—literally. Issy made herself eat so she could take some ibuprofen to ease her throbbing temples.

Sapphie tossed her sandwich in the trash and looked around the crowded, noisy, waiting area. "Newark Airport is looking more appealing by the second. Do you think it'll work if I click my sandals and say 'There's no place like home'?"

"Probably not, since you don't actually have a 'home.'"

"Good point, darn it."

"Try 'Beam me up, Scotty' instead," Issy suggested. "Beaming us back to Jersey sounds pretty good right now."

Before her friend could respond, the speakers crackled and their flight was announced for boarding. As they walked out to the plane, the waves of heat from the tarmac combined with the smell of aviation fuel made Issy feel queasy.

Once in their seats Issy adjusted the winged headrest, leaned against it and closed her eyes. She welcomed the soothing stream of cool air from the vent above her head. The noise of people finding their seat was soon replaced by flight attendants slamming closed the overhead lockers and the drone of the safety announcement. The vibration of the engines firing up exacerbated her sickness.

Issy drank some more water, then tried to fall asleep. But despite the tiredness that washed over her in waves, she couldn't drop off.

After takeoff, her nausea eased a little. But it returned full-force when the meal service started. The smell of coffee made her stomach roll.

Oh, no. She was going to be sick.

Issy jumped up and dashed for the toilets. She barely got the door closed before she threw up.

Welcome back to reality, Isabelle Brandine.

CHAPTER FIVE

"GOOD TO SEE our Millionaire Ice Boy still gets his hands dirty."

From wading in the Caribbean to wading in cow crap in three weeks: the two sides of J.B.'s life.

He didn't give his oldest brother the satisfaction of a verbal response but continued mucking out the stalls in their parents' barn. Shame the shovel of manure slipped, slewing its contents over Marc Andre's jeans and boots.

"You ass," his brother spluttered, jumping back. "I just got cleaned up to go into town."

"I'm sorry, but what do you expect from a lowly 'ice boy'?" He gave an exaggerated sigh. "I'm out of practice at shoveling crap."

"Perhaps I should get Dad to send you over to my place to do chores, too."

His father would love that. "Nah. Not much call for this skill in my day job."

"Maybe not, but it might improve your aim, kid."

"I'd say my aim's pretty damn good." He grinned

and reached for the hose. "Want me to wash you down?"

Marc Andre laughed and stepped out of the line of fire. "By the time you're done I'll need to change everything, even my underwear, and I don't have time."

"Wouldn't be the first time someone walked around town covered in Eau de Cow Dung. No one will bat an eyelid."

"True. But sometimes even us yokels need to spruce up." Marc Andre punched his shoulder. "It's good to see you, bro. Been too long."

"I know." Guilt twinged his chest. The last time J.B. had come to the farm was back in December when he'd flown out a day early for the team's swing through Western Canada.

Though he knew he should make more of an effort to get home, it wasn't easy to find the time. Unlike the guys who played sixteen games of football and were done by the end of January, J.B.'s season was eighty-two games over seven months. If he was lucky, that was followed by a postseason that took him through to June.

And it wasn't like he took the summer off. Technically, J.B. had three months before he had to report for training camp. But in reality, if he didn't start his workout schedule in the next couple of weeks, he wouldn't be in peak physical condition come September.

He'd tried in the past to draw the comparison

with farming, where there was little downtime in the calendar, but it had gone over his folks' heads.

"This was a tough year for visits, with me being selected for the All-Stars and then our Cup run."

"We understand. Well, Dad doesn't, but the rest of us get it. Who'd have thought a Larocque would be burning up the NHL?" His brother rubbed a hand over his jaw. "It's a good thing, because you suck as a farmer."

"Yeah. So, how come you're going into town during the day, midweek?"

"I've got a meeting with the bank. Now Amelie and I know for sure that baby number four is due in the new year I want to simplify my finances."

"Congratulations." That would make seven nieces and nephews. Another reason J.B. felt like he'd been born into the wrong family. Much as he loved the rug rats, for sure he wasn't ready for one of his own. There was plenty of hockey left to play and life to enjoy, before he settled down and burdened himself with those responsibilities.

"If you weren't so freaking stubborn, you wouldn't have any mortgages or loans. Neither would Pierre Luc."

"I'm not taking your money." Marc Andre's expression was fierce. "You'll need it to live off when you're retired. You sure as hell can't make a living off the land."

J.B. leaned on the shovel to stop himself from using it to knock some sense into his brother. This was an old argument that always ended the same. While he respected independence and appreciated that his family weren't spongers, they were too damn proud. "By the time I'm done, I'll have more than enough for several lifetimes."

"You never know. You could get injured or traded. The team could be sold or go belly-up. And once you're done, you'll still be young, with a long life ahead of you."

Like farming was any more secure. "So take the money as a loan. I bet the bank can't beat a no-interest repayment plan."

"Appreciate the offer, but it's best we don't muddy the family water with money."

Straight out of the mouth of Bastien Larocque. Their father said the same thing often enough.

"Anyway, we're not destitute," his brother continued. "This winter was rougher than usual and things got a little tight. The bank's been great about reworking payments to help ease the pressure."

It burned his butt that his brother preferred help from a bank manager over J.B. "If you won't let me give you the money, at least let me invest in your place. Buy machinery, refurbish buildings or something. It'll give me a tax break."

Marc Andre's jaw set. "Thanks, but I'm good."

J.B. knew that stubborn look. "All right. But if you ever need money badly enough to not care about muddy freaking water, you know where to come. Deal?" He stuck out his hand.

"Deal." Marc Andre shook his hand.

"So, what time's your appointment?"

His brother swore as he checked his watch. "I should get going. See you at dinner."

J.B. brooded about the situation as he finished his share of the chores.

He understood his dad's stance. Even when J.B. couched it as repaying what his parents had spent on his hockey, Bastien had refused to accept his money. In his father's mind, professional athletes were a step above gigolos. Earning money playing sport didn't count.

The old man had spent his whole life working the farm, which had never made much of a living for the Larocques. If not for his mom, J.B. wouldn't be where he was today.

He hosed off the floor, hung the tools on the rack and headed to the house to clean up.

In the kitchen his mom was busy cooking. She always made plenty so that her daughters-in-law—who worked alongside their husbands on their farms, as well as looked after their kids—didn't have to. A good thing since both Amelie and Clare were lousy cooks.

Twelve loaves were cooling on wire racks on the counter, next to a dozen jars of homemade spaghetti sauce. On the table two coolers were filled with foil-wrapped parcels.

His stomach rumbled. It had been hours since breakfast and he wouldn't get lunch until after his mom had done her weekly grocery shop. J.B. sneaked a piece of the potato salad his mom was mixing. "Mmm. Are you sure I can't steal you away to come and cook for me in Jersey? You're still the best."

She patted his cheek. "Much as I'd like to make sure you eat properly—you look a little skinny—I couldn't leave the farm. Besides, I'm not sure I'd be happy where you live."

Like most people who'd never been to the Garden State, his mom thought the whole area was an industrial monstrosity. "You'd be surprised how nice it is, Ma. Come visit and see."

"Maybe later in the year."

J.B. wouldn't hold his breath. Like the discussion about money, this was another old conversation. "Are you ready to go into town?"

"Definitely. If you're still happy to take me." She slipped off her apron.

He grabbed an apple out of the fruit bowl. "For sure. I'll have the prettiest woman in the area on my arm."

He wasn't exaggerating. Ellen Larocque's lovely face and cute figure still turned heads. Her black hair was just beginning to be streaked with gray and her pale skin was barely wrinkled.

She swatted him with a dish towel. "I don't

think so. Maybe if you brought one of those women you're always photographed with…"

He kissed her cheek, breathing in her familiar scent: a mixture of her floral perfume and cooking spices. "None of them can match up to you, Ma."

"You always were the charmer. I'll just grab my purse and my shopping list."

On the half-hour drive, his mom chattered away about the latest happenings with friends and neighbors. J.B. didn't know half the people she talked about and was relieved to pull into a parking spot outside the diner.

Though they only had a block to walk to the grocery store, progress was slow with people stopping them every few yards. A few he recognized, but most he relied on his mom's clues as to who they were. It was the same at the store and the diner.

He was grilled about when he was coming home for good. Those who followed hockey were keen to discuss his career. J.B. gave bland answers, his smile becoming more strained with each one. He accepted good-naturedly the usual ribbing about how he should play for a Canadian team, then posed for photos and signed napkins and scraps of paper thrust at him. He never turned down a request, especially from kids.

By the time they got back into the car for the

drive home, J.B. was wrung out, as if he'd played triple overtime.

Only a few more days, he told himself as he did the evening chores. It was pathetic that he'd barely been home twenty-four hours and he was already counting down to leaving. He loved his family, but he didn't fit here. New Jersey was more his home than this small town.

Luckily, he couldn't brood for long because his brothers and their families arrived for his welcome-home barbecue.

Dinner was a rowdy affair. His dad sat at the head of the picnic table, while everyone else squeezed down the sides. His mom sat opposite her husband, beaming, clearly thrilled to have all her chicks under her roof.

"Welcome home, bro." Pierre Luc raised his bottle in salute. "Congratulations on making the Finals. Tough loss."

"You'll get 'em next year." Marc Andre clinked his beer bottle against J.B.'s.

"Damn—darn straight," J.B. said.

"I'm sorry we couldn't make any of your games." His mother frowned. "Finding someone to look after the farm is difficult."

"Jean-Baptiste knows we can't up and travel at the drop of a hat."

J.B. bit back his irritation at his father's words. Other families—even other farmers—managed it. He understood it wasn't easy, but his dad didn't want to make the effort.

"No worries, Ma." J.B. smiled at his mom. "Maybe next year."

"Did you get the mess with that woman in the nightclub sorted out, Jean-Baptiste?" his father asked.

Why couldn't his old man ever call him J.B.? He forced a casual tone. "She got hold of Coach Macarty and explained that it was an unfortunate accident. She told the media, too, but the truth wasn't appealing and the story got buried."

His father huffed. "Your team can't have been happy. It's not like this was the first time you've been at the center of a scandal."

Although that wasn't quite true—Jake had taken the fall before—J.B. didn't bother to correct his dad. He wouldn't listen, anyway. "Once they had the facts, they were cool."

"It's time you started being more responsible. You're not a kid anymore." His father loaded his plate with more potato salad. "Speaking of which, while you're here, Jean-Baptiste, I'd like you to survey the fences. You should keep your hand in the farm."

J.B. exchanged wry looks with his brothers.

"Give the kid a chance, Dad," Pierre Luc said. "He just got here."

"He hasn't even had a chance to stop by our places yet," Marc Andre chimed in.

"They're right, Bastien," his mother chided. "Our boy's only here for a few days. He should rest, not ride the fence line. He works hard enough. He's earned a vacation."

"He just had a week on a beach."

Before J.B. could react, his mother laid her pale hand on his father's dark one. As it had for as long as he could remember, the action calmed his dad.

Later that night, as J.B. sat out on the front porch, nursing a beer, he thought about his parents' marriage. The gentle former teacher and the rough farmer seemed to fit together perfectly; to complement each other. His brothers' marriages were strong, too.

Bella popped into his head, as she had every day since he'd returned from Antigua.

Never before had a woman had such a lasting impact on him.

J.B. shook his head. It didn't matter. Their relationship was over and he was good with that. He didn't have the time, energy or inclination for commitment. Being back here only emphasized his feelings. His family's responsibilities weighed heavily, as if he were the one suffocating under the pressure.

Bella was…had to be…nothing more than a pleasant memory.

"IF WE CAN'T paint the town red, then watching Colin Firth isn't a bad alternative."

Relieved that Sapphie didn't mind their last-minute change of plans for the Labor Day weekend, Issy sighed. "Thanks. I really don't feel up to a dinner cruise tonight." The thought of putting on a fancy dress and heels, and spending the evening on a boat on the Hudson made her stomach pitch. "I promise I'll make it up to you on your next visit."

"You'll get that chance sooner than you think. Part of the reason I wanted us to go out was that I'll be spending a lot more time on the east coast over the next twelve months."

"You got the contract with Marty Antonelli?"

"Starting Tuesday, I'll be evaluating the basketball team he bought and advising him on how to make it a more financially viable enterprise."

"Congratulations!" Issy squealed as she jumped up and hugged her friend.

This was a major coup for Sapphie. She'd worked hard to get her foot in the door with the technology billionaire who'd recently acquired several sports franchises.

They danced around like lunatics for a few minutes, then collapsed on the sofa, laughing.

"I know you like hockey and football. What do you know about basketball?" Issy asked.

"Not a lot. But I used that to my advantage. I told Mr. Antonelli that he didn't need someone with preconceived ideas about the team."

"And he bought that?"

"Of course." Sapphie blew on her nails and polished them on her top. "That, and my impressive track record."

"I'm so proud of you."

Sapphie had always found a way to make things work more efficiently and effectively while squeezing a quart out of a pint-pot budget. She'd put herself through college with her projects on the side for local companies. It hadn't been a surprise when Sapphie had formed her own management consulting firm.

Issy couldn't help being envious of the way her friend was able to improvise and adapt, to achieve whatever she set her mind to. If she'd had even half of Sapphie's talent, Issy would have been made head of department before, instead of being passed over for 'more experienced candidates' the past two times the position had become vacant. Certainly she wouldn't have had to jump through hoops for one more year to prove to Farlingdale Academy's board that she was capable of taking over the retiring head's position.

She frowned at the snack foods on the coffee table. "We should be celebrating with something fancier than popcorn, chips and sodas."

"Trust me, this is great. I get enough fancy food at work. Besides it's the company and—" Sapphie indicated the *Pride and Prejudice* DVD "—the entertainment that makes this a real celebration."

"I promise I'll rebook that riverboat cruise when I'm feeling better."

Sapphie put the back of her hand against Issy's forehead. "You've been sick a lot recently. Have you seen a doctor?"

"It's not worth it. I don't think I've fully recovered from whatever hit me on the flight from Antigua. You know stomach bugs can linger."

"A good reason for you to get checked out. Our trip was over two months ago."

"But the nausea comes and goes. It's worse when I've been busy, so it's probably a low-blood-sugar thing, too."

"You did redecorate your apartment single-handed." Sapphie didn't look convinced. "Promise me that if you're not better by Friday, you'll go to the doctor."

"Yes, Mom. In the meantime, Mr. Darcy eagerly awaits the pleasure of our company."

"I'm more than ready for him." Sapphie loaded her plate. "Mmm, your No-Olive Seven-Layer Dip—my favorite. Are you sure you can eat something so spicy?"

Issy nodded. "It's one of the few things that doesn't turn my stomach these days. In fact, I can't get enough of it."

"How strange." Sapphie sighed, distracted by Bingley and Darcy riding into view on-screen. "Tell me again how this is work."

"Since my class is studying *Pride and Preju-*

dice, I'm having them compare the book with film and TV adaptations. Then I broadened the project to include films based on the story."

"I bet your pupils love your classes. I wish we'd done stuff half that interesting."

Issy warmed to the subject. "Forcing them to study a book that doesn't do anything but sit on their desk can be challenging. I know people are precious about not sullying the books by showing adaptations, but I find it helps engage readers."

"Works for me. And it's a prime example of why Farlingdale's board of trustees should give you that way-overdue promotion."

"From your lips to their ears. Hopefully my classes' results this year will seal the deal."

"I have faith in you." Sapphie leaned over and patted her hand. "It's a tough job, but as I'm such a good friend, I'll watch all those different versions of *Pride and Prejudice* with you. I'm glad we're starting with my favorite one."

"Mine, too." Issy grinned.

They watched the first three episodes of the TV series, then stopped for a break.

"That reminds me." Sapphie rummaged in her purse and pulled out an envelope, which she handed to Issy. "This is for next time I'm in town."

Issy's heart stopped when she saw the snow leopard logo embossed on the strip of card within. "What's this?" she asked, even though it was obvious.

"A ticket to an Ice Cats preseason game," her friend said brightly. "As part of my season ticket package, I get free extra seats to some games."

"We can't watch them on TV?"

"Sure, but you get a much better sense of the game—the speed, the action, the skill—watching the team play live."

She suspected Sapphie's gift had little to do with building her appreciation of the sport. "I thought we agreed we wouldn't see Taylor and J.B. again."

"*You* agreed. I said I might." Sapphie refilled her plate. "There's no guarantee they'll actually be playing on that night. Coaches use the preseason to test their younger, less experienced players. Plus, because the Cats went all the way to the Cup Finals, they had a much shorter off-season than usual. Their stars have earned a rest."

"But they'll still be at the arena, even if they're not playing."

"Probably."

Issy bit her lip. "Seeing J.B. would only complicate things."

"They don't have to know we're there. I just thought it might be fun, having met them." Sapphie held up her hands. "You don't have to come if you don't want to."

She hadn't been able to forget about J.B. since coming home from Antigua. Not a day had passed that she hadn't thought about him, relived their time together or wondered what he was doing. Had he thought about her, too, or had he forgotten her the minute he'd left the resort?

She'd even begun reading the Ice Cats' blog, hoping to see him mentioned. She'd wanted to see if he was the same in his normal life as he was on holiday. Was he genuinely the nice guy he'd seemed? Or was he like the other professional athletes she'd heard about?

Unfortunately the hockey media went on hiatus over the summer. And all she'd learned from social media was that he was as sexy in a tux as he was in his swim shorts.

Over the past month regular blog posts had begun again, but any mentions of J.B. had been solely to do with his preparation for the new season.

Perhaps if she saw him again, away from the idyllic setting where they'd met, she'd get him out of her head.

Before she could change her mind she said, "You're right. I should give hockey a try."

"Are you sure? You don't have to."

"As you say, J.B. won't know I'm there. Besides, I would like to see a hockey game."

"Okay, great. I can't wait."

Issy refreshed their drinks. "Are you ready for the next episode?"

"Definitely." Sapphie settled back on the sofa,

giving Issy a strange look. "Seriously? Buttered popcorn and hummus? Eww."

"Don't knock it until you try it."

"No, thanks. That looks gross."

"I can't get enough of anything dipped in hummus. Strawberries, melon, even cheese."

Sapphie wrinkled her nose. "No wonder you feel sick. Your poor stomach doesn't know what's hit it. The last time I heard anything that weird was when my PA was pregnant and she craved pickles dipped in peanut butter. Yuck."

"That's disgust..." Issy's voice trailed off as her friend's words sank in. "Pregnant?"

Why hadn't that occurred to her before?

"Yes, last year. She had a baby girl—" Sapphie stopped. "You can't be pregnant. Can you?"

"Of course not." Issy gave a shaky laugh. "It was one night."

"And you were sensible about protection."

"But...the condom split."

"That's happened to me before. Enough that I always use the pill as double protection."

"So it should be okay, right?" Issy didn't feel reassured.

"Yes. I'm sure this is all to do with those disgusting sandwiches at the airport."

A terrible thought occurred to her. "Food poisoning could have affected the pill. I was ill for almost a week. Can sperm live that long?"

Sapphie got out her cell. "One way to find out."

She tapped the screen then looked up, her expression apologetic. "Damn it."

Issy's heart sank. "Oh, my God. I *could* be pregnant?"

"It's a *possibility.*"

"What am I going to do? This wasn't supposed to happen." Issy stared horrified at her flat stomach, as if it would suddenly start growing. "I knew I shouldn't have made an exception with J.B."

"Stop." Sapphie sliced her hand through the air. "You don't know anything definitely, so don't borrow trouble. We'll go to the drugstore and buy a pregnancy kit."

"I can't do that." Issy jumped up and began to pace. "What if someone from the school sees me? Or one of the parents?"

"Okay, I'll buy one."

"But they know you're my friend. What if they make the connection?" Hysteria bubbled up inside her. "Farlingdale's morality clause is so strict."

"Whoa. Easy." Sapphie put her hands on Issy's shoulders. "I'll drive to a store several towns away." She grabbed her purse and headed for the door. "I won't be long."

While Sapphie was gone, Issy kept busy by cleaning up. Unfortunately it didn't stop her from thinking. She gave up and sank down onto the sofa, dropping her head into her hands.

It wasn't fair. She'd been so careful. She hadn't been drunk; she hadn't forgotten protection. She wasn't like her parents or her sister. And yet, the result had been the same.

Tears streamed down her cheeks. Forget the promotion. If she was pregnant, she'd lose her job. Without her job, her carefully planned life would fall apart. Everything she'd worked so hard to build for herself...

By the time Sapphie returned, Issy was a mess.

Her friend dumped the bags on the closest table and moved to sit beside Issy, putting her arm around her. "It'll be okay," Sapphie said repeatedly as Issy sobbed.

Eventually, Issy dried her eyes and blew her nose. "I'm sorry."

"No need to apologize. You're not feeling well and this has been a shock." Sapphie stood and brought the bags over. "You still don't know for sure that you're pregnant. You could be worrying over nothing."

Issy didn't think so. "Did you buy out the store?"

Her friend smiled ruefully. "I wasn't sure which kit was the best, so I got one of each. And don't worry. I went to three different drugstores in three different towns."

As she lined up the boxes on the coffee table, Issy stared at them helplessly, overwhelmed. "What am I supposed to do?"

"Don't you just pee on a stick? But...we could be smart and read the instructions."

Issy managed a half smile.

They each picked up a pack, opened it and pulled out the thick pamphlet of directions. The devices and the way they showed the results were all slightly different, but they worked the same way.

"It says the best time to test is in the morning," Sapphie said.

Issy shook her head. "I can't wait that long. I have to know now."

"Sweetie, I know it's hard, but you need an accurate result, not just an answer."

"That's hours away. I could do one and see what it says, then do another in the morning to be sure."

"How will that help? A false reading—positive or negative—is no good to you."

"I suppose so. But it's still a long time and I won't be able to sleep."

"We'll pull a *Pride and Prejudice* all-nighter and watch as many as we can, until we either fall asleep or the sun comes up."

Issy hugged her. Sapphie always stepped up and made things better. "But you don't have to do it with me."

"Sure I do." Sapphie held up one remaining bag. "Did I mention I also brought ice cream? Mint chocolate-chip, strawberry cheesecake and cookie dough. All your favorites."

"You're the best."

"Serve up, while I put these kits in the bathroom. Out of sight, hopefully out of mind." Sapphie gathered up the boxes. "I can't wait. Still to come...Colin Firth in a wet shirt."

Issy gave a theatrical, lovelorn sigh. "I think we should watch that particularly closely to ensure it's suitable for my class. Don't you?"

"Definitely. We should probably review it several times to make sure we don't miss anything inappropriate."

Issy's smile faded when Sapphie headed to the bathroom. As she got out bowls, she tried to quiet her fears. No point panicking until she knew for sure there was anything to panic about. Easier said than done when the consequences of being pregnant were so severe.

The two friends finished the TV series then giggled their way through the silliness of *Bride and Prejudice*, the Bollywood version. Sapphie fell asleep halfway through the Keira Knightley and Matthew Macfadyen film. Issy sneaked a plate of seven-layer dip as she watched to the end. Her eyelids drooped during the Olivier and Garson movie, finally giving in to sleep as Mr. Darcy proposed in the garden.

Despite her assertions otherwise, Issy slept dreamlessly, waking only when she heard Sapphie moving around. The smell of brewing coffee made her stomach roil and she sat up quickly, breathing through her mouth and hoping she wouldn't throw up.

"You look green." Sapphie gave her a glass of orange juice. "Feeling sick again?"

Issy nodded. "It's okay. It'll pass. I ate too much spicy food late last night."

"Of course." Sapphie didn't say what they were both thinking.

Issy sipped her juice. Now that the moment of truth had come, she was strangely reticent.

Sapphie hugged her. "Whatever the result, you won't go through this alone."

"Thank you." That was one thing she could rely on without question.

"Okay. Let's get this over with." Issy rose slowly. As she walked to the bathroom, her steps grew more purposeful. She stopped in the doorway. "Wish me luck."

CHAPTER SIX

TWO PINK LINES. Two blue lines. A pink + and a blue +. A freaking smiley face.

Last, but not least, the damning word in black and white. Pregnant.

With a trembling hand, Issy added the final test device to the array of white strips and gizmos in front of her on the bathroom floor and sat back on her heels. Not a single negative among them.

Although her eyes burned, the tears didn't fall.

What a mess.

All because of one night. A single, lousy night.

Not a *lousy* night. The best night of her life.

Still, she'd mortgaged her future, everything she'd fought so hard for over the past twelve years, for that one amazing night. And she'd done it intentionally. Even though she'd known it could be a mistake, she'd assumed she'd stacked the odds enough in her favor to escape the consequences. The costliest assumption she'd ever made.

A knock on the bathroom door interrupted her thoughts.

"Can I come in?" Sapphie asked.

"Sure. Join the party." Issy's attempt at humor fell flat.

Sapphie opened the door and came to sit next to her on the floor. "Are you okay?"

"Peachy." Issy waved her hand at the devices. "The jury reached a unanimous verdict."

"I'm sorry." Her friend looked miserable. "It's my fault."

"Don't be silly." Issy swept the used tests into a plastic bag.

"You'd never have got together with J.B. if I hadn't pushed you."

"I'm a big girl." Issy jabbed her thumb against her chest. "I make my own decisions."

"But I forced you beyond what you were comfortable with."

"I *chose* to sleep with J.B." Issy smiled sadly. "For once, I wanted to walk on the wild side. I should've known it would come back to bite me on the butt."

"It's not fair. You were really unlucky."

"How many times have I heard that?" Issy's lips twisted. "My parents and sister will laugh when they hear I've been hoisted by my own petard. Rosabelle always said karma was a bitch and I'd get mine for being 'so all-fired holier than thou.'"

"Rosa was dumb enough to believe the high school quarterback when he said they didn't need protection." Sapphie took a calming breath. "Anyway, she's changed her tune since she had to become responsible for your parents. And Tinka started acting out. Rosa's finally begun to appreciate everything you did for her."

The sisters had grown closer in recent years. Close enough to avoid a triumphant I-told-you-so? Issy doubted it. "The fact remains. I followed the family tradition and got caught."

"You did your best to prevent this happening."

"As our pastor used to say—the best protection is abstinence."

Sapphie snorted. "The one caught giving naked dictation to the church secretary?"

"Just because he didn't practice what he preached doesn't mean he was wrong."

"Doesn't mean you were wrong, either."

"Even though it's turned into a disaster, I don't regret that night with J.B.," Issy admitted.

Sapphie hugged her. "It's not a disaster. It wasn't in your plan and it seems like the end of the world, but you'll get through this. You're a strong, smart woman."

Issy didn't feel strong or smart. "I wasn't supposed to get pregnant until I was married and everything in my life was as stable and secure for a child as I could make it."

"We both know things never happen when we want them to." Sapphie stood and grabbed the bag. "While I toss this in the garbage, you get cleaned up and prepare for a day of action-planning. You have decisions to make and I'm really good at project management."

"How many accidentally pregnant women have you project-managed recently?"

She shot Issy a stern look. "The process of dealing with an issue is the same, whether it's making a brand more profitable, a department more efficient or a dear, pregnant friend feel calmer."

"I don't see how."

"You don't need to. Leave it to me." Sapphie pulled her to her feet. "Now wash your face and get your backside in gear."

"Jeez, you're bossy... Thank you."

"You'd do the same for me."

"Like you'd be caught after one night."

"You never know. The important thing is we stand together, no matter what."

"The awesome twosome," they said together as they fist-bumped.

"You have five minutes," Sapphie warned before leaving the bathroom.

Issy was out in three.

Feeling as though the walls were closing in on her, she went to stand on the balcony. The sun warmed her face, though the crisp edge to the breeze signaled fall was coming. Issy breathed deeply, letting the smell of cut grass soothe her jagged nerves.

"We'll work out here." Sapphie set a tray laden

with drinks and snacks on a small ironwork table and then sat.

"Now we know why I've been craving hummus and seven-layer dip."

"At least your taste buds will return to normal at some point." Sapphie took a legal pad and red pen off the tray.

"They're the only thing that will."

"Stop that. No miserable thoughts. You need a positive attitude."

"All right." Issy sighed. "Do your worst."

"That's positive?"

"It's the best I can do right now."

Sapphie arched an eyebrow but didn't press. "Let's begin." She wrote on the pad. "First on the list is an appointment with the doctor."

"I know the drill from when Rosa was expecting Tinka. At least 'no alcohol' won't be a problem." Issy bit her lip. "Do you think it's safe to use my gynecologist? The last thing I need is for someone from school to see me at her office."

"If you like and trust her, stick with her. You could be there for any number of reasons."

"I suppose so." Issy sipped her juice. "What's next?"

"Informing the school, your family and J.B. Not necessarily in that order."

Her stomach tightened. "I'm not looking forward to those conversations."

"I know. Remember, you don't have to say anything right away."

"I don't?"

"It's your news. You decide who you tell and when. Your parents certainly don't need to know now. They've shown zero interest in your life since you left and won't be any help."

"That's a no-brainer. But I'm not looking forward to telling Rosa."

"I suspect she'll be more supportive than you think. Feel her out next time you speak and if you don't feel comfortable, hold off until you're ready."

It sounded so simple when Sapphie put it that way. "Unfortunately, I'll have to tell Farlingdale Academy as soon as possible, since it'll affect my classes and they'll need to find a replacement."

"Not so fast." Sapphie held up her pen. "You don't owe them anything."

"They're my employer."

"Will that stop them getting rid of you when they find out you're pregnant?"

The ultraconservative board of trustees would never allow a single mother on their staff. "I have to give them a semester's notice as part of my contract."

"The notice period won't matter. They'll fire you on the spot, based on that stupid morality clause."

"I can't hide my pregnancy from them forever."

"But you don't have to tell them *now*. Get as much salary out of them as you can. Don't forget, you won't be able to work right before and right after the baby's born."

Issy definitely needed the money. Buying this apartment had seriously depleted her savings. She could get by, but not for long. "You'd better add 'find a job' to the list. Although who'll hire a pregnant woman?"

"Not everyone is as straitlaced as Farlingdale. With your track record, you'll find another position quickly. If not, substitute teach or tutor."

She'd rather have the stability of a permanent job, but part-time work was better than none. "That would give me more flexibility."

They discussed how and when to inform Farlingdale, and what Issy could do in the interim to cushion the blow of being fired. Sapphie offered to help financially, but Issy didn't want to borrow from her friend.

She'd try to delay informing the school until Thanksgiving. She'd be wearing a lot of loose clothes in October and November. Meanwhile, she'd investigate employment possibilities and create a résumé.

Finally, there was only one topic left: J.B.

"I should tell him. But I can't help thinking that it's not fair to ruin his life, too."

"You're having a baby," Sapphie said drily. "That's hardly ruining anybody's life."

"But he was clear about not wanting to be tied down. You can't have anything more restricting than a child."

"J.B. still has a right to know. He can then decide how involved or committed he wants to be, if at all. If you don't tell him and he finds out, he'll be angry."

"But I'd be keeping it from him because I doubt he'd want to know."

"What he wants right now and what may happen in the future are two different things. At some point he may change his mind and want children. If you kept it from him, he might try to sue you for custody."

Issy wasn't sure how she felt about the new life growing inside her. Yet Sapphie's words spurred a fierce protective instinct. This was *her* baby. No one would take *her* child from her. Least of all someone who considered them a millstone around his neck.

"Let him try."

"The thing is, you don't know how he'll react. He could say he wants nothing to do with either of you."

"Fine. I don't need him, anyway."

"Or he may want to be part of your lives. This isn't the concept of a baby. It's the real deal. He may feel differently once he knows you're carrying his child."

Issy couldn't see that happening. "I don't want J.B. in my life because it's the right thing to do. No father is better than a bad one."

Sapphie didn't argue. "Unfortunately that doesn't mean you can keep this from him."

"I know." Issy lost her appetite. "That'll be a fun conversation—not."

"On the upside, you can control the timing of that conversation. There's no reason why you have to tell him now, or even before the baby's born."

Issy suspected the longer she delayed, the harder it would be. "Maybe I should bite the bullet and get it over with. It's not like I don't know where to find him."

Sapphie snapped her fingers. "I'll call Taylor and arrange for us to bump into J.B. at the preseason game. We'll gauge J.B.'s reaction to seeing you again and that'll help us decide how to play this. Okay?"

Issy's heart leaped at the thought of seeing J.B. again. "Yes."

"Good. The game's on the twenty-third, so we have two weeks to figure out how to make this meeting appear casual and unplanned."

Then Issy would know whether J.B. was the man she hoped he might be or the man she was very much afraid he really was.

THE PUCK LAY on the ice behind the goaltender's leg.

While the Cats battled the Islanders' D-men and poked at the netminder's pads, J.B. leaned over the melee and pushed the puck home with the heel of his stick.

The red light flashed, the horn sounded and the fans' goal chant began.

J.B. shot his arms into the air and roared, "Freakin' A!"

His line-mates swarmed him, clapping him on the back and shoulder.

Mad Dog grabbed him in a bear hug. "That's what I'm talking about."

"Sneaky move, kid." Bad Boy knocked helmets with him. "Hope you've got a few more of those up your sleeve this season."

"I'm just getting started, old man." J.B. grinned, then skated over to the bench for a victory pass, slapping gloves with his teammates before heading through the gate to sit.

He puffed out a relieved breath. His first game back and he'd had a hard time getting his legs moving. Even though he'd been skating short shifts, each one had been like plowing through molasses. He'd kept trying to force his body to respond quicker, but with his muscles burning and nothing left in the tank, he'd been sucking major wind by the end of the first and second periods. At least he'd got the scoring monkey off his back. Hopefully things would be better next game.

"Great job." Patrick "Paddy" Mullroney, who was playing second line tonight, bumped his shoulder. "I thought we weren't going to break their new goaltender again. He's on fire right now. Five wins out of five."

"Yeah. Let's see how he performs when the games mean something."

Kenny slid next to J.B. on the bench. "Man, I'm glad we weren't shut out tonight. Two games in a row with no score would have been brutal."

"We're all a little slow getting our skates under us." Paddy leaned on his stick, not taking his eyes off the play. "Happens when you go deep in the postseason. Your body doesn't get enough time to recover a Cup hangover."

"We just need to work through it and make sure we're smart about downtime so we can go the distance again." J.B. squirted water into his mouth. He had to be extra careful. He couldn't afford an off year. For sure he couldn't afford to be plagued with injuries.

"Last minute of play in the period."

J.B. relaxed as he watched the final seconds of the game tick away, knowing Ike would ensure the score held up. The Cats' veteran goaltender had been in the zone all night. Nothing was getting through him.

Sure enough, the horn blared for the end of the

game, with no further scoring. The team poured over the boards to congratulate Ike.

J.B. touched helmets with the goaltender. "Nice game."

"Nice goal," Ike replied as they skated back to the gate. "Could have used you scoring earlier, though, to take the pressure off me."

"Aww. Are you getting too old to handle the young bucks shooting at you?"

Ike swore at him. "These preseason games used to be a breeze when I started playing. Guys took their time to bed in and learn the league. Now every new kid in the show has to prove themselves from day one."

"I hear you." J.B. had already started looking over his shoulder. He still had plenty of good years left in him, but there was always someone gunning for his place in the lineup. Just like when he'd come up from the minors at eighteen, ready and eager to pick off an older, slower guy. "We've got a few days off before the next game and I plan to take it real easy."

"After you hit the clubs tonight," Ike said drily.

"You're just jealous."

The goaltender laughed. "Not even close. I'm going home to my lovely fiancée."

As much as J.B. liked Tracy and was pleased she and Ike had finally got together, he wasn't the least bit envious. He wasn't ready for the whole pipe, slippers and going-home-to-one-woman-every-night thing. Not when he had New York on his doorstep. He could take his pick—blonde, brunette or redhead, tall or short, thin or curvy.

"Ike, second star. Larocque, first star." One of the trainers pulled them aside and made them wait in the tunnel for the official call of the night's three stars of the game as chosen by the attending media.

J.B. skated out when his name was announced and raised his stick in salute. Then he searched out a teenage boy who'd sat behind the bench with his girlfriend, and tossed him a puck. The kid gave it to the pretty gal and earned himself a smooch. J.B. grinned, then gave his stick to a cute little girl with dark ringlets, blue eyes and a precocious grin. Damn, but she reminded him of Bella.

Where the hell had that come from?

J.B. shook his head sharply, as if that would get her out of his head.

"You okay?" Ike studied him. "That hit from behind in the second period was late and you landed against the boards hard."

"It was a bonehead play, but I'm okay." The Islander defenseman had been given a game misconduct for the dangerous check and had been ejected.

"Are you sure? The last thing you or the team needs is concussion problems."

"I'm fine." He squinted at the goaltender. "Although...do you always have two heads?"

Ike cuffed him on the back of his helmet. "One day, you'll have to grow up."

"Maybe when I'm as ancient as you." He ducked out of Ike's reach.

"You'll get yours, bro, and I'll enjoy watching."

"From your bath chair."

The two of them continued to exchange insults as they walked to the locker room. Along the way, J.B. was congratulated by the Ice Cats' back-room staff.

The buzz lasted through his shower and his teammates' razzing. J.B. humbly accepted the player's award for being the hardest-working player on the ice—a headband with black-and-white cat ears—which he dutifully wore during the postgame interviews. He was looking forward to dinner with the guys, followed by closing down his favorite club in the city.

"First round's on you." Paddy punched his shoulder. "You'll have to open an account if you play like that this season."

"And leave a hefty deposit." J.B. took off the cat ears and placed them carefully in his locker, ready to award next game. "With luck, there'll be plenty more nights like tonight."

Paddy snorted. "Luck, my ass. Hard work's the only thing that brings success."

For a guy who looked like an Irishman and had such an Irish-sounding name, Patrick Mullroney was a real grouse when it came to anything to do with superstition.

"Yeah, yeah." He wouldn't let the guys down again. They'd be lifting the Cup next June. He'd make sure of it.

Kenny and Mad Dog sauntered over.

Kenny hitched his thumb at J.B. "The only thing this man works hard at is increasing the notches on his headboard."

"Hey. I put in my hours at the gym and on the ice," J.B. protested.

Mad Dog nodded. "You also put in your hours at the bar and on the dance floor. It's a good job you don't need much sleep. Must be those farmer genes."

"They've got to be good for something." J.B. laughed. "Anyway, all work and no play would make Jean-Baptiste a very dull guy."

"That would be bad." Kenny slung his duffel over his shoulder. "So, are we going to stand around yakking or get that drink you owe us?"

J.B. shrugged into his jacket and grabbed his own bag. "I'm ready."

Taylor and Paddy chorused their approval.

The teammates were heading out of the locker room when Mad Dog's phone rang.

He frowned at the number. "You guys go ahead. I've got to take this."

"I'll wait with you." J.B. waved the others on. "Make it quick. I could murder a plate of quesadillas."

Mad Dog answered. "Hey. How are you?" From his tone, the caller had to be female and someone he liked.

"You're kidding," Mad Dog said. "Where are you? Sure, I'm up for that." He listened then shot J.B. a look. "I'll ask." He put his phone against his thigh to muffle their conversation. "That's Sapphire. She and Bella are at the arena. They've been watching the game. Do you want to say hi?"

Bella. Here. Now.

J.B.'s heart beat hard against his ribs. Part of him wanted to rush out to see her. The other part was more circumspect. They'd said everything they'd needed to say in Antigua.

"Come on, man. It's just hello, not a freaking marriage proposal," Mad Dog said. "If you're not up for it, I'll tell them you've got other plans."

J.B.'s stomach twisted at the thought that he'd miss this chance to see Bella. There was his answer.

"I'm cool with seeing them."

Mad Dog nodded approvingly and gave Sapphire directions to the lower levels of the arena. "I'll get security to let you down here. We'll meet you by the elevator and give you a backstage tour."

As the two of them sauntered over to the bank

of elevators, J.B. said, "I thought you hadn't spoken to Sapphie since we got back."

"I never said that. I said I hadn't *met up* with her. She's been traveling a lot. We've emailed, texted and had a couple of phone calls." Mad Dog lifted his hands in a what-can-you-do gesture.

J.B. wouldn't ask if Bella's name had come up. If she'd asked about him.

The moment the doors opened J.B.'s gaze was drawn to Bella. When she stepped out of the elevator, his pulse raced like he was on a short-handed breakaway.

Man, she looked good. He'd thought she was hot in that polka-dot bikini and those flirty dresses, but she was sizzling in a curve-hugging red sweater and black jeans tucked into tall suede boots that emphasized her legs. Her cheeks had a healthy glow from the cool temperatures of the arena.

Her blue eyes lit up as she saw him. Then the light faded and she gave off the same uptight vibe as the first time he'd seen her.

What was with that? It wasn't like they hadn't danced together or kissed. She'd come apart in his arms—not once, but four freaking times— and all he got was a polite smile and a nod hello? Seriously?

He pulled himself up short, disgusted at the direction of his thoughts. He shouldn't be disappointed—he knew what the rules were. What happened in Antigua...

"Hey," J.B. said coolly. "Welcome."

"Hi," Bella said a little stiffly. "Congratulations on your win."

"Thanks."

"Great to be here. Nice goal." Sapphie stepped forward and hugged J.B. before going over to Mad Dog and planting a kiss on his mouth. "Looking good, hot stuff."

"Back at you, pretty lady." His friend grinned and tucked Sapphie's arm in his. "Are you ready for your exclusive behind-the-scenes tour?"

"Definitely. Especially the locker room. Will we have to shield our delicate eyes from your teammates in various states of undress?" Sapphie asked hopefully. "I know you guys favor those itty-bitty towels and I don't want to shock Bella."

Bella blushed but didn't respond to the teasing.

"There won't be any naked players." Taylor shook his head. "There won't be anyone left in the locker room but the equipment guys and they do their job fully clothed."

"Spoilsport. I'll try to contain my disappointment." Sapphie gave a theatrical sigh. "At least we've got actual players as our guides."

"You should be honored. People pay a fortune for this privilege."

"Lead on."

Mad Dog and Sapphie strolled ahead, arm in

arm, laughing and talking as if they'd just seen each other on the beach yesterday not three months ago.

J.B. and Bella followed behind, not speaking. They were back to square one. It would have been better if he'd gone to the restaurant and left Taylor behind. Then J.B. could've kept his happy memory of Bella, not this strained silence.

He was tempted not to say a word unless she spoke first, but knew that was childish. Instead he played host, pointing out the features of the arena.

Bella seemed genuinely interested. She asked questions and was keen to see everything, including stepping out onto the ice to get a feel for what that was like. She held on to his arm when they walked out to center ice. By the time they headed back through the tunnel, she'd loosened up enough that they could have a normal conversation.

"What did you make of your first game?" he asked.

"I'm not sure I understood what was happening, but it was fast paced and exciting. I think I'm hooked." Becca smiled. "You played well."

"Thanks. I did okay." Jeez. Next he'd be scuffing his toe and blushing. "It was good to get back on the ice and score."

"Did it erase the bad memory of your last game?"

He was surprised she'd remembered. "That

memory won't ever go away, but I don't let it rule me. If I did, I'd probably never score again. So I put it behind me and move on."

"I wish I could do that."

Before he could ask what she meant, one of the trainers called out, "Hey, Larocque. Got your goal puck here."

"Thanks." J.B. caught the biscuit Steve tossed him, then offered it to Bella. "Would you like this?"

Sapphie came up beside them. "You should sign it." She rummaged in her purse and pulled out a silver Sharpie.

J.B. scrawled his name on the back of the puck and gave it to Bella. "There you go."

"Are you sure you don't want to keep it?"

"I'd rather you had it, as a souvenir of your first game and the moment hockey seduced you into becoming a fan."

Her cheeks coloured. "That's lovely. Thank you."

"My pleasure."

This time the look they shared was definitely heated, if a little hesitant.

Mad Dog broke into the moment. "This is the locker room. Where the magic happens and ordinary guys—"

"Ordinary?" J.B. interjected. "Speak for yourself, bro."

Taylor rolled his eyes and continued. "—turn into fearsome warriors of the ice."

"Is this like Superman's phone booth?" Bella asked.

"I like to think of it more like Batman's cave," J.B. replied, enjoying her teasing tone.

"Because Batman had cooler toys." She nodded her understanding.

Maybe she wasn't so different from the Bella he'd known in the Caribbean, after all. Unlike most of the women he knew, she was shy and needed tempting out of her shell. But once she appeared, she was worth the effort. Suddenly, J.B. didn't want to let her go without knowing he'd see her again.

He caught Bella's arm and held her back, letting Taylor and Sapphie walk ahead of them into the locker room. "Do you want to get dinner sometime? Nothing fancy, no strings."

Bella looked startled and paused, considering.

Unreasonably disappointed that she didn't respond enthusiastically right away, he added, "I won't be offended if you'd prefer not to."

"Dinner would be nice. Weekends are better for me now that school has started."

"Okay, good. How about Saturday night?"

"This Saturday?"

"We don't play again until Monday, so it's a good night for me."

"Uh, yes. I'm free. What time?"

"I could pick you up at seven."

She bit her lip. "It would be better if I could meet you somewhere."

For a moment J.B. wondered if his impulsive invitation had been a mistake. Was this all going to be too difficult?

Then she smiled ruefully. "Nothing personal. I don't like being dependent on anyone else to get home. I spent too many years scared out of my skin by my dad driving after too many drinks."

Her honesty eased his concern. He liked that there was no artifice with Bella. She was upfront and didn't play games. "No problem. Where would you like to eat?"

"As long as the food's not too spicy, I'm good with wherever you choose."

"There's a great steak house down by the river in Weehawken."

"That sounds perfect."

Bella opened her mouth to say something else, but Sapphie stuck her head out of the locker room.

"Come on, you guys. You're missing all the fun."

J.B. and Bella exchanged amused looks and followed her inside.

Not long after, the women went home, and J.B. and Mad Dog headed to the restaurant.

As the steaming platters were delivered to the long table, J.B. looked around at the guys. Over the past few years a number of players had married. The ones he was closest to—Bad Boy, Ike and Tru—had shown him that settling down wasn't such a bad thing.

But it wasn't for him. Not yet, anyway. Relationships took work and time and energy. This year would be a tough one, both mentally and physically, so he wanted to focus his efforts on hockey, not anything personal. At least until he'd lifted the Cup again. He drained his beer.

If there was a woman he could have a future with, it would be Bella. It was a shame he'd met her now instead of in a couple of years.

J.B.'s gut churned. He wasn't prepared to make a commitment, so he should be happy that Bella might get what she wanted with someone else. Just as she'd be happy for him to win the Cup.

At that moment, Lise, the new queen of the puck bunnies, and her entourage entered the private dining room. The three women were carbon copies of one another with their long, sleek, blond hair, figure-hugging Ice Cats T-shirts and skintight blue jeans tucked into spike-heeled boots. They walked around the table, greeting the players.

He and Lise had got together early in his career. There hadn't been any chemistry between them, so he knew she wouldn't be looking for a repeat performance tonight, despite his winning goal. But one of the other two was bound to want to end the evening with him.

Sure enough, Lise congratulated him warmly and moved on to Paddy.

Susie, the newest recruit, trailed her hand across his shoulder before leaning down and murmuring in his ear, "Want to give me a private performance of those slick moves?"

Bella was forgotten as J.B. pulled Susie onto his lap. "Honey, you ain't seen nothing yet."

"WHAT A SURPRISE to find you at Grey's, Miss Brandine."

As if Issy wasn't intimidated enough by walking through the imposing glass doors of the fancy restaurant J.B. had suggested, she had to bump into the parents of one of her pupils. Worse, it had to be the woman who always made Issy feel inferior.

Refusing to reveal how much Mrs. Allardyce had knocked her already shaky confidence, Issy did what she'd always done and acted as though she belonged. Hoping her voice sounded cool, she said, "Nice to see you. Do you dine here often?"

"We're regulars. We know the owner, Grey." The elegant blonde gave Issy's outfit a critical once-over. "Cute dress. You're lucky you're young enough to get away with that style and color."

Issy resisted the urge to wipe her damp palms down the pencil skirt of her pink wiggle dress at the backhanded compliment. "Thank you."

"I wouldn't have thought a Farlingdale teacher would eat at Grey's."

Unable to think of a polite way to respond, Issy was relieved to see J.B. rushing up to the restaurant door. "Please excuse me—my friend's here. Have a lovely evening."

Mrs. Allardyce nodded sharply. "Enjoy your meal."

"Sorry I'm late." J.B. kissed her cheek. "I had to do a PR thing for the Cats and it ran over. I hope you haven't been waiting long."

"I only just got here myself."

The maître d' greeted J.B. like an old friend and showed them to their table by the floor-to-ceiling windows. Issy noticed J.B. slipped him a pair of tickets before he left. She couldn't help smiling when the Allardyces were led to the table next to them.

"Who's the battle-ax giving us the evil eye?" J.B. asked once they'd ordered their drinks.

She explained the connection. "Her daughter's a sweetheart. A pleasure to teach."

"I doubt there's much about the mother that's a pleasure." He leaned forward, lowering his voice. "Her husband probably agrees with us."

Issy bit her lip to hold back a laugh. "He's a really nice guy. Whenever I meet them, I wonder why they're together."

"Probably too expensive to divorce her." J.B. picked up his menu. "Let's talk about something more pleasant or you'll have indigestion before you've eaten a bite."

"That would be a shame when I've been looking forward to eating one of Grey's famous steaks all week." She'd been concerned that the queasiness she'd been suffering would be a problem, but it had faded over the past few days. Instead she was always ravenous.

"I'm going 18-ounce rib eye, rare, with all the trimmings." J.B. patted his flat stomach. "I've earned it after a bear of a week at practice. Can't waste away."

"I couldn't manage that much meat if I'd had a bear of a *month* at practice." Issy laughed and opened her menu. "There's no fear I'll waste away."

"You're perfectly proportioned as you are."

Her cheeks warmed. Unsure how to respond, she focused on the menu and stifled a gasp. The prices made her eyes water. The appetizers alone cost more than any meal she'd ever ordered.

Any thoughts of offering to pay half the check vanished.

As if he'd read her mind, J.B. said, "Order whatever you like. I chose the restaurant, so I foot the bill."

"Thank you. That's very generous."

"You're doing me a favor. I hate to eat alone and you've given me the excuse I needed to come here."

She smiled wryly. "I'm sure there are plenty of women who'd have accompanied you."

"Yeah." J.B.'s grin faded. "But they'd expect something in return. Whereas we both know where we stand, so I can enjoy a great meal, in great company, without worrying about hidden agendas."

"When you put it like that…make mine a filet, medium-rare, with a fully loaded baked potato and some creamed spinach."

Despite her light retort, guilt tugged at Issy. She'd certainly had an ulterior motive in agreeing to meet J.B. for dinner…

Telling him about the baby in a public place might temper his reaction.

J.B.'s voice broke into her thoughts. "Is everything okay?"

"I was expecting something a little more… casual," she admitted. "Which is silly, given Grey's reputation."

"We can go somewhere else. But you'll miss out on one of the best meals you'll ever eat."

"I know."

"Don't worry about the other diners. They may think they're special because they're rich or famous, but they put their pants on one leg at a time."

Once again he'd read her mind. How was that possible? She couldn't imagine J.B. feeling awkward; he was so sure of himself. "I suppose so."

"Trust me, I get it. My first season up from the minors I felt like I didn't belong. Even though I was already earning more than my parents will probably see in their lifetime, I was still just a farm boy from Nowhere, Canada." He gave her a self-deprecating smile. "Probably why I over-compensated and was a total jerk."

"I can't believe that." Though from what she'd read on the internet, she knew it was true.

"I promise I'm almost grown-up and mature now."

"I'm sure you are…most of the time."

J.B. laughed.

The waiter arrived to refresh their drinks and take their order.

Once he'd gone, J.B. asked, "What have you been up to since Antigua?"

He couldn't know what a loaded question that was.

Issy dropped a slice of lime into her sparkling water to buy a little time. She had to lay the groundwork over dinner for her big revelation. Starting with how everything had gone wrong. "For the first week, not very much. I was really sick on the flight home. Food poisoning, I think."

"Man, that sucks." J.B. frowned. "Was it something you ate at the resort?"

"I think it was a sandwich at the airport." She forced a light tone. "Once I was better, I did those things I put off during the school year—redecorating my apartment and going home for a visit."

He winced. "How did that go?"

"The same as always. Nothing changes, except everyone's a little older."

"I know that feeling. I went home, too." He raised his glass and clinked it against hers. "Families—can't live with them, can't bury them in the backyard."

Issy laughed. "Especially as I don't have a backyard."

As dinner progressed, in many ways, it was as if there had been no time apart since Antigua. Under the starry tropical sky, they'd learned a lot about each other's pasts and pain. Here, they shared things people talked about on first dates—movies, music, books and food. Their disagreements were good-natured and there was a lot of banter.

Issy shouldn't have been surprised that the attraction was still there. She'd secretly hoped it would be; that it hadn't merely been a function of the sultry Caribbean nights. She'd also hoped it wouldn't, because it might be easier to tell him her news if her body didn't hum with pleasure every time their fingers brushed.

After dessert, J.B. suggested they take a walk along the riverfront.

They strolled the tree-lined, brickwork path

along the banks of the Hudson. Across the water, they could see the lights of Manhattan.

Under other circumstances, it would have been romantic.

Issy's guilt deepened. At least they weren't holding hands. Although J.B.'s hand rested at the small of her back.

She didn't want to spoil the evening. She knew she was being a coward, but it was a shame to ruin things. It wasn't as if the baby was due imminently. Another day or two wouldn't hurt.

Or would it?

"Penny for your thoughts."

Her gaze shot up to meet his. There was nothing but mild curiosity in his dark eyes.

"Oh...they're not that important," she hedged.

"You look like you're doing some pretty heavy-duty thinking there." He pulled a handful of change out of his pants' pocket. "I can up the ante to a dime or even a quarter."

His teasing smile only made her feel worse. "Really, it's nothing you want to know about."

He quirked an eyebrow. "Now you have me intrigued."

Her laugh was a little shaky. "You'll be disappointed, trust me."

"Let me make up my own mind on that."

Damn it. She should have made something up. School worries. Decorating worries. Anything.

Instead she'd painted herself into a corner. He wouldn't give up until she told him.

"It's hard to talk about. Personal."

He didn't say anything for a moment. "We shared a lot of personal stuff in Antigua. Why is this any different?"

Her throat ached at his gentle tone and the understanding in his eyes. She had no choice. The time had come to tell him.

"Why don't we sit on the bench over there?" he suggested.

"All right." She sighed inwardly.

No sooner had she sat than all the carefully prepared words she'd come up with during the week vanished.

"I'm pregnant."

CHAPTER SEVEN

DEAFENING SILENCE.

That phrase had always seemed silly, but as Issy waited for J.B. to respond to her announcement, it described the moment perfectly. The air felt thick and heavy. The sky darkened as a cloud passed over the moon. Even the crickets seemed to stop chirping.

Her gut twisted as she watched his expression transform from concerned to stunned to furious. The light in his eyes turned off as if he'd flicked a switch. His lips flattened from a caring smile to a hard line. A muscle twitched in his rigid jaw.

"If that's your idea of a joke, it's not funny." His words were clipped, forced out through gritted teeth.

She swallowed hard. "I'm sorry, but it's not a joke."

"What kind of freaking game are you playing? You can't be pregnant." Just for a second, something flashed in his dark eyes, pleading with her for it not to be true.

"Trust me, I would love to say I'm not, but I am." She struggled to keep her voice calm.

J.B. rose and began pacing as he tried to process the information. He stopped in front of her. "If it's true, then the baby sure as hell can't be mine."

Shocked, Issy jumped up and stood toe-to-toe with him so there would be no doubt about what she was saying. "It most certainly is."

She'd expected him to be unsettled, upset and angry. She'd also expected him to turn those emotions onto her. To blame her. The one thing she hadn't anticipated was being accused of trying to pass off someone else's baby as his.

"How dare you? You know I was practically a virgin when I slept with you."

His lip curled. "So who did you screw next?"

Stung by his cruel words, she spat out, "No one."

"Yeah, right."

Now she was the angry one. "Get over yourself. You weren't *that* good."

"Not what you said the next morning."

"Seriously? You think I was so impressed that I had to rush out and find another man to sleep with right away?"

"I don't give a damn what your excuse is." He shrugged. "We both know the baby can't be mine. We went overboard on protection."

"The condom split." She refrained from adding "you jerk," but only just.

"You said you were on the pill."

"I *was* on the pill. I told you I was sick for a week after I got home. The doctor thinks that weakened the effectiveness."

"A very convenient explanation."

Her jaw dropped. "Not really."

"This was your plan all along, wasn't it? Set me up, get pregnant and then claim paternity so you could get money out of me."

How had she ever thought J.B. might be understanding? Even laughably, in her craziest moments, imagining that he might work with her to figure this thing out?

"You think I not only wanted to get pregnant but I *planned* it?" Her voice rose in pitch with each word. "For your *money*?"

"You wouldn't be the first." Disgust edged his tone. "You won't get a penny from me without a DNA test."

"After everything I told you about my family, you can't believe I'd resort to that." Tears burned, but she refused to let them fall. "I don't need your precious money."

"Great. We're agreed. And whatever the test results, you won't get my ring on your finger."

"As if I'd want to marry you. You're an immature jackass." She laughed bitterly. "You don't need to worry. I know only too well what it's like to have crappy parents."

"Make sure you stick to that story when it comes to signing the legal paperwork."

Disappointed and disgusted—he'd turned out to be the worst kind of arrogant sports star—she'd suddenly had enough of the conversation. "I've done my duty by informing you. If I never see you again, it'll be too soon." She stalked off, head high.

Issy was grateful that the brick path went around the side of the restaurant so she could walk directly to the parking lot. It was hard enough to keep from breaking down without everyone staring at her.

She'd almost made it to her car when she caught her shoe in a rut, snapping the slender heel in two and turning her ankle, making it painful to walk on. She pulled off her ruined shoes, which were her favorite. The icing on a totally crappy evening.

"Do you need help?" J.B. asked over her shoulder.

Damn it. Well, his car *was* parked in the same lot.

"Not from you." She continued to hobble to her car.

He caught up to her and put his arm around her waist for support. "Come on. You're clearly struggling. The last thing you need, in your condition, is to hurt yourself further."

"*Now* you believe I'm pregnant," she snapped, wrenching herself away from him.

"Yeah, just not that I'm the father."

A loud gasp made them both stop.

Even before she turned, Issy knew who'd overheard them.

Sure enough, Mrs. Allardyce stood at the valet station.

So much for keeping the news of her pregnancy quiet until she was ready.

"Don't worry, it's not catching," Issy said as the woman stared at her.

Issy didn't know where the sarcasm came from. She should be begging the woman not to say anything about what she'd heard, not pissing her off further.

It was just that the security she'd worked so hard to achieve and which she'd been so close to achieving had fallen apart. And with it the life she'd dreamed of having for so long. Between J.B. and Mrs. Allardyce, there was no way to put the crushed pieces of her dream back together.

Issy turned, wincing as pain shot through her ankle, and limped to her car.

J.B. held the door open for her. "Will you be okay?"

His loaded question, showing he understood the implications of what had happened, was the final straw.

"I'll be fine. I made my choice and now I have to live with the consequences." When he started to speak, she thrust her hand up to stop him. "Don't worry. I won't bother you again."

Issy pulled her car door from him, slamming it shut, narrowly missing his fingers.

He jumped back as she reversed out of the parking space.

She didn't look in her rearview mirror until after she'd pulled onto the road. J.B. remained standing where she'd left him, staring after her.

"It's his loss," she said aloud. She glanced down at her stomach. "We'll get through this, I promise."

Issy wasn't sure how, but she'd find a way. Her child would never know anything but love and security, and she sure as hell didn't need a father for that.

DID HE HAVE *gullible* tattooed across his forehead?

J.B. slammed his front door. He kicked off his shoes and took the stairs up to his bedroom two at a time, tearing off his jacket as he went.

There had to be a manual for women that read "bat your pretty blue eyes when you tell your sob story and Jean Baptiste Larocque will fall for your plan."

What other explanation could there be for how many times he'd fallen for the same freaking setup? Other than that he was a total idiot. He tossed his jacket on the bed and stripped off the rest of his clothes before pulling on a T-shirt, workout shorts and his Nikes.

He wanted to hit something. No, he wanted to pulverize something.

Grabbing his boxing gloves, he stalked to the in-home gym across from his room. Not for the first time he thanked Ike—whose town house he rented, along with Kenny and Mad Dog—for installing a state-of-the-art fitness center on the second floor. Including a punching bag that hung from a reinforced ceiling bar.

J.B. taped his hands—no way was he dumb enough to damage his most precious tools right before the season started.

He'd been stupid enough to believe tings had been rolling along nicely. Sure, Bella'd had that uptight thing going again, but he'd put that down to nervousness. Once she'd loosened up a little, she'd been the other Bella. And he'd made the mistake of relaxing.

He tugged on his boxing gloves. During J.B.'s rookie season, Bad Boy had taken him along to his fitness boxing sessions with his trainer, Prince, as a way to burn off extra aggression. It hadn't taken long for J.B. to see how much it helped improve his agility, balance and overall conditioning, and he'd taken it up himself. Anything to give him an extra step on the ice and some added spice to his shot.

Tonight, though, pounding the bag was all about relieving anger.

One, two, one. Right, left, right. Over and over. Harder and harder.

He'd barely begun to break a sweat when he acknowledged the truth: the baby had to be his. Bella may not be as innocent or naive as he'd once thought, but he couldn't see her trying to pass off another man's child as his. He swore.

One, one, two, two. Right, right, left, left.

He was going to be a father.

Hellfire and damnation.

Why now? This was supposed to be *his* season. Cup number two. Proof he was one of the elite players. The team was in great shape. With some key acquisitions over the summer, the Cats were faster and stronger. They'd go all the way to the Finals again, only this time they'd bring home the Cup. He felt it deep in his gut.

But J.B. had to do his part and do it well. More importantly, he had to do it consistently. He had to bring his A-game every night. For that, he needed to be in the best shape of his career. That was tough enough when he'd had the whole summer to recover, let alone when he'd come off a grueling Cup run. He'd have to be careful about his body, his fitness and his stress levels.

This was not the time to have to think about a baby or responsibility. Or commitment. Or anything but reaching his goal.

J.B. pummeled the leather bag until his arms and body ached, and his skin was soaked. Finally, he could punch no more and he bent over, gloves on his thighs, his breath rasping.

"I think you killed him." Kenny leaned against the doorjamb of the gym.

"What?" J.B. ripped off his gloves and wiped his face with the back of his taped hands.

"Whoever it is that you were beating the crap out of." His friend frowned. "I don't think I've done anything to warrant that. Not lately, anyway."

Kenny never took anything seriously. He opened the small fridge and tossed J.B. a bottle of cold water. "Who's the unlucky culprit and what have they done?"

J.B. drained half the bottle before answering. "I wasn't punching anyone. Or if I was, it was myself."

"Come again?"

"For being such a dumb ass."

"What have you done this time?"

J.B. wasn't sure why he hesitated. The whole world would know soon enough how Jean-Baptiste Larocque had screwed up again.

"Hold up." Kenny pointed at him. "Weren't you supposed to be seeing the woman you met in Antigua tonight?"

"Yup. Bella."

"I take it the evening didn't go well."

"She's pregnant." It sounded even worse when he said it out loud.

Kenny laughed. When J.B. didn't join in, Kenny sobered. "You're not kidding."

"Wish I was."

"How the hell did that happen?"

"The usual way."

"Funny. What I meant was, you're always so careful."

"I was this time, too. I didn't take account of a split condom and a freaking bout of food poisoning." He explained what Bella had told him.

"Ouch." Kenny grimaced. "Double whammy. And the kid's definitely yours this time?"

Kenny was the one who'd questioned the last woman who'd claimed to be pregnant with J.B.'s child. He'd also uncovered the truth—that she'd been thrown over by the real father and decided to make a quick buck by latching on to J.B.

"I'm sure. Although I'll insist on a DNA test."

"Still, that sucks."

"Yeah."

"I'm not sure there's a way out of this mess."

J.B. nodded at the punch bag. "That's why I was punching Jason." They'd nicknamed the bag after the villain in a series of horror movies who wore a hockey mask. "I'm happy with my life the way it is. I'm twenty-five years old, have enough money to do whatever the hell I want and I don't have to answer to anyone. What's more, I want to keep on enjoying my life while I'm still young enough to have the choice. I'm not ready to be tied down. For sure I'm not ready for formula and diapers. If I have sleepless nights, I want them to be because I'm tearing up the sheets with a hot babe, not pacing the floor with a screaming baby. I'm more than happy to leave the domesticity to my brothers."

His brothers… They'd expect him to man up and do the right thing. His mom would be thrilled, of course, though she'd prefer him to be married to the child's mother. His father would be disappointed—nothing new there.

"Who says you need to be tied down?" Kenny waved his hand dismissively. "You pay child support, see the kid on weekends and carry on living. Hell, if you really want, you can sign away your rights, pay a lump sum to ease your conscience and never have to be involved with Bella or the kid again."

The second option should have sounded like the perfect solution. Instead it sounded cold. Besides, could J.B. know there was a child with his blood in him and not have anything to do with him? He didn't think so. That didn't mean he wanted to do the whole "doting daddy" thing, either.

"I'd have thought you'd be pushing me to step up, given what happened with your dad."

"I don't believe parents should always be together, especially if they don't want to be." Kenny shrugged. "The most important thing is you make a decision you can live with. Otherwise, you'll make everyone involved miserable. Not least, the kid. Has Bella said what she wants?"

"All she said was that she'd done her duty by telling me."

"So she doesn't expect anything. Do you think she'd be amenable to a deal, if you were to make her an offer?"

Amenable? Ha. That's the last thing Bella felt toward him right now. But he knew how important security was to her. Would she listen to something that might help protect her—their—child's future?

"Possibly."

"It's simple, then. Make her an offer she can't refuse. But make sure you also outline your terms clearly."

The front door banged and footsteps thundered up the stairs.

"Sounds like Mad Dog's home early, too." Kenny gave him a look. "Does he know about this?"

"I'm not sure." He couldn't remember his friend's plans. Was he meeting Sapphie?

One look at Taylor's face as he appeared in the doorway of the gym told him that not only did his friend know, he was pissed.

"You jackass." He lunged for J.B. but Kenny grabbed him and held him back.

The best form of defense was offence. "Did your

date end early because Bella went crying to her BFF when I wouldn't play along with her game?"

"Real classy." Taylor shot him a disgusted look as he shook off Kenny. "My date ended early, but not because Bella was crying. The opposite."

"What the hell does that mean?"

"Bella texted to say she'd gone to bed early. That's when Sapphie knew things had gone badly. Bella insisted we didn't need to interrupt our evening, but eventually spilled the whole miserable story." Taylor shook his head. "Sapphie's gunning for you and I don't blame her. I can't believe you'd be such a jerk. You really are lower than whale crap."

"Back off, man," Kenny interjected. "Bella being pregnant isn't great news, but it's hardly J.B.'s fault."

Mad Dog turned on him. "I bet numb nuts here hasn't told you he denied the baby was his and accused Bella of trying to pass off someone else's child as his."

"It's not like it hasn't happened to him before," Kenny said in an effort to be peacemaker.

J.B. was grateful for Kenny's support, but he knew that would probably waver once he heard the whole story of how the evening had gone down.

"I know. I even got why he accused her of getting pregnant deliberately. I defended him to Bella." Taylor's lip curled. "Until she told me he announced her pregnancy in front of one of the parents of her pupils—which will cost Bella her job."

"Hey, I didn't do it deliberately." J.B. felt terrible. "I didn't see the woman."

"Nothing's ever your fault, is it?"

Mad Dog's remark spiked J.B.'s irritation. "Why would I want Bella to lose her job?"

"What have you done to put it right?"

"What can I do?" J.B. shot back.

"Taking responsibility for your actions would be a good start."

"I was completely open with Bella about not wanting a relationship. Nothing's changed just because she's pregnant."

"As usual, someone else has to clean up your mess." Taylor threw up his hands. "This time, it won't be me."

"Afraid it'll screw up your sessions with your little bed buddy?" J.B. sneered.

"When will you grow up?" Mad Dog scoffed. "Bella's better off without you. She doesn't need to take care of two kids," he tossed over his shoulder as he left.

If Bella was so much better off without him, why the hell was everyone so ticked that he didn't want to get involved?

Kenny crossed his arms over his chest. "Not your finest hour."

J.B. puffed out a frustrated breath. "I can't get

it right tonight, whichever way I turn. All I've tried to do is be honest, but I'm damned if I do and damned if I don't. Hell, the only reason that stupid woman overheard us was because I tried to help Bella when she twisted her ankle."

"Emotions are bound to run high," his friend said sagely. "It's not like Bella can walk away from the pregnancy."

"Sure, she can. She can give it up for adoption." Even as he said it, he knew that wasn't an option. "Scratch that. She isn't like that."

A strange sense of relief tugged at him.

"You're right. It's harder for her than it is for me. Worse, if the school fires her."

"Right. But all of that works in your interest, because it makes her more likely to accept money from you. Which means you can dictate your terms. So what do you want?"

"I don't know. She only told me tonight. Why am I expected to have answers already?"

"Because you usually have a smart-assed response to everything?"

J.B. glared at his friend. "Not helping."

Kenny held out his hands, palms up. "You don't have to make up your mind tonight. Bella will be pregnant for at least six more months. The key is that you have the right to make a decision about the child's future and your involvement in it."

J.B. could feel the chains of responsibility

winding around him tighter and tighter, almost suffocating him.

Kenny continued. "That kid is your son or daughter, too. It's an indisputable biological fact. The only way Bella can cut you out of his or her life is if you want it. Similarly, if you want to be included in your child's life, she can't stop you. The ball is in your court."

His friend's words triggered a moment of realization. The baby was J.B.'s, too. *His* son or daughter. Somehow, until that moment, the significance of that fact hadn't really registered.

Kenny was right. It didn't have to be all or nothing from day one. If—when—the Cats finished their successful Cup campaign, the child would be less than a year old. If they tried to go back-to-back, the kid still wouldn't even be two. What could a child know about his father at that age? Surely it was more important for J.B. to be around as his child grew older.

In a few years J.B. might be ready for a commitment. He'd be able to find the time to teach his kid to skate or toss a ball, go to a game, take a trip. Stuff they'd both enjoy.

All he had to do was buy himself time while keeping his options open. The best way to do that was, as Kenny had said, to provide Bella with an offer she couldn't refuse. Easy. Financial security. That, conveniently, was the one thing J.B. was more than happy to give her.

Problem solved. He'd work out the details tomorrow.

J.B. clapped Kenny on the back. "I've earned a beer. Want one?"

"Sure."

As they walked downstairs, Kenny said, "Tell me about Bella. I know she's a teacher and that's it. Does she have a last name? Where does she live?"

J.B. stopped dead and swore. "I don't know."

CHAPTER EIGHT

FARLINGDALE ACADEMY MIGHT have moved slower than an impending Ice Age about Issy's promotion, but they'd been slick as greased lightning about firing her. From the moment she'd told them—Issy had preempted Mrs. Allardyce and gone straight to the principal before school had opened on Monday morning—to the moment she'd left her classroom for the final time, on Friday afternoon, everything had moved at warp speed.

"Hypocritical jerks," Sapphie raged as she paced Issy's living room on Saturday evening. "Like those board members are perfect themselves. You should fight to get them to reinstate you. I'll back you and we'd win."

Issy had seen how vicious previous fights with the board had been and how badly it had affected the teachers who'd stood up to them. The thought turned her stomach.

"Even if I could afford to take them on, it's not worth the stress. They don't trust me and I don't trust them. Plus, I don't want to work for a school that doesn't value me or my work. I'd rather put this behind me and move on. I have to—for my sake and the baby's."

Sapphie sat next to Issy on the sofa and put an arm around her shoulder. "I don't blame you. Nonetheless, the whole thing sucks. Private school or not, that morality clause is freaking archaic. Hollywood of a century ago, not modern-day New Jersey."

"When I signed my contract, I never believed in a million years I'd get caught out by that clause. Especially not this wa-ay." Issy's voice broke on the last word.

"You've survived worse. You'll get through this, too."

Sapphie's unwavering support kept Issy from spiraling into despair. The uncertainty of her future terrified her. Not only because she'd lost her job, her only source of income and the bedrock of her security—though that was scary enough— but also because this was the first time she had no clear direction for her life. The plan she'd laid out for herself when she'd left home.

Worse, she no longer had only herself to worry about.

Issy started to lay her hand on her still-flat stomach but stopped. The superstitious side of her believed she should get past the critical date at the end of the first trimester before creating an emotional bond with her baby. Foolish really, because she'd already acknowledged the reality of her pregnancy and was committed to bringing this child into the world. Still, she couldn't bring herself to make that simple physical connection.

"What am I going to do?" She fought to keep the panic out of her voice.

"What do you want to do?"

"I suppose I need a plan."

"That I can help you with." Sapphie switched instantly into business mode. "Before you create a plan, you need to decide what your goal is."

"That's the problem. What *do* I want to achieve?" Uncertainty shrouded her future like an impenetrable fog.

Sapphie thought for several moments. "Stability. Security. And you want to give your baby the loving, happy, stable and secure childhood you never had."

Instead of making her feel better, the task ahead seemed overwhelming. "How on earth am I supposed to achieve all that?"

"One step at a time. One issue at a time."

Sapphie's calm, confident tone eased some of Issy's panic. No wonder her friend's business was so successful.

"Where do I start?"

"With the thing that worries you most."

"I don't have a job. Without it, I have no money." Her voice rose in pitch as her words spilled out faster and faster. "Without money, I have no secur—"

Sapphie held up a hand, interrupting her. "Whoa. Stop a minute and breathe."

That didn't stop the problems careening around in her head like bumper cars at a fairground.

"So the biggest issue is financial security," Sapphie said. "We've already talked about you finding another job or part-time work. At least the principal at Farlingdale promised to give you a good reference."

"To be fair, she stood up to the board and defended me, too, but was ignored."

Sapphie's wry look gave her opinion of that. "The point is that you are in a good position to find the work you want. That means we only have to think about how to ensure you have enough money to last you through the interim."

"I have a small amount left in my savings. It won't last long. Not with mortgage payments and bills. Getting a bank loan will be almost impossible."

"You know I can—"

"I'm grateful, but we've been through this before. I won't take your money."

"Promise me that if things get tight, you'll let me lend you what you need."

Knowing Sapphie wouldn't rest until she promised, Issy agreed. "But only if I'm desperate. And I'll want to repay every penny."

"Naturally. I'm not a charity."

Bold words, but Issy knew her friend would be

as stubborn about accepting repayment as she was about loaning it. "I'll hold you to that."

Sapphie paused. "There's another source of financial support you should consider."

"No way." She'd rather be destitute than ask him for help. "I don't want anything from Jean-Baptiste Larocque. He made it clear how he feels about me and the baby. I can't believe you'd even raise it after the way he reacted."

"I know he was a real jerk, but now that he's had time to get his head out of his backside, he's had a change of heart."

"Puh-lease." Issy's laugh had a cynical edge. "You'll tell me next he's sprouted wings and a shiny halo."

"No, but he has been trying to find out how to get hold of you. Apparently he doesn't have your contact information."

"We never exchanged details."

"And you never told him your name isn't Bella."

Issy avoided her friend's gaze. "What does he want?"

"To apologize. He also wants to try to find a way forward for you both."

"*Now* he wants to be involved in my baby's life?"

"I don't know if he's only thinking of financial support or more than that, but he wants to talk. It's up to you."

Issy was about to say no, but Sapphie's expression held her back.

"What have you got to lose?" Sapphie pressed. "If you don't like what he has to say, tell him to get lost."

"What if what he says makes sense?" Could she stand having J.B. in her life? Knowing his feelings about responsibility and commitment, what kind of role could he play? Given they had no possibility of a future together, did she want him to play any role?

Sapphie added, "If nothing else, J.B. could provide you with financial security. Even if only in the short term."

Issy had barely started to get used to the idea of being a single parent. "Let me think about it… I suppose Taylor's the one who talked you into raising this with me. What's going on with you two?"

"We're friends." She shrugged. "With benefits."

Issy didn't understand how that worked. It wouldn't for her. She couldn't envision seeing anyone regularly, let alone sleeping with him, and not wanting more. Look at how quickly she'd fallen for J.B. "Wouldn't you like it to be more?"

"Not really." For the first time a hint of uncertainty appeared in Sapphie's eyes, but she quickly masked it. "No," she said firmly. "Not with my lifestyle—my work, the travel. My business is too important. And Taylor feels the same way about his career. That's why this works. For both of us."

Issy thought her friend protested a little too much.

THE PUCK CLANGED off the pipe and onto J.B.'s stick.

He shot a crisp pass to Juergen on the right-hand side of the blue line, who then flew up the ice, with J.B. and Kenny flanking him, on a three-on-two. Monty, the backup goaltender, shifted to the edge of his crease, anticipating Juergen's shot. But the Swede used a no-look pass to drop the puck back to J.B., who slotted it home through Monty's five-hole.

Before he could celebrate with his linemates, J.B. was knocked on his butt by a late check. He didn't need to look up to know who'd laid him out. This was the second time in the past half hour.

"What the hell is your problem?" J.B. snarled as he got up.

When Taylor didn't respond, J.B. skated up and got in his face. "Spit it out, dickhead."

"Just finishing my check." Taylor shrugged.

"Bull crap. The puck was long gone. It was already in the back of the freaking net and you know it." J.B. shoved Mad Dog.

"Stop being a wuss." Taylor pushed him back. "I barely touched you. I can't help it if you lost your footing and landed on your candy ass."

"This is a *practice*. It. Doesn't. Freaking. Count."

He jabbed Mad Dog to emphasize each word. "Are you trying to injure me before tomorrow night's game against the Leafs?"

"Do *not* poke me." Taylor swiped J.B.'s hand away. "Ass hat," he muttered as he turned to skate to the bench.

J.B. grabbed his friend's sweater and pulled him back. "What did you say?"

Taylor wrenched away from J.B.'s hold. "Get your freaking hands off me."

"Why are you being such a jerk?" He didn't understand Mad Dog's attitude. J.B. thought they'd moved on from their argument in the gym the previous week.

"You can talk."

"Enough." J.B. smacked Taylor in the logo. "Tell me what your freaking problem is or back the hell off."

"I told you not to touch me," Mad Dog growled before ripping off his gloves.

J.B. dropped his gloves, then threw the first punch, catching his friend on the jaw. The work he'd been doing with his fitness boxing trainer, Prince, was paying off, he thought just before Mad Dog's right hook smashed into his left cheek.

J.B. narrowed his gaze, raised his hands slightly to protect his face, then hit out again, harder this time. His fist connected with Mad Dog's jaw with a satisfying thud, making his friend's head snap back.

Taylor wobbled on his skates but recovered quickly. He retaliated by swinging wildly at J.B., landing a punch to the side of his head.

The rat-tat-tat of sticks tapping against the boards echoed around the rink as their teammates stopped what they were doing to watch.

The two of them circled each other slowly, exchanging blows, watching for the moment to take the other man down.

Coach Macarty blew his whistle. "Knock it off. Whatever problems you've got, fix them on your own time." He glared at both players. "And if you can't get it straightened out by tomorrow's morning skate, don't bother showing up, because you'll both be healthy scratches. *Capisce?*"

"Yes, Coach," Taylor and J.B. said together.

Macarty pointed to the bench. "Get your asses off the ice and let the grown-ups work."

J.B. and Taylor picked up their gloves and sticks, skated to the bench and parked their backsides away from the rest of the team. Mad Dog grabbed a bottle and squirted water over his head. J.B. drank from his own bottle before resting his chin on his arm, which was propped on the butt end of his stick.

"Thanks for that, numb nuts." J.B. heaved a sigh. "The best practice I've had in weeks and you blew it for me."

"Yeah, yeah. As usual, it's all about you."

"What have I done to piss you off?"

"Like you don't know."

J.B. racked his brain but came up with zip. "I don't. You weren't this ticked about how badly I screwed up Bella telling me she was pregnant. What could be worse than that?"

"If you care so much about doing right by Bella, how come you spent last night screwing Susie again?"

Realization dawned.

And it was true.

He'd fully intended to spend the night taking advantage of the former cheerleader's flexibility with some hot gymnastics, but he hadn't been able to go through with it.

The whole situation had felt weird. Wrong. Like he was cheating on Bella.

"It wasn't like that," J.B. said quietly. "Nothing…happened."

Mad Dog barked out a laugh. "Right. Nothing happened between Jean-Baptiste Larocque and a woman."

That made him angry. "Keep your damn voice down." J.B. elbowed him. "What does it matter, anyway? You won't give me Bella's phone number or address. Hell, you won't even tell me her full name. So if I sleep with other women, that's nobody's business but mine."

"That's exactly why we're protecting her from you." Taylor snorted. "We don't trust you."

"Keep your damn voice down."

Taylor and J.B. stared at each other from their opposite ends of the bench.

Finally his friend shrugged and broke eye contact. "Looks like you'll have a shiner on that eye."

J.B. turned to watch the players on the ice. "How's your mouth? Did I shake any teeth loose?"

"Nah." Out of the corner of his eye, J.B. saw Taylor wiggle his lower jaw. "I'll survive."

Coach Macarty gave a double blast of his whistle. "Good job, everyone. Hit the showers. Larocque, Mad Dog, stay behind." He beckoned them to center ice.

J.B. and Taylor climbed over the boards and skated across to the coach.

"You ladies kissed and made up yet, or do you need to do a bag skate?" Macarty's gaze moved between them.

J.B. slowly looked at Mad Dog, who nodded but didn't smile. "We're good, Coach."

"Sorry for screwing up practice," Mad Dog added.

"You're supposed to be setting an example for the younger guys." Coach Macarty grunted. "Save your fire for the game. Now get out of here."

Relieved to have been let off lightly, J.B. and Taylor headed to the locker room. They endured some razzing from their teammates as they showered and changed, but didn't reveal the cause of their fight.

Bad Boy, who still mentored J.B., took him

aside and asked if everything was all right. Since he didn't know about the whole Bella fiasco—and this wasn't the time or place to fill him in—J.B. assured him it was under control.

Kenny waited until he, Taylor and J.B. were walking out to their cars to grill them about the fight. "I know it's to do with Bella. I swear, whenever there's a woman on the scene, normal guys start acting like idiots."

"You won't get any argument from me," Taylor said.

"Right, because you've got it together so well." J.B. flipped him the bird before saying to Kenny, "It's a long story."

"Sounds complicated and messy." Kenny gave an exaggerated shudder. "I'm better off not knowing. This is why I avoid relationships."

"Your turn will come, bro."

"When it does, I'll handle it like a champ, having watched Jake, my brothers and now you flopping around helplessly like fish on a deck."

"With friends like you two, who needs enemies?" J.B. unlocked his SUV and tossed his bag in the back. "I've got stuff to do. I'll catch you later."

Before J.B. got into his car, Mad Dog handed him a folded slip of paper.

"What's this?"

"You can read, can't you?" Taylor unlocked his own car and shoved his bag onto the seat.

J.B. opened the note. "Isabelle Brandine." He looked up. "Bella?"

"Issy to her *friends*."

Ignoring Taylor's dig, J.B. said, "Thanks."

"Don't thank me. Sapphie convinced Issy to give you one more shot. Good luck." Taylor got into his SUV.

J.B. sat in his car after Kenny and Taylor drove away, staring at the paper, wondering what he should do next.

Before he could second-guess himself, he plugged her address into his GPS. Thirty minutes later, which included a detour to a local florist, he pulled up outside Bella's—Issy's—apartment complex.

She'd been this close all along.

It was a nice-looking, two-story, U-shaped building, with a couple dozen apartments. Each had big windows, with dark red shutters, and their own balcony or patio. Rolling lawns, lots of trees and flowerbeds and a central lake. Similar to the apartment he'd had when he'd first come up to the show, only his had been down in Edgewater—in the hub of the bustling riverfront community and a ferry ride from Manhattan—instead of a suburban small town.

A stark reminder of how they wanted different things from life. Which was all well and good, but those lives were now indelibly intertwined and he couldn't see how either of them could get what they wanted.

J.B. turned off the engine, picked up the bouquet and got out of the car. Judging by the number, Issy lived on the second floor, but her front door was at ground level. He crossed the parking lot and stood outside her door.

What was the worst that could happen?

He pressed the doorbell. Part of him hoped she'd be out.

His breath hitched as he heard her door unlock.

"Oh. It's you." Her icy tone and inscrutable expression weren't encouraging. She didn't exactly throw the door open for him, either. Crap.

"Hi." He thrust the bouquet toward her. "These are for you."

She didn't accept the flowers. "What do you want, J.B.?"

Okay. He could cut to the chase. "To apologize. For the other night."

When she didn't say anything, didn't even blink, he exhaled heavily. Looked like he was in that worst-case scenario. "Can I come inside? I don't really want to discuss this on your doorstep. I'm sure you don't, either."

Wariness crept into her eyes as she studied his face.

"Please, just hear me out," he added.

Finally she stepped back and opened the door wider. "You'd better come in."

CHAPTER NINE

J.B. WAS IN her living room. All gorgeous and broody.

Issy's heart pounded. She'd forgotten how big he was; how tall and broad. He made her apartment seem small. He filled her cozy living room and made her lovingly restored flea-market-find furniture appear delicate and fragile.

She hadn't expected him here so quickly. Issy had thought he'd call first. Give her time to steel herself.

J.B. cleared his throat. "Nice place."

"Thanks. It's the perfect size for me, two beds and two baths, and ideally situated." She groaned inwardly. He didn't need a Realtor's sales spiel.

They stared at each other. J.B. seemed uneasy; lacking his usual self-confident swagger. Issy wasn't sure how to start the conversation they needed to have. She decided to take her lead from J.B. If he ever spoke another word.

He held out the flowers again. "I remembered you liked daisies and mums."

Don't be impressed.

He probably had a little black book with all that information recorded.

"Thank you," she said finally, taking the bouquet. "I should put them in water."

J.B. followed her into the kitchen.

"They're lovely," she acknowledged as she strained to reach the top shelf.

"Which vase would you like?"

J.B. leaned past her and his freshly showered scent surrounded her. "Uh, the cut-glass one, please."

She stepped back, not wanting to be affected by his closeness. "They didn't build these cupboards with short people in mind. They must expect everyone to be tall." She rolled her eyes at her own babbling.

"Maybe they think most people never need stuff they put on that top shelf." He smiled. "Feel free to call me anytime you need something."

"Not exactly convenient."

For several seconds they said nothing, just looked at each other.

Issy broke the connection first, turning away to deal with the bouquet. She filled the vase, snipped the ends of the stalks and arranged the blooms. Then she carried the vase through to the living room and placed it on the mantel.

J.B. walked over to her patio doors and looked out. He didn't seem to know what to do. He shifted uneasily from foot to foot. "Great view."

"One of the reasons I bought this place. They do a great job of making it look pretty all year round." Enough with the chatter already! "Can I get you a drink?"

"I'm good, thanks."

Silence. He shoved his hands into his pockets.

Issy waited. And waited. Finally she sat in her rocking chair. "Have a seat." She indicated the sofa.

"I'm okay standing."

Silence again. At this rate, it would be dark before he said what he'd come here for.

He began to pace. "I'm not proud of my reaction. I was shocked and took it out on you. I'm sorry." He stopped in front of her, crouching so their eyes were level. "I know I'm the father of the baby. It's not the way I wanted to have a child, but then, it's not like you planned it this way, either."

Issy's jaw dropped. She quickly recovered. "Definitely not."

J.B. rose and resumed pacing. "The problem is… I don't want to be tied down. I don't want to be a husband or significant other."

Even though she'd expected as much, she couldn't help being disappointed.

He halted in front of the patio doors again. Staring out, he said softly, "I'm not ready to be a father."

"Our baby doesn't need a halfhearted dad."

His back stiffened and he turned to face her. "I'd never half-ass it. For sure, not with our child."

Issy said nothing, but she was sure he could read her skepticism.

He continued, his words clipped. "Just because our definitions of commitment aren't the same doesn't mean we don't want the same thing. Doing the best for our kid doesn't mean we need to be married or even living together."

Her disappointment grew. "Why are you here? You've said you're sorry. Apology accepted. You believe the baby's yours. Great. Other than that, nothing's changed."

"Sure it has. I'm prepared to support you one hundred percent, so that you can have this baby with no worries."

"What exactly does that mean?" Issy wanted him to spell it out.

"I'll cover your medical expenses. I'll put you and the baby on my health insurance. Once the kid is born, I'll pay you a generous monthly allowance—all signed and legal—so you don't have any financial concerns."

Money.

She should have known. She *had* known.

"You won't have to work, unless you want to, until our child is in school." He rubbed his jaw. "I'm sorry you lost your job. I didn't mean to sabotage you."

"I know you didn't."

"Anyway, you won't have to worry about money or security."

Damn him. For knowing what mattered—for her and, more importantly, for her child. No uncertainty. No fear about where the next meal was coming from or whether there would be a roof over her head.

"I appreciate your offer. Thank you."

His gaze narrowed. "What's the problem?"

He really didn't get it. He didn't understand that security included emotional stability and certainty, too. Knowing you were cared for, loved. Knowing someone was there for you, every day. "There's more to being a father than sending a check every month."

"I know. And by the time the kid is old enough to need a father—to toss a ball with or to go to a game with—I'll be ready. I'm just not ready now."

She wanted to smack him. "There's also more to being a father than that. Don't you want to be there to help your child learn to walk and talk? To watch them develop a personality?"

"I can do all that without putting a ring on your finger." He began to pace again. "I can't give you what you want. This is the best I can do."

"This isn't about *me* wanting to get married." She clenched the arms of her rocker. "It isn't about *me* at all."

"Then what is it about?"

"The two of us providing a strong, nurturing environment for our child."

"Isn't that what we're doing? You don't have a job. Without that, you won't be able to hold on to this place. Without the financial security I'm offering, you won't be able to provide our child that strong, nurturing environment at all."

That he was right only fueled her anger. She jumped up. "It's not fair to our child for you to pick and choose which parts of his or her life you want to be involved in. You have to make your mind up, J.B. Either you're committed fully, from day one, or you aren't. Make a decision and stick with it."

He stopped in front of her, arms crossed.

"I won't hold it against you if you choose not to be involved, J.B. Frankly, I'd prefer honesty over doing what you think you should."

"So it's your way or the highway? No compromise, no negotiation." His lip curled.

"I don't see much compromise from you. Just 'hey, babe, let me shower you with money so I don't have to be a grown-up.'"

"At least I'm not insisting on a lie. You don't want to marry me any more than I want to marry you."

"We don't have to be married or even live together." She threw up her hands in frustration and spun away before turning back to face him. "We have to be *committed* to being parents."

"I don't see the difference."

Issy rubbed her temples, trying to ease the headache that was building. "You can't flit in and out of this child's life when it suits you. To be a proper father, you have to be involved in every part of this child's life, from birth until they're an adult."

"What if I don't want that?"

"Then get the hell out of both of our lives and stay away."

"IF I WALK away for good, the money's off the table."

As soon as the words left his mouth, J.B. wanted to snatch them back. He didn't mean what he'd said.

The tack Bella—Issy had taken had knocked him on his ass, and he'd reacted without thinking.

Jeez, why was it every time he opened his mouth he dug himself a deeper hole?

Issy walked to the stairs. "The front door's that way. Please use it." Her tone dripped with disgust.

J.B. shook his head. "This conversation isn't over."

"There's nothing left to talk about." Issy tilted her chin. "I'm glad we've clarified what you mean by 'one hundred percent support.' Whatever it takes, my baby and I will get through this without your money. So you can leave with your bank balance and your precious lifestyle intact." She gestured for him to get going.

My baby. As if his presence in the kid's life could be wiped away as easily as a Zamboni cleaning chippy ice. That stung, as though he'd been speared in the gut.

"Hold up." J.B. spread his hands in a gesture of appeal. "Let's take a step back. I'm sorry. I didn't mean what I said."

Issy rolled her eyes. "Which part didn't you mean this time?"

"About cutting off the money. Whether I'm involved like you want me to be, or not, I'm sending you money."

She shrugged. "Well, it *is* only money and you have plenty of that. It's not like you have to give up anything important, like time."

"That's not fair." Damn it! He couldn't win for losing.

"No, it isn't."

"You can't deny that financial security is important to you."

"No," she acknowledged. "But it's not the only kind of security."

"I would never intentionally let our child down," he protested. Even as he spoke, he felt the noose tightening around his neck.

"My parents 'intended' to have food in the house. Unfortunately alcohol was stronger than their intentions."

"You can't compare me to them."

"It'll be hard for you to give up everything you still want to do because a child needs you." She laid her hand on his arm. "That's okay. Really it is. But just because I understand, doesn't mean a child will. And they shouldn't have to."

Why couldn't he grab the easy way out she was offering him?

If he was honest, J.B. wasn't sure what he wanted. He only knew what he didn't want: to have to decide whether to give up his lifestyle or his child. The problem was he didn't know how he could have both.

He needed time to think.

"You can't expect me to make such an important decision just like that." He snapped his fingers. "This isn't only about the next few months, or even years, but my whole future."

"Because it's all about you."

"Yes, it is. You were pretty quick to decide what you wanted, so you're all set. The baby doesn't get a whole lot of choice in the matter. The only person who still has to make a decision is me. And I won't be rushed into anything." He held out his hands, palms up. "Look, I'm only asking for a little more time."

"Why, when we both know what your answer will be?" She jammed her hands on her hips.

Her ready assumption about the route he'd choose pissed him off. "You may have wonderful clairvoyant skills, but as a mere mortal I'd prefer to work things through for myself." He took a deep breath, trying hard not to lose his temper. "The least you can do is give me a week."

Issy's gaze narrowed. "Once you sign the papers, there will be no changing your mind. I can't live with the uncertainty. I won't keep looking over my shoulder, wondering when you're going to storm back into our lives. Or worse, decide to sue me for custody."

He stiffened. "I wouldn't do that."

"So you say. You can't guarantee you won't change your mind on that, too."

J.B. opened his mouth to argue, then snapped it shut. She was right. Even if he couldn't imagine a scenario where it would happen, he couldn't guarantee it wouldn't. Knowing his luck, fate would throw something at him to screw with his best intentions.

"This is a huge decision that will have a monumental impact on both our lives."

"If you care even the littlest bit for me, you won't make me wait."

"All I'm asking is for a week. Please."

She sighed heavily. "All right. One week."

"I promise I'll make a decision and I'll stick to it."

Issy nodded, then led the way to the front door. Their goodbye was stilted.

He wasn't sure what to make of the fact that

she waited until he was in his car before closing the front door.

As J.B. drove home, his cell beeped several times with texts from his teammates asking where he was.

A group of the single guys usually hung out at a local sports bar the night before a game. He'd found it a good way to relax and prepare for the following day.

By contrast, the married guys went home to spend time that was so precious during the season with their families.

Two sides of the very coin he had to toss.

Was he ready to give up his single lifestyle? To make a decision he'd be happy to live with… forever?

The alternative was to give up his child.

If only he could delay making a decision until this season was over. He'd be another year older. He'd be one year closer to retirement. He might even have won the Cup. Or he might be seriously injured, like Ike had been last year, and have hardly played. All of those things would make a difference.

But the baby wouldn't wait and neither would Issy.

He had seven days to make up his mind, so he'd better figure things out fast. Especially with the home opener coming up, followed almost immediately by a weeklong road trip out west.

J.B. smacked his hand on the steering wheel. He knew what to do. Instead of pulling into the parking space outside his town house, he did a one-eighty and headed back out.

JAKE'S VICTORIAN HOUSE was gorgeous, but it was the epitome of tradition and longevity. And family.

J.B. preferred modern, easy maintenance. A place that didn't require him to be a slave to its upkeep. One he could walk away from without a backward glance.

He rented Ike's town house because he wasn't ready to put down roots. Besides, he could be traded to another team at any point.

Still, Bad Boy's house was a great place to visit: warm, welcoming and homey. J.B. felt more comfortable there than he did at the family farm.

Maggie answered the door, with Joe holding one hand. The kid's face was covered in orange goo. "Hi, J.B. Come in."

"Hey, beautiful." He kissed her on the cheek as he stepped inside. He eyed the grinning toddler warily. "Whoa, bud. That stuff looks nuclear."

Maggie laughed. "Puréed carrots. He loves them. As much as mushy peas." She wrinkled her nose at Joe. "I've never liked them, but he eats a bowlful like it's custard. I get tins of the stuff shipped over from England for him. My dad loved them, too."

"Must be in the genes."

"Hopefully that's the only thing Joe gets from the English side of the family."

Maggie's parents had been difficult and, like Issy, she'd left home to escape them.

After an abusive first husband, a professional soccer player, the last thing Maggie had wanted for her and her daughter Emily was to fall in love with a playboy pro hockey player.

Yet, they'd overcome the odds and were a living example of happily-ever-after.

Abruptly, J.B. shook away the strange twinge of envy for Jake. While he was pleased things had worked out for them, that wasn't what he wanted for himself. Not right now, anyway.

He ruffled Joe's hair. "Your kid definitely got his good looks from you and not that ugly dude you married."

Maggie grinned. "Always the charmer."

Yeah. With everyone except Issy. "Is Jake home?"

"He's helping Emily practice her shot in the back garden. They've been at it for a while, so I'm sure he'll be glad of the interruption. You know the way. I'll bring you a beer once I've cleaned up young sir."

"Thanks." J.B. wandered through the house and out the back door. He stood on the deck and watched as his friend patiently explained to his thirteen-year-old stepdaughter how to get more power in her shot.

If J.B. hadn't known Emily's background, he'd have thought she was Jake's natural child.

Emily squealed when she saw J.B. She dropped her stick and rushed over, throwing herself into his arms.

He caught her easily, swinging her around. "One of these days you'll be too grown up to do this, Em."

"Never. It's my favorite thing. Next to hockey."

"Glad to hear it."

Jake put his hand on Emily's shoulder. "Tidy your gear away, then go get washed up for dinner."

Emily dashed off.

"I wish I had half her energy." Jake sighed. "Let's grab a seat on the deck. I ache all over. I swear these preseason practices are getting harder."

"You're getting old, man."

"I know." Jake rubbed his thigh. "Plus the pins in my leg are telling me there's rain coming. I swear it's a better weather forecaster than that Doppler on the Weather Channel."

As they sat in the Adirondack chairs, Maggie brought them out some beers and a tray of chips and dip. "Would you like to stay to dinner, J.B.?"

"If I wouldn't be intruding."

Maggie smacked him on the shoulder. "Don't be silly. You're part of the family."

"Thanks. That'd be great."

"It's all made. I'll keep it warm in the oven until you're finished. In the meantime, I'll supervise Joe's bath."

J.B. watched her drop a kiss on Jake's lips, then go inside. "She's way too good for you."

Jake grinned. "I lucked out there, for sure." His expression turned serious. "What's up?"

J.B. felt strangely embarrassed. It wasn't as if Jake hadn't known him at his worst. Still, he hated to see his friend's disappointment. Jake always saw the good in him. Encouraged him to be better.

"How bad can it be?" Jake asked, understanding in his ice-blue eyes.

"Possibly a new low."

"I doubt that. You're not a bad person."

"Remember that woman I met in Antigua?"

"The one who came to the game with her friend? Bella something?"

"Isabelle. Issy." J.B. nodded. "I got her pregnant."

"Okay." Jake arched an eyebrow. "Tricky. You're sure it's yours?"

"Yeah. This time it definitely is." J.B. sighed. "It's not my fault. Or hers. We were careful. There was a perfect storm of bad luck and now I'm stuck in a situation. I don't know what the hell I'm supposed to do."

"You want to tell me the rest of it?"

Reassured by Jake's lack of judgment, J.B. told him the whole story.

Jake whistled through his teeth. "That's a tough one. There's no right or wrong answer. Except what's best for you."

"That's the problem. I don't know what's best for me. Not true. I know what's best right now, but how do I know that'll still be the correct answer twelve months from now? Or two years or five or ten?"

"You don't. All you can do is make sure you don't put yourself in a position you can't get out of, if your feelings change down the line."

"Issy made it pretty damn clear—it's all or nothing."

Jake tapped his beer bottle against his mouth. "I understand why she said that, but it's not practical to set anything in stone before the baby's even born. Because the moment you hold your kid in your arms that first time, everything changes."

"If I sign away my rights, I won't have to worry about that. I won't ever see the baby." There was that weird tug in his chest again.

"Is that really what you want to do? I'd get it if you didn't like kids, but you do. You love your nieces and nephews, and you adore Emily, Joe and Tru's twins. Take that and multiply it by a zillion for your own child."

J.B. could feel himself being sucked in. "I

guess. It's not like I don't want kids ever. Just not right now."

"It's not the worst thing in the world. Trust me."

How hard could it be? Especially if he did it part-time? That's how divorced parents did it. He could see himself finding a little time here and there to spend with his kid. Perhaps he could have his cake and eat it, too?

Jake continued. "And giving up the lifestyle won't be a hardship, because you'll want to spend any available time with your kid."

Jake's words pricked J.B.'s confident bubble.

Like the older, married guys, he'd be rushing off after every game, every road trip, to fulfill whatever parental obligations he'd agreed to with Issy. His free time would be consumed with worrying about important decisions and key stages in their child's development. His life and his time would be dictated by and revolve around someone else's requirements. Not someone he could blow off, either. Nobody would understand him catering to his own needs.

Crap. Maybe it would be easier, better, all around, if he didn't get involved from the start.

"Do you care for Issy?" Jake asked.

"Sure." That J.B. didn't hesitate told him something. But it didn't solve anything.

"So, if this hadn't happened, would you want to keep on seeing her?"

"More than likely. Why?"

"Because this can't just be about the baby. It has to be about the two of you, as well. If you decide to be involved, you'll spend a lot of time with Issy. Equally, if you go the other route, you wouldn't just be letting your baby go, but her, too."

As if it wasn't a tough enough call.

"I can't be what Issy wants, and the baby needs me to be, at the moment. I don't want the responsibility of a serious relationship or fatherhood."

His admission seemed to lift a weight from his shoulders that he hadn't realized he'd been carrying. "I have too many other priorities, some important goals to achieve, before I think about settling down."

"I get that it's a daunting prospect at the moment, J.B. What with the new season starting and the new-look team settling down after Scotty's retirement and the moves over the summer, but that makes it even more important that you don't make a decision you'll end up regretting later."

J.B. ran his thumbnail over the label on the beer bottle, working one edge free from the glass. "I can't commit to something that isn't right for me because I'm scared of what might or might not happen down the line. It's not just Issy who wants this settled quickly. I do, too. I don't want this decision hanging over my head."

Jake didn't say anything for a moment. "You're sure there's no room for compromise? It has to be all or nothing, right now?"

"Yes."

"For your sake, and to avoid any regrets, I think you should at least see your baby before you make any firm decisions. For sure, delay signing any paperwork until after the baby's born."

"I guess I could make that work. It's only six months. It'll probably take that long to formalize any agreement between us, anyway."

Maggie stuck her head out the screen door. "Are you ready to eat?"

Jake looked at him. "I think we are. J.B.?"

Now that he'd figured out a plan, he was starving. "Yeah, I'm all set." He pushed to his feet. "All this serious talk has made me hungry."

"Dinner will be on the table in five minutes."

As they walked into the house, J.B. said, "Thanks, man. I appreciate the advice."

"Anytime. I don't have all the answers, but I do know you should always think twice before closing any doors for good. Forever is a hell of a long time."

And that, J.B. thought, was exactly the problem. Especially if he made the wrong decision.

CHAPTER TEN

ISSY EYED THE array of spirits lined up along the dark wood bar of the Exeter Diner and wished she drank. Not that she'd ever liked the taste of anything stronger than white wine. Even the smell of bourbon turned her stomach; her parents' trailer had always stunk of it. Still, a little tot might help settle her nerves as she waited for J.B.

It wasn't an option. Her developing baby's health took precedence over jangled nerves. She sipped her sparkling water and checked her watch. Five minutes later than when she'd last looked, and five minutes ahead of when she and J.B. had agreed to meet at six o'clock.

For about the millionth time since his call the previous evening Issy wondered what decision he'd come to. Would he commit or walk away? She wasn't sure what to read into the fact that he'd only taken one of his allotted seven days before phoning.

"You'll know soon enough. What will be, will be," Issy muttered to herself.

She picked up a dog-eared menu but couldn't focus on it, so put it down again. Her stomach churned. The last thing she wanted to do was eat.

She'd chosen the local hole-in-the-wall because it had great food and a clientele that kept to itself. The dim lighting and the high-sided booths had an almost clandestine feel and gave the illusion of privacy. Perfect for the conversation ahead.

She straightened the cutlery and rearranged the condiments to avoid checking her watch again.

Issy started as J.B. slid into the booth and sat opposite her. She picked up her drink and took a sip, but the sparkling water went down the wrong way and she began to cough and splutter.

"Are you okay?" he asked.

Unable to speak, she nodded. Unfortunately she couldn't quite catch her breath and her embarrassment seemed to make things worse.

J.B. came around to her side of the booth, sat beside her and slapped her on the back.

Whether it was the shock of his thigh pressed against hers or the pounding, her airway cleared and she was able to drag in a rasping breath.

"Better?" J.B.'s hand remained on her upper back, rubbing in slow circles.

"Yes, thank you." Her voice sounded scratchy. "I'm fine."

"Can I get you a drink, sir?" A gum-snapping waitress, with *Shirley* embroidered on the bib of her uniform, cocked a hip and waited for an answer.

"Issy?" J.B. asked.

When she shook her head, he gave the waitress

one of his charming smiles and said, "Diet cola would be great, thanks."

"Sure. The specials are on the blackboard. I can recommend the moussaka. I'll be right back with the cola."

As Shirley walked away J.B. returned to the other side of the booth. He picked up a menu, then put it down almost immediately without opening it. "So, uh, thanks for meeting me."

Issy was surprised by his uncharacteristic hesitance. If she didn't know better, she'd think he was as nervous as she was.

He gave her a half smile. "I thought it would be easier to talk about this if we were in neutral territory."

"And having people around would keep it from getting too emotional."

"That, too. No one likes to see a grown man cry."

Reluctantly she smiled. "Some women think it's good to see a man who's in touch with his feelings and isn't afraid to show them."

He gave an exaggerated shudder, then tapped the menu. "Would you prefer to have food first or talk?"

"Why don't we get this over with?" She winced inwardly. She hadn't intended her response to sound so harsh. "What I mean is…"

"That's okay. I get it." J.B.'s dark eyes were shuttered.

"You've come to a decision."

"Once I'd had a chance to consider the issues, the solution became clear."

"What's your solution?"

"I'm prepared to give you full custody."

Her immediate relief was tinged with disappointment. Issy had what she'd wanted. So why wasn't she happier? She might be a romantic, but even she couldn't pretty up what J.B. was. Happy families simply weren't part of his makeup.

"I have one condition."

Damn it. "Which is?"

"I won't sign the paperwork renouncing my parental rights until after the baby's born."

Her heart sank. "Why not?"

"I want to be absolutely sure."

"Of what?"

"That I'm doing the right thing." He sighed heavily.

"I see."

"I need to be free to do whatever it takes to win the Cup," he continued. "I can't afford to be firing on anything less than all cylinders, mentally and physically. I know it's possible to juggle team and family—I have several teammates who thrive on it—but I need to be more than good enough."

How could a sports trophy be more important than his own flesh and blood? He must think her a fool to believe it was just about that precious Cup.

"What about the parties, clubs and women?" she asked sarcastically.

He fiddled with the frayed edge of the menu. "That's just blowing off steam. Once we get into the grind of the season, there isn't a whole lot of time for any of that. We play two or three games a week, sometimes on consecutive nights. Which is why I only party when I know it won't affect my play, and when I date, it's no strings attached. You can see why a family doesn't work with that."

How had she ever thought he might be the kind of guy she'd want a relationship with? "If you're so certain about all of that, then why the delay?"

"I'm sure about the custody arrangement and the financial support. No matter what happens, that won't change. What's harder for me to gauge is signing away all rights to my son or daughter."

"In case you feel like stopping by to play ball once in a blue moon."

He acknowledged her jab with a tilt of his head. "I'm told that once I see my child, I'll feel things I've never felt before. I don't know that I believe that, but what if it's true? What if I regret taking myself completely out of his or her life before it's even begun?"

"The easy answer would be not to see the baby at all. Just forget we exist. We'll be nothing more than a line on your bank statement every month."

He frowned. "You must think I'm a coldhearted bastard. I'm just trying to be honest."

As Shirley served his drink, Issy thought about what J.B. had said. He had a point. She didn't have to like it, even if she was prepared to admit as much.

Once the waitress had gone, he said, "I promise, I won't do anything that will hurt you or the baby."

"I know." He might be self-centered, but he wasn't cruel.

"And it's not like you want to be stuck with me, either."

Issy wasn't prepared to settle for a man who thought *commitment* and *responsibility* were dirty words. "That's true."

For a moment something flickered in J.B.'s dark eyes. Then it was gone.

"I don't want to close any doors until I'm absolutely sure I won't want to open them again," he said. "Wouldn't you want the same if our positions were reversed?"

She felt a little guilty. Perhaps her demands had been a little unfair. She'd got the most important thing: control over her child's life with no interference from J.B. Even if she didn't trust him, she could make sure that she was covered legally, every which way, to prevent any nasty surprises down the line.

"All right. I'll get a lawyer to draw up the custody agreement and, separately, the paternity rights papers."

"Great." J.B. mimicked wiping the sweat from his brow. "I'm glad we got through that without any bruises or bloodshed."

"I can't promise that'll be the case if you re-nege on this, J.B."

"I won't. I know it's not exactly what you wanted, but I think it'll work out okay." His gaze met hers. "I'll make sure it does."

Strangely she could believe he would. "All right."

He grinned and then picked up his menu. "Now that's sorted, I'm starved. What would you like to eat?"

Despite her earlier concerns, and her intention to leave once their discussion was over, Issy found herself hungry, too. What harm could it do to have a meal with him?

"I think I'll give that moussaka a try."

"CAN I GIVE you a ride home?"

J.B.'s question, as they walked through the diner, after their meal, shouldn't have surprised Issy. After a stilted few minutes, while they'd waited for their dinner, they'd both relaxed enough to enjoy their evening. For the next couple of hours they'd forgotten the issues that separated them, as they'd enjoyed each other's company. It was almost as if they'd been transported back to Antigua.

Issy had been reminded of how much she'd

liked being with J.B. How easy he was to talk to, because he actually listened to her. He respected her opinion, even if it differed from his, yet wasn't afraid to go toe-to-toe with her. She'd forgotten how passionate he was about issues that mattered to him; he hated cheats, in sports or other walks of life, and admired people who were creative and innovative. And how often he made her laugh.

Under other circumstances, it would have been the perfect date.

Pushing aside that thought—she *really* did not want to go there—she smiled. "I appreciate the offer, but it's only a short walk from here."

"It's dark out. At least let me escort you home."

J.B. leaned past her to push open the heavy door. Briefly she felt his hard muscles as they pressed against her from shoulder to thigh. Memories of how she'd run her hands over his smooth, caramel-brown skin popped into her head. She remembered clearly how she'd trailed her tongue over every mound and dip of those same muscles, which had rippled in response to her touch.

Another couple wanting to enter the diner snapped her back to reality. Issy was grateful for the brisk autumn air that cooled her heated cheeks and reminded her that they weren't in the romantic tropics, but in down-to-earth New Jersey.

As the door swung closed behind them, J.B.'s hand settled at the small of her back.

"That's really not necessary. I do this all the

time. This is a safe town, well-lit and with plenty of traffic and people around."

"I'm sure it's okay, but I'd still prefer to make sure you get home with no problems. Besides, my mom would kill me if she knew I'd let a woman— let alone a pregnant woman—walk home unescorted."

She didn't want to be affected by his corny line or his cheeky smile, but the man was hard to resist. "Well, I wouldn't want you to get into trouble with your mother. You've probably given the poor woman enough gray hairs already."

Issy began walking across the parking lot.

J.B. fell into step alongside her. "Hey, Mom adores me. I'm her favorite son. She doesn't tell everyone that because she doesn't want to upset my brothers, but I know the truth."

Issy laughed. "Favorite or not, I bet you're the one she worries about most. Especially since you don't live close by."

Yeah." His smile faded. "That's been hard on her. I haven't lived at home since I was in my early teens. Like most young hockey-mad kids, I went where I could learn to be the best and stayed with billet families until I came up to the NHL."

"You're kidding. She was okay with you living away so young?"

"Not okay exactly, but she knew I was never going to turn into a farmer. Mom understood my passion for the ice and enrolled me in the local hockey program. Later, when my coach suggested sending me out west to play in one of the junior leagues, Mom backed my play and convinced my father to let me give it a shot."

His mother sounded like a wonderful woman, Issy thought with a touch of envy. "It must have broken her heart to send you away."

"My brothers told me she cried after I left. One of the best moments of my life was bringing the Stanley Cup back to our small town and showing it off to everyone." He reached into his back pocket, pulled out his wallet and handed her a dog-eared picture of him with his arm around a smiling woman with the big, silver trophy in front of them. "Even my brothers will admit I was the favorite son that day."

Issy was touched by his obvious love and affection when he spoke about his mother and his brothers. A stark contrast to his attitude toward his father. Was that part of the reason why he didn't want to be a father himself?

"It must have been weird living with strangers. Weren't you homesick?"

"I missed my mom and my brothers, but I didn't miss living on the farm. The chores. The hard hand-to-mouth living. I was lucky that my billet families were really nice and made me feel like I belonged. Plus, everyone around me was like me, they lived, ate and breathed hockey. I wasn't the odd one out anymore."

As they walked, J.B. told her stories of his time in billets. Though he spoke fondly of the people he'd lived with, she ached for the young boy who didn't fit at home and who'd found his place in the world thousands of miles away from his family.

No wonder he didn't want any ties or responsibilities. He'd been independent for so long. Hockey had become his family and his home.

It struck Issy that although their childhoods shared similarities, they'd both had to be self-sufficient from a young age. Both she and J.B. had learned early to focus on their dreams, and they'd had to leave home to get what they'd wanted.

But just as she and Sapphie had responded differently to the circumstances of their childhoods, so had Issy and J.B. He'd turned out more like Sapphie than her. Eschewing family ties, connections and permanence while striving for his career. Perhaps he'd have been better off with Sapphie.

Was it wrong to feel a little smug that he hadn't?

Besides, if J.B. had wanted her friend, he'd have gone after her. That much she knew for sure about him; he'd have found a way.

As if this situation with J.B. wasn't complicated enough. The last thing she needed was to let sympathy cloud the issue, let alone remind her of how attracted she was to the man walking beside her. That was how she'd ended up in this mess in the first place.

"It was years before I could eat anything with tuna." J.B. made a gagging sound.

His billet mother's tuna-surprise casserole prompted Issy to share the tale of her first attempt at that same dish, when the only things in the store cupboard were gherkins, olives, maraschino cherries and cornflakes. She felt a rush of pleasure when J.B. roared with laughter.

As they walked through the gates of her complex, Issy began to feel nervous. She stopped and turned to him. "I can make it from here."

She tried to forestall any argument by adding, "My building's straight ahead and you can see my front door."

It didn't work.

J.B. took her hand and hooked it through his arm. "You're getting the full-service escort to the door and that's final."

"Pushy, much?"

"I like to think of it as determined. I wouldn't be able to live with myself if something happened to you on the last leg of this journey." His tone was pure drama queen and he struck a pose to match, with the back of his hand against his forehead.

She laughed. "I don't think there are wicked villains hiding in the shrubbery. At least, I've never spotted anyone tall, dark and dangerous lurking. Hmm. Maybe I should look more carefully, just in case."

He squeezed her arm against him in retaliation.

"Leave the surveillance of nefarious characters to me, my lady. The only tall, dark and dangerous you need to worry about is me."

"And that's supposed to reassure me? That's like putting the fox in charge of the henhouse," she said, to cover the little kick of delight his insistence gave her.

His teeth gleamed white as he grinned.

Issy left her arm linked with his as they resumed walking.

At her front door, the awkwardness returned. Issy wasn't sure what to say.

As she pulled out her keys and unlocked her door, she fell back on good manners. "Thank you for dinner and the escort home. You can tell your mom that you did her proud."

"My pleasure. All part of the service."

She looked into his eyes and couldn't look away again. Her pulse tripped.

"Good night." Damn it. Why did her voice have to sound soft and husky?

"Good night, Bella."

Using the name she'd given him in Antigua gave her a clue as to what was coming. She didn't move when J.B. leaned down and kissed her.

The touch of his lips against hers was fleeting at first. Yet the brief, hot contact sent a bolt of lightning through her. She barely had a chance to drag in a jagged breath before his mouth settled more firmly into place.

He pulled her close, wrapping her tightly in his embrace as she wound her arms around his neck. Her soft curves molded to his hard body. She parted her lips and his tongue took advantage of the invitation.

By unspoken agreement, as they kissed they moved inside. Neither flinched when J.B. kicked the door shut. They were too engrossed in the moment and the opportunity to taste and touch, when they'd assumed they'd never see each other again.

He tasted even more delicious than she'd remembered.

Her fingertips tingled as they found their way beneath his shirt to smooth, hot, bare skin.

Deep within her body throbbed. Issy was back where she belonged.

Except she didn't belong with J.B.

Issy broke off the kiss and wrenched her body out of his embrace. She shivered, even as waves of embarrassment washed over her, making her cheeks burn. She couldn't bring herself to meet his gaze. She wrapped her arms around herself, rubbing her hands up and down her goose bumps.

She raised her eyes to look at him. His jaw was set, his mouth a thin, hard line. His gaze was shuttered; cold and dark. If she didn't know better, she'd assume that he hadn't been as affected by their kiss as she had. Only his uneven breathing and the muscle working in his cheek gave the truth away.

Issy tried to soften her rejection. "We haven't figured out how any of this is going to work. This isn't the time to do…this." She waved her hand back and forth between them.

"Cool your jets. It was just a kiss. I'm not going to deny it was a great kiss—we hardly need any more proof that we connect on a physical level—but it wasn't a marriage proposal or anything."

His words sliced through the remaining haze of desire left from their kiss.

"It would take one hell of a kiss to make me forget your stance on anything to do with commitment and, nice as it was, it wasn't that great."

She hadn't thought his jaw could get any tighter.

"I want to make one thing clear," she continued. "Whatever role you decide you want to play in our child's life, there will be nothing physical between us."

"You won't get any argument from me."

She dug in her purse, pulled out a notepad and pen and handed them to him. "If you put your contact details on there, I'll forward the legal documents to you once they've been drawn up."

"I'll get my financial guy working on a suitable support package and I'll talk to the team's insurance people about adding you to my healthcare policy."

Issy wanted to argue that those steps weren't necessary, but she wouldn't cut her nose off to spite her face. Or her baby's. "Thank you. If you let me know what information they'll need, I'll make sure they get it promptly."

He opened the door. "Thanks for an...entertaining evening."

She cleared her throat. "Good night."

Issy watched him saunter down the path to the gate. Just when she thought she had everything under control, J.B. had to blast through her plans like one of his cannon-shot pucks.

CHAPTER ELEVEN

J.B. WAS WEARING the furry cat ears again. He'd had a four-point night—two goals and two assists—as part of a boat-race win over their hated rivals, the Rangers. The perfect way to end the preseason. He just hoped his run of good form would carry over into the regular season, which was less than a week away.

He felt good. Scratch that—he felt great. Everything was clicking. This was going to be his season. He knew it, deep down inside. Just as he had his first year in the show, when the Cats had won the Cup. Last season, when the feeling had been missing, he'd put it down to the fact that he was older, wiser and more experienced. Sadly, his gut feeling, or lack of one, had been proved right.

"You're buying the first round again," Paddy said as he toweled off after his shower. "I told you you'd have to run a tab."

J.B. zipped up his pants and slipped his wallet into his pocket. "Yeah. I'll have to speak to Delilah behind the bar and put down that deposit. This could be an expensive season."

"Here's hoping you have to take out a loan." Kenny shrugged into his sports coat. "I want to go all the way again."

Paddy nodded. "But this time I want to be drinking out of Lord Stanley's trophy instead of drowning my sorrows."

"I hear you." Mad Dog combed his wet hair. "Man, does that champagne have a special taste when you drink it out of the Cup."

"I'll take your word for it." Paddy hadn't been with the Cats when they'd last won the championship. "I hope that's not because Kris Draper's baby pooped in it back in '08."

Kenny laughed. "The guys who look after it clean it up real well every night."

"Before they sleep with it," J.B. added.

"There's a visual I don't need." Mad Dog gagged.

"Is that why they wear white gloves when they handle the Cup?" Kenny mused.

"Hell, I don't care. I can't wait for my turn." Paddy tossed his towel into the laundry bag. "I don't want to be one of those sad old guys who retire without ever having won it."

"I'll be a sad, old, starving and thirsty guy if you don't get your ass in gear." Kenny sat in his stall and rested his feet on his gym bag. "Come on, man. Get dressed already. There's a beer and a plate of burritos with my name on it."

"Keep your hair on. Larocque's not done yet, either."

"At least I've got my pants on." J.B. pulled on his shirt and began buttoning it.

Paddy's retort, involving an off-color reference to J.B.'s sexual preferences, was interrupted by a ringtone playing Twisted Sister's "We're Not Gonna Take It."

J.B. grabbed his cell from his locker. He didn't recognize the number. "Hello?"

He couldn't make out the reply because there was a lot of crackling and background noise. From the announcement, whoever was calling was at an airport.

"Hello?" he said again.

"Hold on…breaking up…moving…better coverage. Don't hang…"

The female voice sounded familiar. "Sapphie?"

Mad Dog's head shot up and he sent J.B. a questioning look.

J.B. shrugged. He had no idea why she'd be calling. Unless… Was there a problem with Issy?

"Just a second, J.B." The interference stopped and the connection became clear. "There, is that better?"

He wanted to yell at her to tell him what was wrong, but he told himself to stay calm. "You're coming through perfectly. What's up?"

"Nothing to worry about. I just need a huge favor."

"Is everything okay? Is Issy all right?"

"We're both fine, though the favor is for Issy."

"Okay, shoot."

"I'm supposed to go with Issy to her first ultrasound tomorrow. Unfortunately my flight out of O'Hare has been canceled because of bad weather and I can't get on another one until tomorrow morning. She says she's fine going by herself, but she shouldn't be alone for something so important. I know you don't want to get involved with the baby, but this is a good opportunity for you to show that you'll step up when it counts."

J.B. hesitated. He'd planned to hit a new club in the city that everyone had been raving about, especially since they had a few days before they had to play again.

He gave his head a shake.

What was he thinking? He could go the club anytime.

"I'll take her. What time's the appointment?"

"Nine fifteen, but she needs to be there at nine o'clock."

"All right. Do you have the address?"

"I'll text it to you. Thanks. I owe you one."

When he hung up he noticed the guys staring at him, clearly concerned.

"What's going on?" Mad Dog asked.

"It's no big deal." J.B. explained about Sapphie's travel hiccup. "It's a pretty easy procedure, with no gore or bodily fluids involved, so I'm good."

"Better take a clean handkerchief, for when you start to cry," Jake said, grinning as he joined the group. "It's a big moment, seeing your baby for the first time. Makes it real."

J.B. couldn't imagine getting emotional over one of those little snapshots he'd seen teammates passing around proudly. Half the time you couldn't even tell it was a baby.

"Just try not to pass out like Tru did," Paddy teased him.

"That was different," Kenny said. "It was all the needles and stuff that made him keel over, not a simple ultrasound."

"Needles?" J.B.'s stomach rolled.

"The needles were for the IVF that Jenny went through, numb nuts." Kenny rolled his eyes. "Issy's already pregnant. There won't be any needles."

J.B. wiped away the sweat that beaded on his forehead. "Okay. Great."

Mad Dog grinned. "I can take Issy if you're not up for it."

"No need. I can handle it."

"Now that's settled, can we please get our asses over to the restaurant?" Kenny slung his bag over his shoulder and headed out of the locker room.

"Somebody give the kid a candy bar so he'll shut up already," Paddy grumbled.

The rest of the guys followed behind, laughing.

J.B. did his duty and bought the drinks, made his obligatory, short thank-you speech and endured the also obligatory heckling. There was another round to honor Jake as their new captain. Bad Boy was already a great leader and a strong veteran voice in the locker room. It was another strong sign for the upcoming season.

Still, J.B. was glad when the shenanigans were over and he could dive into the food. He needed the distraction from his nerves about seeing Issy tomorrow. Which was dumb. What was there to worry about? He was simply playing chauffeur.

Mad Dog leaned toward him and said in a low voice, "You should call Issy and let her know about the change of plans, so it's not a big shock to her in the morning."

The enchilada he'd been eating suddenly tasted like cardboard. "Sapphie will already have done that."

Mad Dog elbowed him. "Call her, numb nuts."

He wasn't sure he liked the way both Sapphie and Taylor were finding ways to push him toward Issy. Treating him like a teenager with his first crush.

He grabbed his beer and headed toward the door, where it was quieter. He paused, his thumb hovering over her name in his cell's contacts list.

"Get on with it," he muttered before tapping the icon.

Issy answered after a couple of rings. "J.B.?" Her voice sounded a little husky, as though she'd been asleep.

He recalled how she'd looked that last morning in Antigua, her cheeks flushed, her eyes drowsy and heavy lidded. Fire headed straight to his groin.

Man, that was not a good thing in a room full of Ice Cats. He blinked to get the enticing picture out of his head, and tightened his grip on his cold beer bottle. Very cold. Icy.

He cleared his throat. "I'm sorry, did I wake you?"

"I think I was half-dozing in front of the TV." She paused, then asked warily, "Is there a problem?"

"Nope." At least there wouldn't be once his erection subsided. *Concentrate.* He rolled the cool bottle over his hot forehead. "Uh…just wanted to check what time I should pick you up in the morning."

"That's not necessary," she said quickly. "Sapphie shouldn't have called you. I'm fine driving myself to the appointment. No need for you to bother."

"It's no bother. So, when should I be there?"

"Okay. Thank you." Her tone became brisk. "The doctor's office isn't far from here, so around eight forty-five should give us enough time."

"Sounds good. I'll see you then." He hung up and walked back to the table.

Mad Dog passed him a platter of tacos.

J.B. helped himself to a couple.

"You're doing a good thing."

"You make it sound like that's a novelty."

"You're a good man, even if you act like a jerk sometimes." Taylor ducked J.B.'s head swat. "Issy seems kind of vulnerable compared to a lot of the women we meet."

"She's tougher than she looks. Surviving what she has isn't for cupcakes."

"Neither's being a single parent," Kenny said. "Just ask my mom."

"She's a saint." J.B. had been taken under her wing in his early days in the NHL. "She had four of you to raise. Five, if you include our new captain."

Jake's parents had helped Karina Jelinek when her rat of a husband had walked out on her, leaving her with four young sons. That's why Jake and the Jelineks were as close as brothers. J.B. was lucky enough to have become part of that group when he'd lived with Jake.

J.B. nursed his beer—he'd lost his appetite—biding his time until he could call it a night. At that point, Lise and her entourage walked in.

He knew he'd be expected to end the night with one of the puck bunnies. He didn't want to play that game. Anyway, it didn't seem right, given what he'd be doing in the morning.

He made up an excuse. "My leg's a little tight and I need to soak my muscles. I don't want to risk an injury before the season's even started."

Lise's gaze narrowed, but she didn't call him on it. Instead she sashayed around the table to Blade, the second star of the game, and dropped into his lap.

J.B.'s life was already changing and the kid hadn't even been born yet.

So FAR, THE MORNING had been an embarrassing exercise in awkward.

Issy tried to concentrate on the dog-eared food magazine that was months out of date and not on the brooding hockey player who sat beside her reading the latest sports headlines on his iPhone, in the ob-gyn waiting room.

It had started when J.B. arrived. He had looked at her like she'd had a snake in her belly, not a baby. Then, as they'd pulled into the parking lot, he'd asked if she'd received the health insurance and child support papers from the lawyers. She had.

The awkwardness had increased during the check-in for her appointment.

"Dad is welcome to accompany you, if you'd feel more comfortable with him there," the receptionist had said.

"I'm not—" J.B. had cleared his throat "—sure that's a good idea."

"That's fine." The woman had smiled, probably having seen countless nervous fathers-but-not-fathers before. "The nurse will call you through shortly."

"I'm sorry," he'd muttered when they'd sat in the only remaining pair of seats.

"No need to apologize," she'd replied quietly. "It's a new experience for me, too."

"I'll go in with you, if you want me to." He'd sounded like he'd rather stick a red-hot poker in his eye.

"That's okay." She hadn't been sure what the scan involved and wasn't comfortable with the thought of being naked in front of him. Which was silly given how she'd ended up in this situation in the first place. "I'd prefer to do this alone."

"Whatever you want." The edge of relief in his voice had been tangible.

Issy's nerves were ragged. It didn't help that J.B. fidgeted like a child who couldn't sit still—puffing out a breath and shifting his position every few minutes. Not that she blamed him. As the only man, surrounded by pregnant women, she could just imagine how out of place he felt.

It was also hard to ignore the obvious signs that several of the women were whispering about her and J.B. Probably just him; they were more likely to recognize J.B. than her.

The door opened and a beaming patient came out. The smell of disinfectant wafted into the waiting room behind her, turning J.B.'s skin a little green.

"Isabelle Brandine," the nurse called.

Both she and J.B. jumped.

Issy reached for his hand at the same moment he reached for hers.

He squeezed hers. "Are you sure you don't want me in there with you?"

She was touched by his offer. "I'll be okay, but thank you."

She rose and walked over to the nurse.

The scan went smoothly. The only moment of hesitation was when the technician asked whether she wanted to know the sex of her child. Issy wanted it to be a surprise but wondered whether J.B. would want to know.

While it had been good of him to come with her today, that didn't change anything. This baby was hers. Once the paperwork was signed, it would be official. So it was her decision.

"Please don't tell me," she said.

The technician smiled. "No problem. Let's see what Baby's up to this morning."

Getting a clear picture was tough as he or she moved around. A lot. Issy was relieved to hear that everything looked good. How the woman could tell, when it looked like a peanut with a blob sticking out of it—apparently an arm—Issy didn't know, but she was grateful all the same.

Suddenly the picture changed and Issy could see the clear shape of a baby lying on its back, its little arm waving.

Her heart squeezed so hard she almost couldn't breathe.

My baby.

Her throat tightened and her eyes welled with tears. She watched the screen, searching out every detail. When the baby moved again, turning back into a blobby peanut, she was disappointed. She wanted to stay there all day, waiting for another glimpse of her unborn child.

It was a shame J.B. had missed this.

"Here you go." The technician handed her a small, black-and-white printout of the screen shot. "I managed to catch Baby at the right moment, so you have a nice, clear picture."

"Thank you so much." Issy held on to the photo carefully. "Would it be possible to get a second print? For the father."

"Sure. He'll want to put it in his wallet and show it off to his friends."

Issy smiled noncommittally, knowing that was unlikely.

She managed to walk sedately out of the room and back toward the waiting area. Her head felt as if it was surrounded by sunshine and birds, like in a Disney movie. For the first time Issy actually felt pregnant. The nausea and aching breasts she'd experienced so far didn't count. Now, she felt complete.

J.B. stood as she came through the doors. His concerned look made Issy want to laugh.

"Everything okay?" His hand rested lightly at the small of her back, as if he was afraid to touch her.

"Perfect. I'll show you in a minute."

"Great…?"

His uncertainty made Issy want to laugh even more.

He hovered protectively while she set up another appointment. She was surprised when he checked the date against his calendar.

"That won't—" she started.

He cut her off. "I know it's not necessary. I'd like to bring you."

She wasn't sure what to think about this change in him. What did it mean? "Okay. If you're sure," she said hesitantly.

"I am."

Issy waited until they were walking across the parking lot to fill him in on the scan. "Everything's as it should be at around four months."

"Good. Did you find out what you're having?"

"No. I want it to be a surprise."

"I agree," he said. "It's like knowing what's inside your birthday presents before you open them—spoils the fun."

"Exactly. Though it will make painting the nursery a little more difficult. I wasn't going to do the whole pink or blue thing, but I would like to put some cute pictures up. I suppose I'll go unisex and choose animals."

He opened the car door for her. "When are you planning to decorate?"

"Over the next few weeks. Better to do it now than when I'm carrying a big bump." She sat in the car and put on her seat belt.

J.B. came around to his side. "Is it safe? Paint fumes and stuff?"

"As long as I keep a window open to let the room air."

"What about climbing ladders? That doesn't sound like something a pregnant woman should be doing." He frowned as he turned the key in the ignition.

"I painted the rest of my apartment myself and the doctor said I could do what I'd normally do. I'll be careful."

"Tell me when you plan to do it and I'll come round and paint for you. And before you start with the whole 'it's not necessary' thing—I know. But I can get a couple of the guys to help and we'll be done in no time. You can order us around."

His offer appeared to surprise him almost as much as it surprised her. He turned away and focused on driving out of the parking lot.

Issy bit back her instinctive refusal. She was

used to having to do everything herself. "Only if I can provide the food and drinks."

"Deal."

"Great. I'll scout out colors and borders and get back to you."

He nodded.

They were back to awkward.

She babbled about the scan. "The way Peanut kept moving around made me wonder if he or she would be a hockey player."

"Peanut?"

She explained about how their baby had looked like a peanut. "That reminds me. I have a copy of the scan for you." She dug around in her purse for the spare. "If you'd like it?"

He was quiet for a moment before he said, "Sure."

Once he'd parked, she handed him the picture.

He stared at it. "Definitely a peanut."

"What do you mean? You can see clearly that it's a baby. Look, there's its head and—" She broke off when she saw his lips quirk. "Very funny. Wait and see how you react when one of your teammates says something about Peanut."

"I'll be cool...then I'll introduce them to the business end of a hockey stick."

Issy laughed as J.B. got out of the car and came around to open her door. Whatever his faults, J.B. was always a gentleman.

When she got to her front door, she started to

worry about how to say goodbye. How to avoid more awkwardness.

He solved the problem by leaning to give her a brief kiss on the cheek. "You know where to get hold of me if you need anything."

Before she could answer, he turned and went back to the car. He'd driven off by the time she had her front door open.

Once inside, she pulled out the scan and fixed it to the refrigerator door with a heart-shaped magnet. Then, running her fingers over the image of her baby, she said, "Welcome home, Peanut."

Oh, my God—I'm having a baby!

What did she know about having a baby? Issy's secondhand experience with Rosa's pregnancy had hardly prepared her for having a child. Thoughts of her sister and Tinka brought another, more troubling, question into her head.

What did she know about being a mother and raising a child? She'd done her best to take care of Rosa and look how that had turned out.

Where did I go wrong? Issy had made sure her sister was fed, clean and clothed. Went to school; did her homework. Though there was barely a year between them, she'd tried to provide structure, boundaries and discipline. Rosa had gone off the rails, anyway.

Making mistakes with a child was bad enough, but a helpless, innocent baby? What hope did Issy have of getting it right with Peanut, if she couldn't get it right with her own sister?

She couldn't do this, let alone on her own. What was she thinking? There was a reason why she hadn't wanted to start a family until she was in a secure situation, with a husband to share the responsibility.

The phone rang, interrupting her downward-spiraling thoughts.

Issy grabbed the phone and answered it.

She should have checked the Caller ID.

Her stomach twisted when she heard a familiar voice. The very person she just been thinking about.

"Hey, sis. How's things in the big city?"

"Oh. Hi, Rosa." Her sister's timing was impeccable. Issy didn't have the energy to fake being all right, so she simply said, "Good."

"You sound weird. Did I call at a bad time? I thought this was your lunch break."

She really didn't want to tell her sister she'd lost her job. "I'm just tired."

"You have free periods this afternoon, right? Go home and take a nap. You can grade papers later."

"Maybe I'll do that."

"What's wrong?" Rosa demanded. "Something's up. I can hear it in your voice."

Issy closed her eyes, trying to keep the emotional tumult from breaking loose. She cleared her throat. "I'm fine."

"Bull. At least be honest with me."

The hurt in Rosa's voice broke through Issy's flimsy barriers.

She sank to the floor, her legs unable to support her. She couldn't hold back any longer. Slowly at first, then with gathering momentum, the whole story poured out. Words tumbled over each other, sometimes punctuated with an escaping sob. Tears streamed down her face.

Rosa asked an occasional question for clarification, but otherwise listened quietly until Issy ran out of steam.

Issy was wrung out by the time she'd finished. Her body ached, her eyes burned and her throat was raw. At the same time she felt a cathartic relief.

Dragging in a shuddering breath, she braced herself for her sister's reaction.

CHAPTER TWELVE

"WELL, THAT SUCKS."

Not what Issy had expected Rosa to say. Not even close. Maybe "Karma's a bitch" or "How the mighty have fallen." Even "Now you're really one of the family." There wasn't even a sarcastic edge to her sister's words.

"Tough break," Rosa added, her sympathy obvious down the phone line. "Especially as you were so careful."

Who was this woman and what had she done with Rosabelle?

Rosa continued. "The important thing is that you want the baby. You do, don't you?"

Issy's panic hadn't subsided completely. "Yes, of course. But that's not the issue."

"You'll be fine. And even if you make mistakes—which you will, because everyone does—remember that children survive crappy parents all the time. We both did. Although I had you to try to keep me in line."

"No offense, but that's hardly a resounding endorsement."

"None taken." Rosa's laugh was rueful. "You

can't put my stupidity on your shoulders. I was old enough to take responsibility for my actions. I chose not to. Was it a reaction to the boundaries you set? Sure, but then, if we'd had responsible parents, I'd have reacted against them, too. That's me—I hate rules and restrictions."

Issy wasn't convinced. "That wasn't what you said at the time."

"I wasn't ready to acknowledge it before. Maybe it's my age. Or maybe seeing that you're not so perfect, after all, has made it easier to admit."

"I'm nowhere near perfect." Issy was shocked that her sister felt that way about her.

"It's all relative. You've always acted like you had it all together, while I've been a mess." She sighed. "I made some dumb choices and blamed everyone but myself when they went badly. Then, you left. That was a huge wake-up call. I had to step up and look after Tinka because no one else would. I resented it like hell, but eventually I had to grow up. Tinka's turned out okay, in spite of all that. Though, God help me, I'm not sure I'll survive her teenage years. That really is karma coming back to bite me on the ass."

Rosa filled Issy in on her daughter's latest antics and the sisters shared a laugh.

Eventually, though, the conversation returned to Issy's situation.

"Are you coming home?" Rosa asked.

"No. I'm settled here." She didn't want to tell

her sister that returning would be a backward step. That she'd feel like a failure.

"And you don't want to get sucked back into the old issues."

Issy couldn't deny that, either. "I'm sorry."

"Our parents are what they are. I can handle them. But you never know—someday I may take you up on your offer and move with Tinka up to Jersey."

"You're welcome anytime. If you need any help, just say the word."

"Same goes. I don't know what I can do to help you through this, other than to reassure you that you'll be a great mom. Your baby is lucky."

Her sister's support touched her deeply. "I don't know about that."

"I do. And I plan to remind you regularly."

"I have a feeling I'll need reminding."

By the time she hung up Issy was exhausted. As she stood her muscles protested; her body was stiff from sitting on the floor for so long. Yet she felt lighter than she had since she'd discovered she was pregnant.

The joy she'd felt when she'd first seen Peanut washed back over her like the gently lapping waves on that Antiguan beach.

Issy laid her hand on her stomach, finally ready to forge the bond she'd been so wary of. "This may not be exactly as I'd planned, but I'll do my best for you, little one. I promise."

WHO'D HAVE THOUGHT a small, blurry, black-and-white picture would become J.B.'s talisman for the season?

He wasn't one for superstitions—the actions he performed regularly, before every game, were a routine. But as he stood by the boards with his linemates, watching hats rain onto the ice, J.B. was happy to call the scan photo anything the hockey gods wanted, as long as his good fortune continued.

Jake cuffed J.B.'s helmet. "Opening day hat trick. That's what I'm talking about."

"A win on home ice to start the season is exactly what we need." Kenny held up his stick, pointing the blade toward J.B. "Maybe you should kiss this to give me the same luck."

"Only if you kiss my award-winning ass first."

Mad Dog rolled his eyes. "Ever since that local women's magazine voted you the sexiest rear in the area's pro sports, you've been an award-winning *pain* in the ass."

"I can't help it if those ladies appreciate that my talents aren't restricted to the ice." J.B. climbed over the boards, sat on the bench and then swigged from his water bottle.

Paddy shook his head. "Carrying that oversize ego around must make it hard to stay upright on your skates."

"Just trying to deal with what life throws at me, the best way I can."

His teammates laughed and tossed crude but good-natured insults at him. J.B. didn't care. The points on the board were all that mattered.

"Whatever brought you, and us, this good fortune, keep it the hell up." Kenny slapped him on the shoulder. "And tell me where I can find something lucky, too."

"Hard work and single-minded determination are all that matters, kid," Paddy said. "No inanimate object can affect the outcome of a game."

"You'll believe in lucky charms when it affects your play," Kenny shot back.

"I'm going to need more than a four-leaf clover to get me back scoring."

"Maybe J.B. should be kissing *your* stick."

"In his wet dreams."

J.B. tuned out the conversation and tried to focus on the game. There was still enough time left to play in the third period for the Senators to score and even up the game again. A hat trick meant nothing if the Cats didn't win.

Still, not a bad start to the season, he thought as he watched the officials and the ice crew shovel up hats, most of which would be donated to a charity of J.B.'s choosing.

Maybe it was just coincidence about the scan picture, but J.B. wasn't about to mess with what seemed to work, and that photo was the only thing that had changed in his life.

When Issy had handed him the scan of their

child, J.B. had slipped it into the back of his wallet, assuming he'd forget about it. It wasn't like the picture was clear; despite Issy's insistence, the blob was more peanut than baby. And who got sentimental about a peanut?

J.B. had barely reached home before he'd pulled out the picture and stared at it.

A baby. For real.

His baby. Holy crap. He was going to be a *father*.

J.B. had stuck the photo back in his wallet, which was how it had ended up in his locker the following day. Then he'd had the best practice in months, so he'd kept the photo in his wallet.

Today's game sealed the deal.

"J.B., Paddy, Juergen, you're up." Macarty gave them an outline for the play he wanted executed, then sent them over the boards.

"Try for a pants trick," Kenny called after him.

J.B. touched his helmet in response as he skated to the far circle for a face-off.

Ever since a well-known hockey podcast had nicknamed a player scoring four goals in a game as a pants trick—resulting in fans throwing pants onto the ice—the Ice Cats had wanted one. So far, no one had managed it in their barn. There was even a pool on the board in the locker room, with everyone adding bills to sweeten the prize. The first player to score a pants trick would win the pot, which currently stood at several grand.

Not that anyone needed the money. But the kudos of winning kept scorers on their toes.

J.B. didn't register a shot during his shift. The Senators grew desperate as time ticked away. Another goal would kill off the game, so they put their bodies on the line to keep the puck from reaching their net. The second power-play unit didn't fare much better and the extraman advantage expired without a change in score.

Both teams played punch, counterpunch, with the action moving swiftly from end to end and back again. The Cats' defense, led by Jake, was solid, backstopped by Ike. They would not let this lead slip away.

With the clock down to the final two minutes in the game, the Sens pulled their goaltender for an extra attacker. This was the Cats' chance to close out the game with an empty-net goal. But first they had to stop their opposition from scoring.

Play was frantic as white jerseys swarmed the Cats' net. Shots pinged off the pipes and Ike's equipment, but the goaltender stood tall. Shift after shift, J.B. and his teammates poked and jabbed, trying to release the puck from the Sens' possession.

The announcer called the last minute of play. The battle in front of the net intensified, but still the puck wouldn't go in for the Sens.

When it squirted out of the melee to J.B., the crowd roared for him to shoot, but he didn't have a clear shot and he didn't want to risk an icing call with thirty seconds to go. He passed to Juergen, who skated into the zone and slotted the biscuit into the empty net, icing the game and guaranteeing the Cats' win.

J.B. hadn't got a pants trick, but he didn't care. The Cats were on their way; two points closer to another playoff run in April. This might only be the first game of the season, but every point counted.

The celebrations moved to the locker room after the game. Once again J.B. accepted the cat ears and wore them during the postgame press calls.

"Why don't we just put your initials on the damn things?" Kenny mumbled good-naturedly as he buttoned his shirt. "The way you're playing, no one else will get a look-in."

"Sure they will." J.B. placed the cat ears on the shelf in his locker. "This can't continue all season. Besides, there are other valuable players on the team. Our D was solid tonight."

"Maybe your luck will hold, and you'll give Sid and Ovi some competition," Kenny said.

"It's one game."

"Enjoy it while you can," Paddy said. "I wouldn't mind ending my dry spell."

"You always get hot against Western Conference teams, so you'll come good on our road trip."

The Cats would be leaving immediately after their next game for an eight-day, five-game swing through California, returning via Detroit and Nashville. It was a tough start to the season, but at least it got the trip out of the way early on. Hopefully their good play would continue. J.B. knew what he'd be taking along with him to help.

"See you guys at my place," Jake called before leaving the locker room.

Since the Cats' home opener was an afternoon game, Jake and Maggie were hosting a buffet dinner to celebrate the new season and Jake's captaincy. Wives, children, partners and extended family were all invited. Parties at the Badoletti's were always great, so the whole team was looking forward to letting off some postgame steam.

J.B. usually went stag. It was easier all around and meant he avoided any searching questions from the two moms—Jake's mother, Tina, and Kenny and Ike's mother, Karina. The best friends who'd kind of adopted him as an extra son during his early days as an Ice Cat, fussed over him, much as they did their own children. In turn, he teased and flirted with them.

The party this evening was different; Issy would be there.

Though Jake had told him to invite her, J.B. hadn't wanted to send the wrong message—to her and everyone else. Before he could wrap his head around it, Taylor had stepped in and invited both Sapphie and Issy.

They'd accepted.

Impatient to get going, he chirped at Paddy who, as usual, was the last to be ready. "Come on, man. Your ugly face isn't getting any prettier as you mess with it."

Paddy tossed his wet towel at J.B. "You're just jealous. Women like your ass, but they love my face."

Kenny laughed until J.B. dropped the towel on his friend's carefully combed hair. "Hey, don't mess with the goods."

Mad Dog shook his head. "If you're ready, ladies, it's time to party."

A short time later the group strolled into Jake's house and made their way through to the big kitchen where everyone had gathered.

Instantly, J.B. felt at home, not to mention a familiar twinge of guilt. Was he as pleased to see his folks as he was to see Jake's mom and dad? Or Aunt Karina and her husband, Rory? The sobering answer was that he loved to see his mom, but not his father.

J.B. spotted Sapphie and Issy almost immediately, by the heavily laden kitchen table, having an animated conversation with the two moms. Aunt Karina and Aunt Tina were probably grilling the younger women with the subtlety of the FBI questioning a murder suspect.

He sauntered over and put his arm around the two older women, kissing both on the cheek. "So this is where my favorite ladies are hanging out."

The moms laughed, demurring. Sapphie rolled her eyes. Issy sipped her drink but wouldn't meet his gaze.

"It must be if you're here," Aunt Tina said fondly.

"I always said he's a smart boy." Aunt Karina patted his cheek. "If I was thirty years younger, I'd give you girls a run for your pennies."

J.B. grinned. Although her English was good, it was her adopted language, and Kenny's mom was well-known for mixing up phrases. "Don't you mean a run for your money?"

Aunt Karina waved her hand. "Pfft. Pennies, money. It's the same, no?"

"Of course," Issy said earnestly, shooting J.B. a stern look.

"We understood what you meant." Sapphie smiled.

"*Thirty* years, Karina?" Aunt Tina arched an eyebrow. "More like forty."

Her friend shrugged. "I figured he could handle a tiger."

"Cougar, Ma," Kenny said as he joined the group. "An older woman is a cougar."

"I know what I meant." Aunt Karina winked at her son. "Just ask Rory."

Kenny looked horrified. "Whoa! Way too much info, Ma."

Everyone laughed.

J.B. snagged a beer from the counter. "Here, that'll take the taste out of your mouth."

"Thanks." Kenny drank as though he'd been in the desert for weeks. "On that note, Jake sent me over to tell you we're running low on ravioli, meatballs and potato salad."

"We'll put some more out," Tina said. "Make sure these lovely young ladies get some food, Jean-Baptiste, before it's all gone."

"Yes, ma'am," J.B. said.

She turned to Issy and Sapphie. "The boys are like vultures after a game. If you don't move quickly, there won't be anything left."

"We will," Issy replied. "Everything looks and smells so good, I may need two plates."

"As long as you keep your hands off mine." J.B. steered her over to the buffet. "I know what you're like about stealing food."

Issy's blue eyes twinkled. "You stole the shrimp from my plate."

"What about those chocolate-dipped cherries?"

"You gave those to me."

"So I did." The memory of feeding her made his groin tighten.

"They were delicious." She moistened her lips.

The party seemed to fade around them until it felt as if there were only the two of them in that kitchen.

"Yes, they were." His husky tone left no doubt that he wasn't talking about the cherries.

He stepped closer, until their bodies touched. Even though they were both fully dressed, desire fizzed along his skin as if they were naked.

Her cheeks turned pink. The pulse at the base of her throat fluttered.

He lowered his head. "Let's see if I can find something you'll enjoy just as much."

Her lips parted.

Then someone knocked him in the back and he stumbled forward into Issy's arms.

Startled, her eyes widened as she steadied him.

He took advantage of the moment and held on to her.

Neither of them moved for a few seconds.

Then she stiffened and pulled away, frowning.

J.B. looked over his shoulder at his teammate, Blade.

"Sorry." Blade grinned, clearly unrepentant. "I was trying to avoid stepping on the cat."

A black cat sat beneath the table, washing its face.

J.B. and Issy focused on filling their plates. He got her a drink. She thanked him. She pointed out her seven-layer dip. He gave himself an extra helping. They grabbed a couple of empty chairs in the living room, and conversation ebbed and flowed around them as they ate.

"So I spoke to a few guys—Mad Dog, Kenny, Paddy, Ice Man and Blade—and they'll help out painting the nursery," J.B. finally said. "Between the six of us, we'll get the room decorated in no time."

"That's nice of them. I'll make sure I get plenty of food and drink. Jake's mom was right about how much you all eat."

He grinned. "We burn up a lot of calories during a game. It's harder work than it looks."

"As someone who's never set foot on ice, skating looks like very hard work."

"Maybe I could give you skating lessons sometime."

She surprised him by saying, "I'd like that. But it can't be for a while, obviously."

"Uh, sure. Whenever you're up for it, say the word."

"When do you think you guys will be free for a painting party?"

He explained about the road trip. "We leave right after our next game—the day after tomorrow—then get home to a packed schedule, including a couple of back-to-back games. It'll be early November before we get a decent break, so we can spend the day at your place."

"That's okay. I've got a lot to sort out before then." She sipped her drink. "Who knew a baby needed so much stuff."

"It'll be fine." He laid his hand over hers. "Have you decided what color you want to paint the nursery?"

She smiled. "I've found these really sweet animal wall stickers. They're big enough to make the wall look like a painted mural. So I thought I'd paint the bottom half green and the top half blue, with the ceiling white. Once I've added the animal stickers, it'll look like they're playing outdoors."

"Sounds good. Blade's arty—he could probably paint some trees and stuff."

"Oh, that would be lovely."

Her face lit up, sending a warm glow through him and making him want to offer more to keep her looking happy. "We could help you put the nursery furniture together, too, at the same time."

"That would be a huge help."

"Then we're set. I'll get back to you with some dates and you can choose which suits you best."

"Sounds good. I'd planned to go furniture shopping tomorrow afternoon. Would you like to come with me?"

"I'm not sure I can make it."

Wandering around furniture departments or baby stores, or wherever you got baby furniture from, wasn't high on J.B.'s list of fun things to do on his last free afternoon for almost a month.

"That's okay." The disappointment in her eyes was a kicker. "Don't worry. I'll be fine by myself."

He frowned. "Won't Sapphie be going with you?"

Issy shook her head. "She's got a couple of big new business pitches coming up, so she's flying out to Chicago later tonight and won't be back for a few weeks."

J.B. bit back a sigh. "Maybe I could spare an hour or two."

"Only if you're sure. It's not—" She gave him a sheepish smile.

"I am."

The gratitude in her expression was worth it. And it was only a shopping trip. Nothing between them had changed, he tried to reassure himself. Somehow he wasn't convinced.

"I THOUGHT YOU preferred the four-in-one convertible crib."

Why did J.B. have to challenge every choice she made?

Issy knew he was trying to be helpful. She really appreciated the time he'd spent traipsing from baby store to furniture store to department store with her—especially as she'd steeled herself for him canceling. And, to his credit, though he'd initially looked like he was facing a root canal without anesthetic, he'd valiantly helped her navigate the vast array of baby items on offer; from bassinets and dressers to baby monitors and diaper disposal units.

But he was slowly driving her nuts.

They were sitting in a funky little café-cum-bookstore in her neighborhood. J.B. wanted their baby to have everything top-of-the-range and had no concept of budget.

"The standard crib is good value and it has a nice matching dresser with a changing-table topper." Issy sipped her tea, trying to shore up her patience.

"But the other one can be converted into a toddler bed, then a sofa, and has the dresser built in."

"It's also three times the price of the crib and dresser combined."

"It'll save you money in the long run, because the kid can use it longer."

"I can't afford to spend that much on one item, even if it is multipurpose. I have so many other things to buy and I haven't even started looking at high chairs or strollers or car seats." The thought of what she had to do to prepare for her baby was overwhelming.

J.B. looked thoughtful. "If money were no object, which crib would you prefer?"

He was annoyingly persistent. "You know the answer."

"What if I buy the furniture for you?"

Issy bristled. Why was money always his solution? "Babies have survived for centuries without fancy cribs. In some European countries, babies sleep in a box. Peanut will be fine with a standard crib."

"Whoa." J.B. held up his hands. "That didn't come out right. I meant that if I topped up your budget, you could get the crib you really want without strapping yourself."

"You're giving me enough money already."

"How about if I match your budget and you decide if you want to spend the money on that four-in-one crib or something else?"

Issy knew throwing money at problems kept him from having an emotional connection to them. Well, she wouldn't let him buy his way out of responsibility. "I'll accept your generous offer on one condition."

"What's that?"

"You're involved in the decision-making."

His laughter had a nervous edge. "I'll put the furniture together and I'll help you research the specifications. Isn't that involvement enough?"

Issy looked at him steadily.

"I trust your judgment." He gave her his famous charming smile. "Anyway, I'll be busy playing and traveling. I won't be able to go on more shopping trips with you. As much fun as this one has been."

Her answering smile was sweet. "I'll email you the links and you can send me your opinion."

"You're not going to give up, are you?" He rubbed his hand over his jaw.

"Nope. Of course, if you don't give me the money, we'll be all square."

J.B. sighed. "All right. I accept your condition."

"Then I'll accept your check."

"And you'll get that four-in-one crib."

She could be gracious in victory. "Thank you. I will."

"And you can buy us both a couple of chocolate brownies to celebrate."

Issy laughed. "Hold up. Brownies aren't baby goods. They shouldn't come out of the baby budget."

"You tell me that when this kid is driving you insane at 2:00 a.m. for the third night running. Ask Jake what Maggie stocked up on for the first six months of Joe's life. Chocolate, chocolate and more chocolate. I'd say they're essential baby goods."

"You're just saying that because you don't want to buy the brownies."

"Aha. So now you're happy to spend my money."

"Chocolate is the exception to any rule." Her lofty tone was spoiled by her grin.

"I wish someone would write these rules down." He rose. "I guess I'd better get some brownies, then. Are you sure you don't want a pickle or some other weird thing with that?"

"My cravings are more savory—seven-layer dip, hummus. Although, perhaps a brownie dipped in hummus…" She laughed as J.B. looked horrified. "Just kidding."

"Are you done for today or would you like to hit some more places?" J.B. asked when they finished eating the brownies.

Issy was hit by a wave of tiredness. "I'm worn-out." She yawned. "I'm sorry. This happens a lot. I'm fine and then, all of a sudden, I need to sleep."

"Let's get you home." He cleared away their stuff. "Am I allowed to say I'm glad? I don't think I can handle looking at high chairs right now."

"Be grateful you'll miss the rest of the shopping. Your road trip is conveniently timed."

"I got the NHL to organize it specially."

"Why doesn't that surprise me?" Her steps dragged as they walked back to his car. She'd barely got her seat belt fastened before she'd fallen asleep.

When Issy awoke she was still in the car, but it wasn't moving. J.B. sat in the driver's seat, tapping his phone. The dashboard clock told her she'd been asleep for almost two hours.

"I can't believe I slept that long." Embarrassed, she straightened and undid her seat belt. "You must have stuff to do before you leave tomorrow night. You should have woken me."

J.B. looked up from his phone. "I tried, but you were sleeping like the dead. You have a cute snore."

"I do not snore."

"How do you know, if you're asleep?"

"Sapphie would have told me."

"She probably didn't want to upset you." He tapped the side of his nose. "Don't worry, your secret's safe with me."

She rolled her eyes. "Pots shouldn't call kettles black."

"Yeah, yeah. Seriously, I did try to wake you, but when I couldn't, I figured it was best to let you sleep. I thought about carrying you inside, but I didn't want to dig around in your purse for your keys."

She laughed even as her cheeks warmed at the thought of being cradled in those strong arms.

She took out her keys. "Thanks for coming with me today."

"You're welcome. It was surprisingly fun."

"Compared with what? Getting stitches?"

He smiled. "I'm serious. I enjoyed being with you."

"I enjoyed being with you, too."

The silence in the car was heavy with unspoken words.

Before it could turn awkward, Issy opened her door. "Have a good trip."

J.B. got out of the car.

She gave him a half smile. "I'll be okay."

"Work with me here."

"All right." She unlocked her front door and slowly climbed the stairs. "There you go. Safe and sound."

He smoothed a loose strand of hair from her cheek. "You have my contact details, right? In case you need to get hold of me while I'm away."

"I do, and I'll be fine. I appreciate the concern,

but there's not a whole lot you can do from California. Just concentrate on your game and not getting injured."

"So you worry about me, too." His cocky grin made her pulse skip.

Damn it. Why couldn't she be immune to him? "How will I get the nursery painted and all that furniture put together if you're laid up?"

"It'll get done. Even if I have to organize things from a hospital bed. Trust me."

Strangely she did. "I can imagine. All those nurses lining up to do favors."

"I meant you could rely on my buds to help you out."

"Still, I'd rather you weren't injured."

"Pfft. Not gonna happen." He waved a hand dismissively. "Email me with how you're getting on. About the furniture and anything else. Take care of yourself and Peanut."

"Yes, Mom."

"Definitely *not* your mother." He pressed a brief kiss to her lips.

Before she could react, he'd gone.

The sound of the front door closing spurred her to move. She touched her fingers to her lips and sighed. She really couldn't fathom him.

She understood the issues with his family and his childhood. It wasn't as if she didn't have her own baggage. But, as she got to know him better, she found it hard to believe that he would abandon his own child.

J.B. was a good person and a loyal friend. She'd seen several examples of the man he was at the party. From the respect and affection he'd shown Jake's parents, to the camaraderie with his teammates, to his indulgent teasing of Emily and Joe. There were definitely more layers to Jean-Baptiste Larocque than she'd first thought.

The more time she spent with him, the more she wanted to find the real man hidden beneath the cocky but charming exterior. She was also aware that, like the proverbial onion, the risk she took peeling away those layers was that she could end up in tears.

But for the sake of their child, she had to try.

Her cell beeped a few minutes later with a text. Put your feet up!

For a man who didn't want ties or responsibilities, he was getting very involved.

CHAPTER THIRTEEN

"Nice postgame interview."

Issy's voice washed over J.B., firing his blood, even though she was talking to him over a crackling phone line from Jersey and he was in Nashville. He sat on the bed, stretching his tired legs out in front of him. Three-o'clock face-offs were hard on the body, especially at the beginning of the season. He hated missing his afternoon nap; it messed with his system. Maybe he was getting old.

No freaking way.

"You saw it?" The thought of her watching him on TV pleased him. "Did you catch the whole game?"

"I did. Another goal to add to your tally. The announcer said you're averaging over a goal a game. At this rate you'll be breaking NHL records."

The admiration in her voice made him feel like he'd already won the Rocket Richard scoring trophy. "Thanks for the vote of confidence, but Gretzky holds the record with ninety-two. The closest anyone has come in the past seventeen years is around sixty in a season."

"Then it's time someone changed that. Why not you?"

"I'd love it to be me and I'll be trying." He searched the internet on his tablet. "Even if I got a goal a game from now until April—eighty-two— I'd still only be fifth on the all-time list."

"Not that you've checked."

"It's always good to know where you stand." He settled back more comfortably against the pillows and drained his Coke Zero. "Anyway, the number of goals isn't as important as the number of wins."

Issy groaned. "I'm glad I don't drink. I'd be totally blitzed by now."

"I don't get it." J.B. frowned, confused.

"Sapphie has a drinking game based on clichés in player and coach interviews. You have to take a shot for every time someone says 'we need to stick to our game,' 'we have to execute our system,' 'we need to be more disciplined' or 'it's not my goal that matters, but the win for the team.' What you said has to be on the list."

J.B. thought back to his comments after the game and winced. "I went four for four."

"You weren't the worst—that guy who stands between the benches is terrible." She laughed. "Like I said, it's a good thing I only drink soda."

"So, did you enjoy the game?"

He didn't know why it was so important that

she liked hockey. He'd dated plenty of women who hadn't.

Since he'd be spending time with Issy, at least until the baby was born, and the situation was fraught enough, it would help if she didn't hate hockey.

Her enthusiasm was a relief.

"I'm finally getting the hang of the rules and can actually follow the play now. It's a lot easier in the arena, where you can see all the action. Of course, no one hears me swear at the officials at home."

"Anytime you want tickets, let me know. I have two seats by the glass."

"Thanks, but the seat next to Sapphie is empty, so I can go with her."

He shoved his disappointment aside. So what if she didn't want his seats? "If the two of you ever want to watch the game from the lower bowl, my seats are yours."

"I may take you up on that."

"Anytime." He changed the subject. "Have you ordered all the furniture, so it'll be ready for our nursery-painting party in a couple of weeks?"

"Everything essential will be here by next Friday. I emailed you the color references for the paint. Let me know what you think."

"I'll check them out later. Did you figure out how many cans you'll need?"

"I did, thanks to that idiot's guide you sent me."

Issy laughed. "You should see all my math. I must have recalculated a dozen times to make sure I got it right."

Issy yawned. "Sorry. It's my bedtime. I should let you go. You probably have a club to hit."

Normally she'd have been right. Nashville was a great city to visit, especially when they had an off day before they played the Predators. He'd always scored more than goals in Nashville and he'd scored plenty of those over the years.

Tonight, though, the partying had quickly worn thin. He'd ducked out early and joined Jake, Ike, Juergen and a few others for dessert at their favorite restaurant, then headed back to the room he shared with Ice Man. The veteran forward was currently out at a blues bar with Mad Dog, Kenny and Blade.

J.B. had wanted to call Issy before she went to bed.

He and Issy had spoken practically every day on this trip. Usually after dinner, except on game days, when they'd catch up before his afternoon nap.

It was a little unsettling. He'd never communicated so much with a woman before. Then again, he'd never wanted to. But, as the trip wore on, he found himself thinking about Issy more and more. He tried not to think about the implications of that. He didn't want to go there.

He'd also picked up a couple of gifts for her

on impulse. While in California, he'd bought a second-hand CD with the song they'd done that crazy dance to—"Oops Upside Your Head"—in Antigua.

"J.B.?" Issy's voice broke into his thoughts. "Are you okay?"

"Tired, too," he admitted rather than explain what he'd really been thinking about. "How's Peanut behaving?"

"So far, so good. I haven't felt a kick yet, but I keep getting a sensation of movement." She chuckled. "It's probably indigestion."

Gross. Sounded like something from a movie about aliens. "Is it weird?"

"Not really. Just different."

"Rather you than me."

"I didn't get much choice in the matter." She yawned again.

"Go. Get some sleep."

"Good luck tomorrow evening."

"Thanks. It'll be a tough game. The Predators have started the season hot and Rinne is like a brick wall in net."

"Lucky that you're just as hot, then." The husky note in her voice suggested she wasn't just talking about his play on the ice.

"Yeah. Sleep well."

"Good night."

J.B. was restless once he'd hung up. He switched on the TV, but nothing caught his interest. He started to read the thriller he'd picked up at the airport, but the plot was too complicated and needed his full attention. He was too wired to sleep.

The hotel was too quiet.

Maybe he'd go down to the bar and get a drink. Some of the older guys might be hanging out down there. Maybe he'd just grab something from the minibar instead.

What's your problem? He pulled himself up short. Jeez, he was acting like he was middle-aged. He should haul ass, get changed and go out. It wasn't that late.

He stalked over to the closet, grabbed some clothes and tossed them on the bed.

Twenty minutes later he strolled into the blues bar and saw his pals at a table in the back.

Kenny wolf-whistled. "Look who finally decided to grace us with his presence."

"Missed me, did you?" Ice Man grinned.

"Like a hole in the head." J.B. motioned the waitress to bring him a beer.

"What changed your mind?" Mad Dog raised his beer bottle in a toast.

"He finished blowing kisses down the phone to the lovely Isabelle." Kenny made loud smooching noises.

"Aw, you lonely for your girlfriend, Larocque?" Blade asked while the rest laughed like a pack of freaking hyenas.

"Funny." J.B. flipped them the bird. "I wanted

a night where I didn't have to stare at your ugly faces, but I realized if I wasn't here, you'd be miserable and boring." He waved his arm around to emphasize his statement. "No one should leave Nashville until they've had a great time. As good as the music is, sitting and listening is *not* my idea of a great time."

His so-called friends responded with a variety of colorful expletives.

J.B. arched an eyebrow. "I'm not hearing any denials. Who's up for a couple of hours in this sweet club I know not far from here? The music's hot and the babes are hotter."

"Let's crank up the volume and party." Ice Man pumped his fist in the air. "I'm ready for some Tennessee action."

The others chorused their agreement and finished their drinks. Chairs scraped back and, en masse, they headed for the door.

THEY MADE IT back to the hotel just before curfew.

A short time later J.B. lay on his back, staring at the ceiling, still unable to sleep. It wasn't Ice Man sawing logs that kept him awake—J.B. had learned to tune that out—but the worrying realization that he hadn't enjoyed the night as much as he should have.

The club had been hopping, as always. The band had been young but enthusiastic and extremely talented. Gorgeous women had flocked around the hockey players like honey bees. Hell, J.B.'d had enough phone numbers stuffed into his pockets to keep him busy until Christmas. The other guys had been in their element.

The evening had been fun, but it had lacked something. J.B. hadn't been interested in a single woman. One dance, one drink, one selfie and he'd moved on. Partway through the night, Blade had muttered that J.B. was being too damn picky. At the time, his friend had had a blonde on one arm, a brunette on the other and a redhead in his lap.

As the bedside clock hit midnight, J.B. admitted to himself that he'd found fault with every woman he'd met tonight because he'd compared them all to Issy. And they'd fallen short.

She'd pretty much ruined them for him.

"I'M CONFUSED." Issy sighed as she opened a pizza box and placed it on the breakfast bar.

Sapphie, on the opposite side of the counter, did the same with a second of eight extralarge pies to feed the hungry men decorating Issy's soon-to-be nursery. "What's up?"

Issy looked over her shoulder, but 80s rock continued to blare from a boom box and there was no interruption in the rumble of deep male voices.

"Don't worry," Sapphie said. "They're still hard

at it. Although the smell of pizza will have them out of there shortly, so spill."

Issy laid out a third box. "Ever since J.B. got back, he's been acting strangely."

"I thought the two of you were getting on well. From the way he's behaved toward you today, he's hooked on you." She gave Issy a knowing smile. "He's superattentive and very touchy-feely. And those looks he keeps giving you..." Sapphie fanned herself. "Phew! Scorching."

"Exactly. If you didn't know better, you'd think there was something going on between us. Except we're not a couple."

"Have you asked him what's brought on this new behavior?"

Issy set a stack of plates next to the pizzas. "It's not as easy as you make it sound, Sapphie. We've hardly seen each other. The Cats' schedule has been brutal since they got back. He's stopped by unexpectedly a couple of times, to see how I am, but he doesn't stay long." She lowered her voice. "And he keeps kissing me."

"Now I'm confused. Kissing is usually a good thing." Sapphie frowned. "Unless they're friendly pecks."

"They're definitely not platonic." Issy's cheeks warmed at the memory of some of J.B.'s short, hot kisses. "But what am I supposed to say to him? 'How come you don't want a serious relationship with me, but you keep kissing me like I matter to you?'"

Sapphie laughed. "That is confusing. He hasn't said anything to explain this new überfriendly behavior?"

"Not a word. I feel as if I'm missing something. Does he assume we're dating?"

"Why not let it ride for a bit and see where it goes?"

"I have to think about Peanut. I need to know where I stand."

"My godchild won't be here for a while yet," Sapphie said gently. "A lot can change in five months."

"I don't want another fling, thank you."

"Then speak to him. You have the perfect opportunity this evening, once we've all left."

"I'm afraid raising the issue will spoil what we've got."

"Which is why, if it were me, I'd let sleeping dogs lie."

"I wish I could, but I can't. I need to know."

"Why?" Sapphie asked. "And don't tell me for Peanut's sake."

Issy was saved from having to find an answer when Taylor came out of the spare room to get drinks.

He grinned when he saw the pizzas lined up

on the kitchen counter. "Great. I'm starving." He stuck his head back into the nursery. "Food's here."

"Beers are in the cooler," Issy called out. "Help yourself."

A chorus of approval greeted the announcement.

Issy smiled. She'd enjoyed having the men here today. Their noise and bustle had filled her apartment. Even now, as they piled out of the nursery, they were razzing each other. This was the first time she'd been around a group of men—her family had been overrun by females.

In no time her small kitchen was crowded with big men loading their plates.

"We're pretty much done. Just a few things to finish off once the paint dries." J.B. tossed his arm casually over her shoulder. "Want to take a look?"

Issy arched an eyebrow at Sapphie. "Lead on."

The nursery was taking shape nicely. The trim gleamed glossy white. Below the line of the windowsill was a soft kelly green, which Blade had turned into rolling hills. Above the hills was the blue of a summer's day. The white ceiling had been textured to look like fluffy clouds, with patches of sky in between. The sun encircled the light fixture and, in the far corner, by the built-in closet, he'd painted a rainbow as if it burst out the doors.

Issy was touched. "I love it. It's even better

than I imagined. I can't believe how much trouble you've gone to."

"It was our pleasure." J.B. squeezed her shoulder. "Blade said he'll come back next time the Cats have a free day to add the finishing touches and help you apply the wall stickers."

"That's so nice of him."

"Yeah, real nice." J.B. snorted dismissively. "The crib and the dresser are assembled, too. We put them in your bedroom, with the rest of the baby stuff, for now. I'll help you move it when the nursery is finished."

She turned her head to smile at him. "Thank you."

Suddenly she was too aware that they were standing alone in the empty room. Of the weight of his arm on her shoulder. Her pulse skipped at the desire in his eyes as they dropped to focus on her mouth.

They'd barely touched when a fluttering sensation in her stomach reminded her of Peanut's presence. And her responsibilities.

She pulled back and slipped away from his arm, forcing a bright note into her voice. "You've earned your dinner. You'd better hurry or your pals will have eaten all the pizza."

He said nothing as he walked back to the kitchen with her, but the message in his eyes said they'd talk about it later.

After they'd eaten, the guys cleaned up and left.

"I'm off, too." Sapphie grabbed her purse. "Early flight to LA. That famous bad-boy chef wants me to look at his business."

Issy accompanied her to the front door. "Aren't you worried he'll yell at you, like he does on TV?"

"If he does, I'll yell right back. Besides, I'll be the one telling him to shape up, not the other way around." Sapphie gave her a pointed look. "Will you be okay?"

"I'll be fine." She hugged her friend. "Either way."

Issy watched until Sapphie's taillights disappeared in the distance before she closed the door and returned upstairs.

J.B. stood in the doorway of the nursery. She couldn't tell what he was thinking. "You guys did a great job."

"That's the beauty of teamwork. Especially when you have a PITA project manager like Blade to orchestrate the whole thing."

"You gave him enough abuse because of it."

"That's the downside of being the boss. One reason I'm glad I don't wear the C for the Ice Cats."

She looked at him curiously. "You don't want to be captain?"

"I don't mind being one of the voices in the locker room that guys listen to, but I don't need the aggravation."

Her heart sank. Another area where J.B. didn't want responsibility. Given how much he valued the team and his career, that didn't bode well for her or their baby.

Maybe she didn't need clarification on where she stood that badly after all.

"Blade's got a real artistic talent." She ran her fingers over the "grass" on the nearest wall, then walked over to the closet to study the rainbow. "And an amazing attention to detail. You can almost see a pot of gold. It's hard to imagine a big guy like him, who throws such punishing hits on the ice, could be so sweet."

"Yeah. He's real sweet," J.B. growled. "Don't be fooled. He's as dangerous as he looks."

"You're not jealous, are you?"

"No, because I know you think my face is prettier than his."

"You're not bad."

"Not bad?" He stepped closer, until he was looming over her. "You can do better than that."

He didn't scare her. She moistened her lips. "I don't know. Blade has such clever hands, too."

"He may be skilled with a paintbrush, but I'm way more talented with my hands than he is."

"Really?" Issy was stepping into dangerous territory. There was only way this flirting would end. Her heart pounded.

Sex with J.B. would mean nothing more than it had in Antigua. He wouldn't magically change his mind about commitment or responsibility. Was she prepared to accept that?

He trailed a finger gently down her face to her mouth, then traced its outline before lingering along the seam of her lips.

She swallowed hard. "I can see that you have a talented touch."

His fingertip left her mouth to caress the edge of her jaw to her ear, then down the side of her neck to the place at the base of her throat where her pulse throbbed.

She couldn't help tilting her head back to give him better access.

He took advantage, pressing a hot, open-mouthed kiss to the spot. "Still need convincing?"

Before she could formulate a coherent reply, J.B. nibbled his way up her throat. He kissed her chin, then his tongue skated along her lower lip, teasing her mouth open. Wrapping his arms tightly around her, he settled his lips firmly onto hers.

This time Issy didn't pull away but locked her arms around his neck and kissed him back.

Their bodies pressed closer, and still closer, until clothing became an unwelcome barrier and they moaned with frustration. She dropped her hands to his waist—to pull the faded Cats T-shirt from his jeans—then slipped them underneath to the silky skin of his back. His arms loosened, so his fingers could skim up her sides to rest on the undercurve of her breasts. Their caresses grew more urgent.

Issy wanted more. Much more. She ached with need. But, in the recesses of her fogged brain, she knew that giving in to that need now would be a mistake.

Slowly, regretfully, she eased back on the kiss.

J.B. didn't object, resting his forehead against hers.

They said nothing but were both breathing heavily.

Finally he lifted his head. He watched her carefully, as if he wasn't sure how she'd react. He didn't release her, but his hold loosened slightly, giving her the opportunity to move away should she want to.

She didn't. Issy cleared her throat. "Where are we going with this, J.B.?"

"Where do you want to go with it?"

"Oh, no. You're not turning that around onto me. You agreed to the ground rules for our being together, then proceeded to break them at every opportunity."

He hitched a shoulder. "I'm not very good with rules."

"You are when you need to be. Hockey has strict rules."

"True."

"So you can abide by rules—when it matters."

"You matter," he said quietly.

She allowed herself to be pleased for a moment. "What does that *mean*?"

He exhaled heavily. "I want to see where we can go with this."

"This, as in 'us'? You want us to be a couple?"

He nodded.

"You know that any relationship will have to include Peanut? We're a package deal."

"Peanut isn't due for five months. That gives us plenty of time to figure this thing out."

His answer set off warning bells. "You want us to sleep together until the baby's born and then you'll decide whether or not you want to continue fishing or cut bait."

J.B. ran his hand over his head. "I don't know how I'll feel when Peanut is born. I only know how I feel right now. There's definitely something between us. You feel it, too. I want to explore what we have, but I won't make false promises."

His honesty should have made things easier, but it did the opposite. Issy also wanted to explore the attraction between them, but she had to be realistic. How could that change his feelings about relationships? About responsibility?

"What's the point? We'd have a good time for a while, but we both know that one of us will be disappointed down the line." She matched his honesty. "We have a child on the way. One who'll be affected by how this turns out."

To give him credit, he didn't back down. "I won't lie to make you feel comfortable. You deserve better than that. All I can say is that I feel differently about you than about any other woman I've dated. I don't know if what I feel is, or can be, anything more. I can only promise I'll always be honest. You need to decide if you can accept that."

She couldn't argue with his sincerity and she appreciated that he didn't play games. The big question was could she take a chance on J.B.?

Issy recalled her earlier thoughts about him. She'd seen a side of J.B. that he didn't understand himself. She knew he was capable of the things he denied—commitment, responsibility—in other contexts. He'd already admitted that he cared about her enough that he wanted to make a change in his life. So if their relationship worked and J.B. made the commitment to her and their child, she knew he'd honor it.

Equally, if it didn't, he'd walk away without a backward glance.

In a moment of clarity, Issy realized she wasn't only scared for her baby. She was falling for J.B. Her bigger fear was that if she agreed to his plan, she'd tumble the rest of the way and he wouldn't. Then she'd be left brokenhearted while he moved on.

But in protecting her heart, was she prepared to miss out on the possibility that they could make this work?

"We've done everything ass backward," J.B. said. "We can't change where we've come from, but we could go back and fill in some things we've missed out. Like, be exclusive to each other."

"You're prepared to give up your precious independence and freedom?"

He didn't hesitate. "This is important to me. I want to do it right."

"Okay."

He continued. "We spend time together and get to know each other better."

"You want to see if familiarity breeds contempt?"

"More like boredom. I don't know if I can do 'serious' with a woman. But if there's anyone I could do it with, it's you."

She studied him. "What happens to our agreement if it doesn't work?"

"Nothing changes. You still get full custody and the financial support."

She had to ask. "And if it does work?"

"I don't know. This is uncharted territory for me and, as I said, I won't make empty promises. But whatever happens, we'll figure out the way forward together."

His gaze met hers. She saw there a vulnerability she'd never seen before. Her decision mattered to him. He was putting himself on the line, too.

That vulnerability tipped the scales.

"All right. Let's do this."

J.B.'s grin lit up the room. He pulled her back to him, lowered his mouth to hers and murmured against her lips, "Let's celebrate."

CHAPTER FOURTEEN

ISSY WAS OVERWHELMED. In a good way.

She'd had a small taste of J.B.'s extended family—the Badolettis and the Jelineks—at the Opening Day dinner, but that hadn't in any way prepared her for their annual Thanksgiving party. The noise, the boisterousness, the number of people and the mountains of food. Not to mention the love, laughter and general good will.

She'd never experienced anything like it. It was every family occasion she'd ever wished she could be part of...on steroids.

This year, the Cats' goaltender, Ike, and his new wife, Tracy, had opened their home for the party. Every room was packed with a mixing pot of family—of which Issy had become an honorary member because of her relationship with J.B.—friends, neighbors and Ice Cats.

As she looked around the packed living room from her spot on the sofa, Issy couldn't believe how quickly her life had changed since she and J.B. had become an item. How easily she'd been absorbed into his world. It was like a fairy tale.

She'd read about such close-knit extended families and seen them on TV. People who cared about each other, looked out for and supported each other, through good times and bad. She'd never believed she'd be part of such a group.

Issy had enjoyed being fussed over by the two moms once they'd discovered she was pregnant. Being teased by J.B.'s teammates, especially his closest friends. Being accepted into the fold by the wives and girlfriends. And, most important, being treated as though she was special by J.B.

"Holy moly, these people know how to have a good time." Sapphie flopped onto the sofa. "I shouldn't sit down. I've eaten so much, I may never get up again."

"I'm glad everyone will assume my bump is due to Peanut and not overeating." Issy touched her stomach, which triggered the now-familiar fluttering sensation. She smiled. "Peanut's saying, 'Thanks for that, Mom.' Either that or it's indigestion."

"Is Peanut kicking again?" Sapphie started to reach out, then stopped. "Can I feel?"

"I don't know if it's strong enough." Issy laid her friend's hand on her stomach. "There you go. 'Hello, Aunt Sapphie.'"

Her friend shook her head. "Hello back, little one. You're missing a great party. Can you believe this time next year, you'll be here with a baby?"

There were no guarantees. "We may not be invited next year."

Sapphie looked at her sharply. "Has J.B. come to a decision?"

"Nothing's been decided. I don't know which way he'll go."

Sapphie linked fingers with her and squeezed. "I thought you said everything was going well."

"It's been wonderful."

For someone who'd been set against a relationship, J.B. had quickly settled into a routine that enabled him to spend time with her, working around his hockey commitments. He'd been attentive and caring, helping her to prepare her apartment and her life for their baby's arrival.

It had gone so smoothly that Issy had started to wonder if she was being silly to worry about the future. How could J.B. walk away from what they had? Especially when he seemed as excited about Peanut's arrival as she was.

He'd even helped her work out a plan for when Peanut was due. Because the Cats had several road trips during February and March, they'd agreed it would be better for Sapphie to be Issy's birthing partner. J.B. had seemed genuinely disappointed that he might miss out on the main event.

And yet...

"I can't believe it'll work out the way I want it to," Issy admitted.

"Don't borrow trouble. How could he fail to want you and Peanut?"

"He hasn't told his family about us." She wasn't

surprised, given what he'd told her about his relationship with them, but it was unsettling nonetheless. "He says it'll be easier to present them with a done deal."

"That he believes there will be a 'done deal' has to be a good sign."

"I suppose so." She wanted—needed—the confirmation.

"You haven't told your parents," Sapphie said gently. "With good reason. Don't read anything into it."

This was the first year that Issy and Sapphie hadn't gone home for the holiday. It had never been a trip they'd looked forward to, because it immersed them in the past they'd left behind. Every year, they questioned why they put themselves through the heartache. As nice as it was to spend time with Rosa and Tinka, and Sapphie's sister, Emerald—and they missed seeing them—it also reinforced that their parents would never change.

Next year, the two friends planned to start a new tradition and ask their siblings to come to Jersey for the holiday.

"You're right." Issy sipped her tea. "I should stop worrying about the future."

"Nice try." Sapphie laughed. "But you like everything planned and organised. You need to accept that you can't account for every variable."

Their conversation was interrupted by Ike calling for the men to head to the kitchen for the traditional all-male cleanup. The women were directed to make themselves comfortable in either the living room, where a Hallmark movie was playing, the family room, where they could watch the latest blockbuster, or the den, where football would reign.

Issy and Sapphie opted to stay where they were.

"I could get used to spending holidays like this." Sapphie sighed happily. "I'm looking forward to your Christmas Day lunch. Are you sure you and J.B. want me there?"

"Of course. Taylor will be there, as will a bunch of other single Ice Cats." Issy had been pleased when J.B. had accepted her suggestion that they host a Christmas meal for his teammates who couldn't get home for the holidays.

"Joint entertaining is a nice sign of togetherness, isn't it?"

"True." Issy curled her legs under her. "Though I'll be doing all the cooking."

"I'll help. How come the guys are skipping their share of the work? The NHL is dark from Christmas Eve to the twenty-sixth."

"Jake's hired the practice rink for a voluntary training session on the twenty-fourth, as well as the day after Christmas. The team can't do anything officially but, as captain, he can arrange a skate and everyone will take part. Hence, the bulk of the prep work will fall to me."

"I hope you insist on the same cleanup roster as today."

"You bet. I'm learning fast." Issy grinned.

"Aren't we lucky to be part of this?"

Issy wondered how long she'd be included if J.B. decided he didn't want to continue their relationship once Peanut was born.

J.B. walked out of the kitchen with a damp dish towel around his neck. He dropped onto the arm of the sofa beside Issy.

"How are you holding up? Can I get you anything?" He'd been hovering around her all day.

Issy wasn't complaining; she enjoyed being pampered. "I'm fine. I couldn't eat another bite. This has been amazing. It's so kind of everyone to include us."

"Yeah. They're a pretty cool bunch. It's a shame Tru and Jenny can't be here. You'd love Jenny. Hopefully, you'll get a chance to meet them over Christmas. They're supposed to fly out, with the twins."

Issy had heard of the former puck bunny who'd married the second oldest Jelinek brother. She wasn't sure what they'd have in common.

"We're almost done in the kitchen. Can you hold out until the end of the Cowboys' game and I'll take you home then?"

"No problem. The movie is about to start."

J.B. pressed a quick, hard kiss to her mouth. "Try to miss me a little while I'm gone."

Issy batted her eyelashes. "I'll be desolate. I'll pine pitifully until you return." She put the back of her hand against her forehead and feigned a swoon.

He snapped her with the dish towel. "Remember, payback's a bitch."

"Ooh, I'm so scared."

"I don't get any respect around here," J.B. said mournfully.

Issy held up her hands. "What can I say? You're a big softie."

He arched an eyebrow. "I'll remind of you that comment later."

Her pulse jolted at the promise in his dark eyes. "Yes, please."

As he strolled back to the kitchen, Sapphie fanned herself. "That man is H-O-T for you."

"That's one area I don't have any worries about," Issy said honestly.

Even if they hadn't slept together yet. She'd checked with the doctor to make sure she wouldn't harm the baby—she was reassured she wouldn't.

A heated debate broke out between the two moms about which movie they should watch, *Miracle on 34th Street* or *It's a Wonderful Life*.

The argument was settled when Tracy put *Christmas in Connecticut* into the DVD player.

Once the movie and the football game were

over, J.B. and Issy departed, laden with enough food to keep them going until Christmas.

"I know I'm supposed to be eating for two, but I'll end up looking like I'm having triplets if I eat all this," Issy said as they drove off.

"Think of all the nights you won't have to cook." J.B. flicked his indicator. "Leftovers are way better than TV dinners."

"Amen to that. Besides, I could eat Karina's stew every night and not get bored."

"You know the moms have adopted you and Sapphie as two more chicks."

"They're a hoot. I adore them." Issy smiled, suppressing a yawn unsuccessfully.

"You're exhausted. You should have said—we could have left sooner." He pushed a button and her seat reclined. "Take a nap. I'll get you home and into bed in no time."

"Promises, promi—" Issy yawned. "I'll rest my eyes for a few minutes."

She awoke when J.B. pulled into the parking spot in front of her apartment and turned off the ignition.

Once inside, J.B. set the bags on the counter. "Take a load off while I put this stuff away. You've been on your feet too much today."

"My swollen ankles thank you." Issy grimaced as she toed off her shoes. "Put everything in the refrigerator for now. Be warned, I'm changing into my pajamas."

"Penguins or cats?"

"Penguins, in honor of the season."

"Perfect." He winked.

Relieved to take off her dress and remove the hated hose, which had become constricting as the day had worn on, Issy slipped into her soft flannel pajamas.

"This is so unsexy." She grimaced at her reflection before walking out of her bedroom.

At least she wasn't waddling yet. That was something to look forward to.

She eased onto the sofa and put her feet up with a heavy sigh.

"Sounds like you need a foot massage." J.B. joined her and lifted her feet onto his lap. "Luckily, I'm an expert."

"Feel free to ply your talents on me. I'm in your hands."

His wicked laugh sent need arcing through her. Her tiredness vanished. Beneath her flannel top, her braless nipples tightened.

As he kneaded the knots in her right foot, she moaned with pleasure. "That feels so good, I may not let you stop ever."

His fingers worked on her toes, one by one, moved on to her arch, then her ankle.

She willed him to go higher. She wanted to feel his touch moving over her calf, her knee, her thigh and higher still.

Even as she had the thought, he switched to the other foot.

Issy bit back her frustration.

J.B. chuckled. "Patience. I don't want to miss a bit."

Her skin tingled. Her pulse points throbbed.

She dropped her head back against the cushions and closed her eyes, savoring the sensations whirling through her.

His fingers slipped beneath the soft fabric to dance over her shin. This time, he made it as far as the tender skin at the back of her knee before stopping.

She swallowed a plea for him to continue. She shifted restlessly, trying to tell him without words what she wanted. Needed.

In one swift move he lay beside her and covered her mouth with his.

Their kisses quickly deepened. Their caresses grew more urgent. Somehow his shirt vanished, along with her pajama top. His hands, then his mouth, worshipped her breasts. Her hands, then her mouth worshipped his chest.

She fumbled with his belt buckle and the zipper of his pants as he slid his hands beneath her pajama bottoms. Then they were naked.

Issy barely had time to wonder if this was another time they'd pull back when he murmured, "Is it safe to continue?"

She smiled brightly and nodded.

"Hallelujah!"

RELATIONSHIPS WERE A piece of cake.

Why had J.B. been against one for so long? So far his life hadn't changed, except for the better. He wasn't restricted or constrained or bored. It hadn't interfered with his hockey and he did pretty much everything he'd done when he was single, except for the partying and the women. And he was okay with that because he had Issy.

He looked at her, seated to his right at his dining table, which was decorated for Christmas, heavily laden with food and surrounded by some of his best friends.

Beautiful. Pregnancy had brought a soft glow to her face and her festive, red sweater dress emphasized the healthy color in her cheeks. Her eyes sparkled as she laughed at something Kenny said.

J.B. recalled his first impression of her and smiled to himself. Uptight. Now it was one of the many things he found charming about her. Her tendency to worry and be a stickler for the right. She calmed him. She made him think twice.

Yeah. She was one special lady.

Special enough that they were hosting Christmas lunch together, at his place. They'd even exchanged gifts this morning. He'd never have done that with another woman; he'd have been worried about sending the wrong message. With Issy, it wasn't an issue. More importantly, it felt good.

For sure, things were changing for him.

He pushed aside the niggling concern that this

was the calm before the storm. He knew things were easy in part because their baby hadn't been born yet. He knew Peanut would definitely be a game changer. He'd seen enough of his brothers and their families to know that his life would never be the same again. But that was still a few months off and J.B. intended to enjoy this for as long as he could.

That was the beauty of his relationship with Issy. He didn't have to worry about expectations and demands. They both knew where they stood. Even though there were still questions about the future, the options were clear and she didn't hassle him constantly about what his decision would be.

It probably helped, too, that the Cats were riding high in the standings; clear leaders in their division and the Eastern Conference. J.B. had managed to keep up his average of a goal a game and was up there with the leaders in the league for top scorers. He was also a lock to represent the Cats at the All-Star Game at the end of January.

Yeah, life was good.

"I never thought I'd see the day that Jean-Baptiste Larocque was tamed." Ice Man toasted Issy. "You are a queen among women."

"Bite me, Kasanski," J.B. said mildly.

"How do you know it isn't the other way around? That he hasn't tamed me?"

Issy's sexy grin instantly made J.B. rock-hard. Damn it. She'd probably given every man at the table an erection. From the way the guys looked adoringly at her, he figured there wasn't a man there who didn't envy him.

As long as they did it from afar.

The thought stopped him in his tracks. He'd never been a jealous man before. But then, he'd never cared as much for a woman before. It made him uneasy.

"I don't know about you guys," Issy said, "but my back's sore. How about we adjourn to the more comfortable seats in the living room for dessert?"

A chorus of approval met her suggestion.

"Since I've helped you peel, slice and chop for what feels like twenty-four hours, I'm putting my feet up, too. The men can take over." Sapphie stood, taking her glass and a half-empty champagne bottle. "Grab your ginger ale and come with me."

"We'll handle the cleanup after dessert." J.B. held Issy's chair as she rose. "You and Sapphie can relax and watch something on TV."

"What about organizing the leftovers?" Issy asked.

"Later. You've worked hard enough creating this fantastic feast."

The guys tapped their knives against their glasses; the dinner-table version of a stick tap. Then, Mad Dog and Kenny offered to clear the table while Ice Man and Blade volunteered to play waiter, serving dessert. Paddy took charge of refreshing the drinks.

"Which leaves me the onerous task of escorting you two and seeing that you're comfortable," J.B. said.

Taylor shook his head as he began stacking and scraping plates. "He always ends up with the girls, while we do the real work."

"Them's the breaks." J.B. grinned at his friend.

"Aw. If you're a good boy and do the dishes, I'll cheer you up later." Sapphie smiled, leaving no doubt as to how she intended to do that.

Was it J.B.'s imagination or did his friend hesitate before saying, "Sounds good."

"Why does everyone always feel sorry for Mad Dog?" Kenny grumbled. "What do I get for helping with the cleanup?"

"An extralarge serving of trifle," Issy offered. "I made it to Maggie's recipe."

"What a woman." Kenny clutched his heart. "If you ever wise up and ditch pretty boy over there, I'm yours."

"Don't hold your breath, Kennedy." J.B. flipped off his friend. "Get your ass in gear and do your duty." He stuck his arms on his hips, elbows out. "Ladies."

They stuck their arms through his, then walked through to the living room.

The men were surprisingly efficient at clearing the table and were soon sprawled in sofas and chairs around the living room, tucking into dessert.

"Man, a New Year's Eve game in Philly sucks." Paddy waved his spoon to punctuate his complaint.

"Not as bad as a flight to Columbus right after the game." Kenny grimaced. "By the time we get there, they'll have rolled up the sidewalks."

"Not true," Ice Man said without looking up from his thick slab of yule log. "When I was with the Avalanche, we did the same thing and the city was rocking on New Year's Eve. Parties in the big hotels and at the casino. There were some half-decent bars and clubs, too."

"Of course, our resident father-to-be will be tucked up in bed at the witching hour," Blade said, grinning.

"No he won't." Kenny shook his head. "It'll be his last chance for a blow-out night with us before the baby arrives."

The razzing was getting a little old, but J.B. dealt with it with a few choice, colorful words.

"Junior doesn't arrive until March. Larocque's got a few more nights out in him yet," Mad Dog said. "All-Star week, for one. I'm sure Raleigh has some decent clubs where he can strut his stuff."

Issy laughed along with everyone else. She didn't seem to resent the time his career took or his occasional nights out with the guys. It was nice to think that his wings weren't clipped. Besides, he preferred spending his spare time with Issy.

He couldn't get enough of her. Ever since Thanksgiving they'd spent most nights together. Usually in her apartment. Even when he'd had a game the next day and he'd only slept with her in the literal sense—he had a strict no-sex-before-a-game rule—he'd enjoyed curling around her soft, warm body and waking with her in his arms.

He thought of the most recent scan in his wallet, which had brought him as much luck as its predecessor. Peanut looked like a proper baby now. Instead of dreading the kid's arrival, J.B. was kind of looking forward to it.

He no longer even considered walking away from the baby. He didn't want joint custody—the thought gave him hives—but he would be part of his child's life. The kid would know J.B. was Dad, and in return J.B. would get visitation rights. Hell, who else would teach the kid to skate?

That kernel of concern resurfaced. "Cleanup time, guys. The sooner we get it done, the sooner we can chill."

Despite the good-natured grumbling, his buds did a great job and the place was shipshape in no time.

"We're heading into the city for a few hours." Kenny shrugged into a jacket. "Our favorite club is open and you get free beers if you turn up in a Santa hat. You coming?"

J.B. was tempted—it was always a good night—but he looked at Issy and lost all interest in loud music. He shook his head. "I'll stay here and relax."

"Getting old, man," Ice Man said before hugging Issy. "Thanks again. Awesome meal."

"Yeah, yeah," J.B. replied. "But I'm still not as old or as ugly as you, Kasanski."

Sapphie grabbed her coat. "I'll head out with you guys, if you think you can keep up with this party gal."

Naturally his pals thought they could. They hugged and thanked Issy, dissed him some more then cleared out, taking Sapphie with them.

Once they'd gone, J.B. and Issy turned off the lights, leaving only the twinkling Christmas tree, returned to the sofa and cuddled while Christmas music played in the background. He tested himself to see if he was bothered by missing out on a lively evening with his friends. Nope. He felt pretty damn good right where he was.

A short time later they decided to make some popcorn and watch a movie. J.B. went for snacks and drinks while Issy selected a DVD.

The house phone rang as J.B. walked back into the living room with a tray balancing a bowl of buttered popcorn and two mugs of hot chocolate. "Could you get that?"

"Okay." Issy lifted the receiver. "Hello?"

She listened. "This is Isabelle." She listened

again. Instantly she looked embarrassed. "Oh. Hi. Yes, he's here. Hold on. I'll get him for you."

She held out the phone. "It's your mom."

They did an awkward swap; phone for tray.

"Hey, Ma," he said cheerily. "Merry Christmas. I planned to call you guys in a little while. How's it going?"

"Merry Christmas, Jean-Baptiste. We missed you."

In the background he heard his old man say, "I don't know why. He never comes home for the holidays."

J.B. ignored his father. "I missed you, too. Thanks for the presents."

They discussed gifts for a few minutes before his mom asked, "Who's Isabelle?"

J.B. looked over at Issy, who was studiously watching a car ad as if her life depended on it. He wasn't sure what to tell his mother. He couldn't spring the information about the pregnancy on his parents over the phone, but he couldn't say she was only a friend, either. Not when Issy was sitting right there.

"We're dating." He hoped his casual tone would stop his mom reading too much into it.

"That's nice." His mother sounded pleased. "Have you been seeing her long?"

"A few weeks."

He read the disappointment in the stiffness of

Issy's body. *Crap.* This was why he didn't like re-lationships. Too many potholes to trip a guy up.

"I hope we'll get to meet Isabelle at some point," his mom said carefully.

"Yeah."

He realized suddenly that he hadn't considered how this situation—Issy and Peanut—would work with his family. His parents would want to know their grandchild, as would his brothers and their families. They wouldn't understand how he could be involved with his child and not be married to Issy. Even if they did, they wouldn't understand why he didn't want joint custody.

Why did everything have to be so freaking complicated?

He hung up a short while later; Issy kept watch-ing the TV. "I didn't want to announce the news to my mom over the phone."

"I understand." She sighed. "Maybe this will all be easier once Peanut finally arrives."

"For sure," he said with a confidence he didn't feel. "Now let's get back to where we were and watch that movie. And don't hog all the popcorn."

"You can talk." Issy grabbed a handful of pop-corn and nestled into his arms.

As the movie started, J.B.'s mind wasn't on the opening credits but on the sinking feeling that once the baby arrived, things would get very com-plicated indeed.

CHAPTER FIFTEEN

ONE MONTH TO GO and Issy was fed up with being pregnant.

The romance of a new life growing inside her had given way to the reality of nagging backaches, swollen ankles, Braxton-bloody-Hicks and having to pee every five minutes. She was as big as a whale and she couldn't stay in any position for too long, because she was too uncomfortable. The wonder of feeling Peanut move had switched to pleas for stillness as the baby kicked almost nonstop.

He or she clearly took after J.B., who was rarely still, even when he slept.

Issy huffed at the television about the bias of pregnancy as she watched J.B. skate up the ice into the Red Wings' zone. "Men have it so easy."

There he was gliding along while she waddled everywhere. She couldn't even see her puffy feet anymore. It was all right for him, climbing neatly over the boards for his next shift, while she struggled to stand, sit, lie or do anything that required moving her behemoth body.

Her back spasmed painfully. Issy rubbed the

base of her spine and debated using the heating pad to soothe the muscles. Maybe when the game was over. She'd have to go through the delights of hoisting herself up from the sofa to pee, anyway.

It was late in the third period of the afternoon game and the Cats had a narrow one-goal lead. She'd learned enough to know that the Red Wings would probably pull their goaltender shortly, for an extra attacker, to try to get an equalizer. She hoped they weren't successful. Not only because the Cats could use the win but, since J.B. had scored the potential game winner, he might feature in the postgame show.

Despite a lot of frantic action around the Cats' net, Ike and his defense held strong and the 2-1 score became a final. Issy cheered as she watched the players congratulate their goaltender. She enjoyed seeing the faces of the guys she knew. It had been a tough road trip through Canada—Vancouver, Calgary, Edmonton and Winnipeg—with mixed-bag results.

Thankfully, it also meant the team was on their way home at long last.

She admitted part of the reason she was feeling down was that she hadn't seen J.B. much since Christmas. Certainly not on consecutive days and no sleepovers. The increased intensity of the second half of the season—road trips, back-to-back games and the All-Star break—had cut into their time together. They'd spoken on the phone and used FaceTime, but it hadn't been the same.

Valentine's Day had been a wash because the Cats had been in Winnipeg. Not that she'd ever been fussed about such holidays, but flowers and chocolates didn't make up for kisses and cuddles. Which she sorely needed. As for sex—ha. Even if J.B. had been around, she doubted he'd want to make love with Shamu.

Seeing J.B. on the postgame interview didn't do much to improve her miserable mood. For a start, he barely looked out of breath after a hard-fought period, while she was winded after walking from the living room to the bathroom and back. Where were the bags under his eyes? Oh, right. He didn't have trouble sleeping.

It wasn't his fault. Actually, yes, it was.

Instantly she felt bad. No pregnancy meant no Peanut.

"I'm sorry," she whispered to her bump, which kicked several times in response. "I'm not wishing you away."

Once the interview was over, Issy plugged in the heating pad. As she eased herself onto the sofa, another spasm jolted through her back. At the same time an ache similar to a really bad menstrual cramp gripped her stomach.

Her breath whistled out through her teeth as she rode out the contraction. "Wow, that was a bad one."

So bad, it made her feel sick and desperate for the toilet. Heaving herself to her feet again, she had to stop for several moments to get rid of the dizziness.

"This can't be good," she muttered, hurrying down the hall to the bathroom.

But by the time she got there, the pain and the nausea had subsided.

"I hope this won't be a feature of the next month, Peanut." She couldn't handle too many more of those blasted Braxton Hicks if they were as bad as that last one. She'd been told they'd vary in intensity, getting worse as her due date approached, but she hadn't expected them to be so bad.

The pain struck again as she splashed water on her face. Not as bad or as long, but still enough to make her catch her breath. She held on to the sink until the contraction had passed.

Perhaps she'd eaten something that disagreed with her. Pretty much everything gave her indigestion these days, so she only ate plain food. She'd have chicken soup from the local deli for dinner—that wouldn't upset her stomach.

Back in the living room, Issy lay on the sofa, trying to think calm thoughts. The dull ache in her back remained. The pain in her stomach had turned into a weird tugging sensation. Peanut was, for the first time, strangely still. Instead of being relieved for the respite, she began to feel nervous. Was something wrong?

She'd give it little longer. If the spasms continued, she'd call her doctor. Issy didn't want to bother her in case it was nothing, but better to get checked out than not.

With the heating pad warming her back and the quilt covering her, she rested her hand on her belly and closed her eyes.

The phone woke her.

"Hey, Bella." J.B. had started calling her that again when she'd complained of feeling orca-like. He said it would remind her that she was beautiful. *Yeah, right.* "How's things?"

"Pretty good, considering." There was no point worrying him when he was so far away.

She gritted her teeth as another spasm took her breath away.

"Is Peanut behaving or practicing kicking?"

"A bit of both," she managed to say.

"Are you sure you're okay?"

"It's not one of the better days, but I'm fine." Trying to distract him, she changed the subject. "Another nice win and a pretty goal."

He took the bait. "Just what we needed after the previous couple of losses. A prolonged slump can be killer, especially at this time of year with the run-in to the playoffs and everyone so tight in the standings."

"Didn't you tell me every team goes through a bad patch?"

"Yeah. Doesn't stop you wanting to win every game and getting frustrated when things don't go to plan. It's all about momentum for the next couple of months. We want to hit the postseason on a high."

Although Issy didn't claim to understand how he and his friends felt, she was beginning to appreciate the pressures and strains of playing professional sport. She was also gaining an insight into the truth behind J.B.'s sunny personality and devil-may-care smile. His fierce commitment to the game, his team and his fitness, the knowledge that he cared deeply, and his rigid discipline had impressed her.

"You will. I bet you'll be glad to get home." The Cats planned to fly back to New Jersey the day after tomorrow, straight after the final game on their road trip in Buffalo.

"For sure. I'll be glad to see you, too. Seems like forever since we were together."

Knowing he'd missed her gave her a warm feeling inside, overriding her discomfort. J.B. was still uncomfortable about expressing his feelings, so she was pleased whenever an admission slipped out. "For me, too. I—"

Pain struck without warning.

Sharp. Piercing. Right in the middle of her stomach.

She doubled over and gasped. The intensity was so severe she didn't know what to do with herself.

Wave after agonizing wave... Bile rose in her throat.

This definitely wasn't good.

"What's happening?" She heard J.B.'s voice as if from far away.

She tried to respond, to reassure him, but all that came out was a long, low moan.

"Issy?"

"Hurts. Bad," she forced out through gritted teeth.

She tried to sit up, to stand, but couldn't. She had to get to the bathroom. Now.

The tugging sensation she'd felt earlier returned but a thousand times worse. Then the pressure released with a pop and fluid began to leak down her legs. She knew what that meant and it was far worse than not good.

She let out a high-pitched cry. "No!"

"Issy? Speak to me!"

"Please. No." Issy closed her eyes as the pain subsided. "Don't let my baby come now."

TERROR GRIPPED J.B.

This couldn't be happening!

Issy was alone and in labor, while he was stuck in an airport lounge hundreds of miles away from her.

What the hell can I do?

He had to get her help. Someone had to go to her. She couldn't be alone.

"Issy, is Sapphie in New Jersey?"

"No-o-o."

Her wailing answer winded him worse than a slap shot at close range.

"Is everything okay, man?" Mad Dog, who sat opposite him, leaned forward.

J.B. shook his head, unable to verbalise his fear. "Issy's in trouble."

Instantly the guys around him were alert.

"Is it the baby?" Ice Man asked.

J.B. nodded. "She thinks it's coming."

"Now?" Jake looked worried. "She's not due for another month."

"I know, but nobody told the freaking baby that."

To J.B.'s relief, the veteran guys took over and started snapping out instructions.

"Paddy, call 9-1-1 and get her an ambulance," Ike said sharply. "J.B., ask Issy if she can get to her front door and make sure it's open for the paramedics."

Numb and as if in a daze, J.B. did as his friend instructed.

"Tell her to do it now, before the pain comes back," Jake added.

"Move while you can, Issy. You don't want them to have to break down your door, do you?" His attempt at humor fell flat.

"But I need a bag. It's not packed. I'm not ready." Her panic crucified him.

"Honey, don't worry about that now. Just grab your coat and purse, and let the ambulance guys do the rest."

"Okay. Don't hang up."

"I won't. I'll stay on the line as long as you need me." J.B. jumped up and started pacing.

Ike continued to bark orders. "Blade, tell Coach Macarty what's happening. Mad Dog, get hold of Sapphire. Kenny, call Tracy and get her to find a way for Larocque to get home. Tell her to charter a plane if she needs to."

Ike's wife ran a service-providing business called Making Your Move, which specialized in relocation, transport and travel. If anyone could find a way for him to get from Detroit to Newark in an emergency, she could.

"Ambulance is on its way," Paddy said.

"Did you hear that, Issy?" J.B. tried to keep his voice calm. "Help will be with you shortly."

Issy's wail of pain stabbed him in the heart.

He couldn't bear it. He wanted to be there with her. Helping her. Not standing in a freaking lounge twiddling his thumbs.

"Not long now, sweetheart. Hang in there."

"What if something goes wrong? This is bad. What if Peanut—?"

"It won't," he interrupted forcefully, even though the same fear was turning his veins to ice. "Everything will be fine." He couldn't add "trust me," even though he desperately wanted to. "You'll get the best medical care possible and both you and Peanut will be fine."

"Tell her Maggie and the other Cats' wives will meet her at the hospital. She won't be on her own," Jake said.

J.B. sent his friend a grateful look and relayed the message, which calmed her a little.

Issy let out another cry of pain. "But Sapphie's my birthing partner. I need her here."

"We're trying to get hold of her."

Mad Dog sent him an urgent look, which had J.B. covering the phone. "Sapphie's not answering. I can't reach her. I've left a voice message and texted."

"Keep trying."

Hysteria built in Issy's voice again. "Sapphie's in California. She can't get here in time."

J.B. tried to sound calm and measured, even though he'd never been so scared in his life. "I'll be there. I'll help you. I won't let you do this alone."

"Promise?"

"Definitely. How hard can it be?" He added in a singsong voice, "Pant, pant, breathe, breathe, push. Rinse and repeat."

She let out a gasping laugh. "Easy for you to say. You don't have to—"

Issy broke off and there was a commotion on

her end of the phone. "The paramedics are here. I've got to go."

He didn't want to hang up but knew he had to. "I'm on my way back to Jersey, so hang tough and do what the medics tell you. I'll be there as soon as I can."

When the call disconnected, his knees gave out and he sank to his seat. He leaned over, putting his head between his knees to counteract the nausea washing over him.

She's in good hands. She'll be okay. He kept repeating the mantra over and over.

Slowly he lifted his head. He cleared his throat, trying to ease the constriction tightening it. "The paramedics have her," was all he managed to squeeze out.

The relief around him was tangible, as if the whole lounge had done a massive exhale.

Kenny strode up, his phone still to his ear. "Tracy's got two options. A private jet can fly you to Teterboro, but it'll take three hours minimum before they can get everything lined up. She's started the clock on one, if you want to go that route.

"The other option is that the Pistons are flying to New York for their game against the Knicks and are wheels up in sixty minutes. If you can get to their hangar ASAP, they'll give you a ride on *Roundball One.* You'll be back in Jersey before you've even taken off with the other option."

No contest. "I'll ride with the Pistons. Tell Tracy thanks."

Kenny gave him a thumbs-up and relayed his message. "She'll get a team rep to escort you over there."

J.B. stood and grabbed his bag. When he saw Dale Macarty walking toward him, J.B. realized he couldn't just leave. He had a responsibility to the team. *Crap.* He hoped his coach wouldn't stand in his way, because whether he approved it or not, J.B. was out of there.

Luckily, Macarty was understanding. "Anything you need from the organization, let me know and I'll get Hardshaw to pull whatever strings he has to."

The Cats' general manager wasn't his favorite person, but he'd walk through fire for his team. He could make things happen. "Thanks, but I think we've got it covered. I'll try to get to Buffalo for the game tomorrow night, but it'll depend on what's happening back in Jersey."

"Don't worry. Do whatever you have to and get to your lady's side. And stay there until she gets the all-clear. We'll manage without you." Coach gave him a half smile. "Even you're not indispensable."

J.B. didn't have to think up a smart retort because a tall guy in a sport coat with a Pistons logo on the breast pocket entered the lounge. "I'll keep you posted."

As he followed the team rep, J.B.'s friends walked with him, in equal measure wishing him luck and giving him a hard time about flying with an NBA team.

The next few hours were kind of surreal—passing both quickly and slowly at times. The ball players welcomed him and were sympathetic about his situation, but gave him space, too. J.B. spent most of the flight silently begging the heavenly powers for Issy and their baby to be safe. If they survived, he'd do whatever it took to look after them from now on.

When he arrived in New York, a limo driver was waiting to whisk him to the hospital. He made a mental note to thank Tracy—she'd thought of every detail.

His heart nearly jumped out of his chest when his phone rang. Tracy.

"Is Issy okay?" The words burst from him before she'd said hello.

"So far, so good." As if she'd read his mind, she continued. "Don't worry. I'm calling to update you. I know being out of the loop while you're traveling is hellish."

J.B. inhaled deeply and exhaled slowly, trying to calm his jerky pulse. "Thanks. I really appreciate everything you've done for me. You've gone above and beyond."

"That's what friends are for. You'd do the same for me."

As he looked out the window at the view from the GW Bridge down the Hudson, J.B. was chagrined, wondering if he would.

Once again she seemed to know his thoughts. "You took care of me the night Ike was injured. You helped me hold it together."

That was hardly in the same league, but he let it go. "What's going on? Did they manage to stop the contractions?"

"No. They haven't been able to do anything and the doctor decided it's causing too much stress both to Issy and the baby. She thinks it's best to get the baby delivered as quickly as possible. Maggie's in with Issy, so she's not alone."

His feet pressed against the carpet, as if he could make the limo go faster.

"They'll be all right, won't they?" He was asking for a reassurance that Tracy couldn't give, but he needed something to hang on to.

She didn't blow smoke up his ass. "Issy's in the best place. They have great facilities and there's an experienced team working their butts off to make sure this goes smoothly. Getting her here as quickly as you did really helped."

He'd never been so relieved to see the Welcome to New Jersey sign. "We're ten to fifteen minutes out."

Tracy told him where to go when he arrived. "I'll meet you and bring you up here."

The last leg of the journey was one where time

slowed. J.B. was practically bouncing off the doors
when the lights of the hospital appeared ahead.
As promised, Tracy was waiting in the entrance.

J.B. jumped out of the Town Car before the
driver could open his door and raced up to her.
She hugged him tight. He gave in to the comfort
for a moment, absorbing her strength, then raised
his head and scanned her face.

She grinned. "Perfect timing. Everything went
well, and mother and baby are fine. They're just
cleaning them both up. You should be able to see
them right away."

He grabbed the back of the nearest chair and
held on until he could move without falling over.
He sent a heartfelt thank-you heavenward.

It was only as they got into the elevator that his
brain cleared enough to ask, "What did she have?"

"I don't want to spoil the surprise," Tracy replied.

The waiting room was filled with Cats' wives
and girlfriends. He was touched so many had
come to support Issy. He accepted hugs and congratulations, but what he really wanted was to see
Issy and Peanut.

Maggie appeared in the doorway. "They're
ready for you now. Congratulations, Dad."

Holy crap. He was a father.

J.B. wasn't able to process the emotions running through him, other than the slight feeling of
panic, as he followed Maggie down the hall. He

should have brought flowers. Maybe something for the baby.

When she stopped at the door of a private room to let him pass, he hesitated. The moment he stepped over that threshold, his life would change forever.

Don't be a nimrod. His life had already changed. Walking into the room wouldn't do anything to him or his life, except prove that Issy was okay. And he'd get to meet their baby. He stepped forward.

For a woman who'd gone through such trauma over the past several hours, Issy looked remarkably well, if a little pale and tired. Her smile when she saw him warmed his heart and started to melt the icy grip that fear had had on him since he'd last spoken with her.

"Hey," he said gruffly as he leaned over to kiss her.

"You're here."

"I promised I'd come."

"Yes, you did."

His gaze was drawn to the bundle she cradled in her arms. "Everything's okay?"

"It is now." She smoothed the blanket around the baby and lifted it so he could see. "Say hello to your daughter."

CHAPTER SIXTEEN

J. B. LAROCQUE HAD never been in love...until now.

One flutter of those baby blues and he was a goner. Perfectly formed—from her shock of dark hair and her pink rosebud mouth, down to her tiny fingers—his daughter was the most beautiful thing he'd ever seen.

And the most terrifying.

She was so small. Looked so fragile. He didn't dare touch her.

For a man famous for his "magic touch," on and off the ice, he was ridiculously nervous about doing something wrong. Tentatively he reached out and caressed her soft cheek.

He almost jumped when she clenched her tiny fists and waved them in the air. He stroked the back of one little hand and was taken aback when she caught his finger in a surprisingly tight grip. She looked up at him and their gazes met for the first time.

Love welled up inside him. His eyes burned. His throat tightened. He wanted to speak, to say something to his daughter, but the words wouldn't come.

"Would you like to hold her?" Issy asked gently.

Hell, no! Hell, yes! He wanted, desperately, to cuddle that precious bundle, but he felt huge and awkward and clumsy.

He cleared his throat. "What if I damage her?"

Issy laughed softly. "Given what she's been through in the past few hours, I think you can safely say she's one tough little cookie."

"Like her mom." He reached out and trailed a finger down Issy's cheek, just as he'd done with the baby. "I'm sorry I wasn't here for you."

Issy covered his hand with hers. "You came as soon as you could. You didn't have to. I can't tell you what that means. Other than Sapphie, no one's ever been there for me before."

"I didn't want you to go through this alone." He hitched a shoulder, as if it was no big deal. He didn't want to admit how scared he'd been.

"It was nice of Maggie and everyone to come here, too. Especially since they don't really know me."

"They know me." He wasn't sure what else to say. "They're a supportive group."

"I suppose being a hockey wife is kind of like being a military wife. Everyone has to stick together and look out for each other to survive."

"Yeah." The topic of wives wasn't one he wanted to explore right now. Not when his emotions were so raw. "Are you okay? You haven't had an easy ride of it yourself?"

"Now Peanut is here safely, I feel wonderful." Her lips twisted. "Though I expect once the drugs they gave me have faded, I'll feel sore and ache all over."

J.B. winced. He didn't need to think about that, either. He was amazed she could even sit up. "How long are they keeping you in for?"

"A few days. Mainly to monitor Peanut. Even though she's early, they think she's developed enough not to need to be in Intensive Care. Her lungs are fine and she's positive on all the other measures. She had a surprisingly good Apgar score, considering everything. Obviously she's got to put on some weight and they want to check how she feeds. But they don't think there will be any problems." She nuzzled the baby. "You're absolutely perfect."

Issy connecting with their child made him feel warm through and through. "You can't keep calling her Peanut. I thought you'd decided on a name."

Issy had tried to discuss names with him before the baby was born, but he'd insisted that was something she should do herself. Now, he kind of wished he'd paid more attention.

"I did, but I wanted to make sure it suited her once she arrived. Plus, I know you said you didn't want to be involved, but I'd like you to at least approve of what I've chosen. She's your baby, too."

His argument died in his throat at her steady

look. "Right now, all I can think of is that she's as beautiful as her mama and she needs a name to fit. A mini you. Bellita."

Issy blushed. "I agree about her being beautiful, but I don't want her name connected with my family. We're all Belles—Isabelle, Rosabelle and Tinkabelle."

J.B. arched an eyebrow. "Seriously? Like the fairy?"

"Spelled differently, but, yes." She shook her head. "We call my niece Tinka."

And he thought his family's Quebecois tradition of double first names was weird. "So what name did you choose?"

Issy smiled down at their daughter. "Sophia Ellen. Sophia is similar to Sapphire. It's what Sapphie used to call herself because she hated her name. She got teased terribly about it when we were younger."

"Because it's a gemstone?"

Issy wrinkled her nose. "Because of the *p-p* in the middle."

J.B. groaned. "Kids are cruel." Then something dawned on him. "My mom's Ellen."

"I know. You told me. She sounds like a special woman, so I thought it would be nice if our baby had her name, too."

"Thanks. That's really thoughtful." He was touched.

And a tad guilty. He'd have to find a way to

tell his parents that they had a new granddaughter. And figure out how to deal with the inevitable questions about his relationship with Issy and the future. None of which he had an answer to. At least not one that would satisfy everyone, let alone himself.

That was for another time.

"Sophia Ellen. I like it. A perfect name for a perfect little girl."

"Would you like to hold Sophia?" Issy lifted the bundle toward him, giving him little choice but to accept.

He froze; his arms stuck out awkwardly. "What if I hold her wrong?"

"You can't. Support her head and backside and you'll be fine."

Issy's quiet confidence broke through the white noise that clouded his brain. If she could trust him to hold the most precious thing in her life, then he should trust himself. It wasn't as if he'd never held a baby before, for crying out loud.

This was different. Way different.

He looked down at his daughter. Sophia's unfocused baby gaze met his. She lay there calmly, unfazed by her father's panic.

Okay. He could definitely do this. J.B. eased down to sit on the edge of Issy's bed, then slowly, carefully, brought the blanket-wrapped baby into his body. He was glad there was no one other than Issy in the room to see him so out of his element.

As Sophia's warmth seeped through to him, he began to relax. Wave after wave of emotion washed over him. Awestruck that he'd been part of creating this beautiful little girl, his heart swelled.

Unaware of what a momentous occasion it was for her father, Sophia yawned and her eyelids drooped. He watched carefully to make sure she continued to breathe. When he was convinced she was simply sleeping, he let out a breath he hadn't realized he was holding.

Jake was right. J.B. could never have imagined he'd feel this way about a baby. Possessive. Protective.

Sophia was his. His daughter. His baby girl. His Bellita.

Holy crap. God or the fates or whoever the hell was in charge of karma was having a big old belly laugh at him.

J.B. had made a mistake assuming he could stay detached from this child. Right now he knew he'd do whatever it took to keep Sophia safe. He was shocked to feel a primal urge to roar and wave his broadsword at all comers. No one would hurt his girl.

His girl? Nice sentiment, but what did that mean?

All he knew for sure was that he didn't want to let Issy or Sophia go.

He laid Sophia in the hospital bassinet beside Issy's bed and tried to figure out what to say.

But she was ahead of the game. "You've changed your mind about custody of Sophia."

He couldn't tell whether she was pleased or disappointed. Her voice and expression held no emotion.

"Yes…no…kind of."

"Well, that pretty much covers every option." Her short laugh had an underlying edge, the only sign of her tension.

"I don't know what I want to do." He puffed out a breath. "I don't want to walk away from Sophia or you. I don't want to sign away my paternity rights. Sophia is my daughter and I don't want to deny that."

"I see." A tiny frown creased her forehead.

"The problem is," he continued, "I don't know how I want things to work. I promise I won't take custody from you. But beyond that I need time to figure it all out."

"I understand it's unsettling," she said carefully. "This is something you've never experienced before. Sophia's turned my world upside down, and I was expecting it, so I can imagine how you feel. I don't have a problem with giving you time to adjust, but what happens in the meantime?"

He didn't have a freaking clue. "Can't we play it by ear?"

"By 'it,' do you mean our relationship or parenting our baby?"

J.B. paced beside her bed, thinking irrationally again that he should have brought flowers. The room looked bare and clinical.

"Both. Look, I know my decision will impact all our lives, especially that little one's. And that we can't chop and change—we'll need to plot a course and stick to it. But there are a bunch of factors to evaluate and I want to do it properly."

"I get that, but what does it *mean*? I need to know what to expect from you."

He inhaled deeply. "We carry on with our relationship as it was before Sophia arrived. You and she settle down at home and we see how I fit into that."

"Don't you mean how *we* fit into *your* life?" Though her words sounded brittle, her tone was matter-of-fact.

"That, too. I need to see if there's a way to make it work, so we're all happy."

He could tell she wasn't convinced but she simply said, "Fine. We'll take it one day at a time and see how it pans out."

"Thank you. I…"

She held up a hand to stop him. "You have until the end of the season to figure it out."

"By 'season,' do you mean the regular season or the end of the Cats' run for the Cup?" he asked lightly, though his gut twisted as he awaited her response.

"Negotiating terms already?" Her tone matched his.

"I want to be clear. Until we win the Cup or we're done in the playoffs, my focus will be on one thing. There are times when hockey comes first. The postseason is one of them. Are you willing to accept that?"

She was silent for several moments, during which he actually felt sick with nerves.

"All right," she said finally. "You have until the day after you win the Cup or your postseason ends."

"Thank you." He leaned closer and kissed her until they were both breathless.

"Now, I'd better leave you to get some rest. I also need to find out whether or not the Cats expect me in Buffalo in the morning." He bent over the crib and kissed his daughter's forehead. "Sleep well, Bellita."

At the door he waved goodbye to his girls. Funny how easily those words came.

Issy blew him a kiss in return.

J.B. went to the waiting room and thanked the women there for supporting Issy. He hugged Maggie and Tracy.

"I owe you both big time." His voice cracked.

Tracy's laugh was watery. "Don't think we won't collect."

"Just remember, we have a vested interest in Issy and Sophia's well-being now," Maggie said sternly. "Mess with them and you answer to us."

"Yes, ma'am."

J.B. managed to keep it together until he was in the hospital lobby. His knees gave out and he sank into one of the chairs in the waiting area. Then, hand trembling, he pulled out his cell and called Mad Dog.

Taylor's hello was drowned out by cheers, cat calls and yelled congratulations. From the raucous response, he guessed they were on the team bus heading to their hotel. He filled his friend in briefly on what had happened, including how he'd left things with Issy.

"What does Coach want me to do about tomorrow's game?"

"It's up to you. He's good, either way."

For the first time in his career, J.B. was torn. He'd never refused the chance to play for any reason, let alone for a woman. Two women, he corrected himself. The game in Buffalo wasn't hugely important; the Cats were so far ahead in the division standings that making the playoffs wasn't an issue. Still, he hated to let the guys down.

The image of that beautiful baby, lying in his arms, her gaze fixed on his, popped into his head. "I'll stay and catch up with you guys when you return."

Once he'd hung up, J.B. took a deep breath and

dialed his parents' farm. Now that he would definitely be part of Sophia's life, he needed to tell them about her and Issy. They deserved to find out from him rather than the media.

When his mom answered, he said, "Hey, Ma. It's your favorite son."

"Marc Andre? Is that you?"

They both laughed at the old joke.

"How are you?" his mom asked.

"I'm good. Are you sitting down? Because I've got some news."

"HAVE I MENTIONED that my goddaughter is the most beautiful child in the world?"

Issy rolled her eyes at Sapphie. "Only a few thousand times."

They were enjoying a rare day together. Sapphie had finished her research and was about to start writing her final report for Marty Antonelli. Frustrated that because of work, she hadn't had a chance over the past month to meet Sophia, Sapphie had flown in for the weekend. She hadn't put Sophia down since she'd arrived—except for diaper changes.

"Mommy's just jealous." Sapphie cast a disparaging look at Issy, who was folding freshly washed baby clothes, then rubbed noses with Sophia. "You look gorgeous in your new candy-striped onesie and matching headband, while she's in faded, baggy sweats with her hair in a scrunchy."

"Mommy's jealousy has more to do with the fact that the little monster's lying peacefully in your arms, instead of screaming the house down as she did pretty much every hour, on the hour, last night." Issy yawned.

"Mommy didn't mean the *M* word."

"Yes, she did." Issy tackled a second pile of baby clothes. Babies created so much laundry. Thankfully, Sophia had received baby outfits as presents and a number of Cats' wives had handed down clothes, or Issy would be washing every day. "I couldn't figure out what was wrong with her and nothing I did worked. At 4:00 a.m. I started to cry along with her. Then we both fell asleep... for an hour."

"Poor thing's finally worn herself out."

Sapphie lowered Sophia gently into the Moses basket next to the sofa. "You must be exhausted."

"I am. I've learned to take short naps whenever I can or I'd be a zombie." She bit her lip. "I hope Sophia isn't coming down with something."

"She doesn't have a temperature and she's eating okay, so I'm sure she's fine."

"It's hard when they can't tell you what's wrong."

"I'm the world's worst at interpreting baby cries. It's a good thing I don't intend to have kids." As if to prevent a discussion on the subject, Sapphie added quickly, "It was probably a blessing that Sophia's daddy wasn't here last night."

The Cats were on a quick two-game road trip to Ottawa and Toronto.

Issy wrinkled her nose. "True. He wouldn't have been happy to have his sleep interrupted like that."

"So J.B.'s still sleeping over?"

"Unless he's on the road or there's an early face-off. He's spent practically every night with us since we came home from the hospital."

"Wow. Almost a month. Impressive."

"It is and I *am* impressed. He's taking this daddy business more seriously than I expected. He even helps out changing diapers. Only the wet ones, but that's more than someone else I could mention."

Sapphie shrugged. "Godmothers are for fun stuff. It's not like I didn't change enough when we were younger. And I would do it, if you weren't around." She wrinkled her nose. "You have clothespins, right?"

"Oh, yes." Issy laughed.

"So Sophia's helped Daddy turn over a new leaf?" Sapphie's casual tone didn't fool Issy.

"She's certainly made him think twice about what's important in his life." Issy folded a tiny Ice Cats T-shirt. "He spends as much time as possible with her. He adores her. Of course, she adores him, too. Her little face lights up whenever she sees him."

"She's not the only one. Her mama's does, too."

Issy didn't bother denying it. "J.B.'s been wonderful. He treats me like I'm special."

"I'm glad. He hasn't said any more about what he wants to do about your relationship?"

Trust Sapphie to spot the one tiny fly in the ointment. "No, and I haven't pushed him. I said he could have until June and I meant it."

"I know. I suppose I was hoping that this new J.B. would put his money where his mouth was and make that final commitment."

"His money isn't the problem." Issy waved a hand around the apartment. "There isn't a thing our daughter needs that he hasn't bought. And a few things she doesn't." She pointed to the enormous stuffed snow leopard beside the sofa. "Him, for example."

"He's beautiful, but he needs his own room." Sapphie laughed. "This limbo would drive me crazy. J.B. stays here whenever he can, but he hasn't actually moved in. He's on the birth certificate as Sophia's father, but hasn't decided whether that means anything legally. He's crazy about you and her, but hasn't done anything to formalize your relationship."

Issy sighed. It wasn't that she didn't want love, marriage, a stable family unit and the security that came with it. She did, very much. But she didn't want to have them because J.B. felt pressured.

The past month had been a taste of what being with J.B. permanently could be like and, despite the stresses of being a new parent, it was great. But she'd also seen how much of a time commitment being an NHL player was. Not only the practices and the games, but the other things that went along with it. Media calls, charity work, workouts at the gym, reviewing film of opposing teams—the list went on.

She'd known J.B. took his job very seriously, but she hadn't appreciated how rigid he was about keeping fit, eating right and doing his homework. He said he had to work harder as he got older, because things got tougher with age. What he'd taken for granted when he was younger wasn't so easy now, even though he was still only twenty-five.

And by rigid, she meant like an iron rod. Totally inflexible. Which took some managing when there was a baby in the house who had the rigidity of cooked spaghetti but who demanded whatever she needed now, now, now. So far, Issy and J.B. had been able to work their way through those issues because Issy had been the one to compromise.

"Am I frustrated? Sure," Issy admitted. "But I can live with it, as long as we're providing the best for Sophia."

Sapphie didn't look convinced. "Sophia's a pretty placid baby and she seems to have settled into a routine fairly quickly. You're lucky."

"I know. Up to now, things have been relatively

easy. Despite being premature, Sophia's developed well and had no problems. She isn't sickly or whiny, and she's usually easy to please. At least until last night."

"Added to which the Cats have been on a homestand or their away games have only been in their division, so there hasn't been a lot of extended travel to contend with."

"Plus, the Cats have been on fire." With less than a month to go in the regular season, the team topped their division and conference level, and were second in the entire league. "J.B.'s been in a good mood and hasn't been stressed out."

"And he's banging in goals like he's trying to catch Gretzky's record. He's neck and neck with Ovechkin for the Rocket Richard Trophy."

Which brought her to the real worry. "It's easy for life to be sunshine and flowers when everything's going well. What happens when they're not?"

"You deal with it. You've dealt with worse."

"I suppose."

"You can't tell me everything's been plain sailing these past few weeks." When Issy shook her head Sapphie said, "So what did you do then?"

"Worked my way around it." Issy hitched her shoulder, trying to sound casual. "I'm not the one with the complicated, strict timetable"

"But you have an important schedule of your own, for Sophia."

"Her schedule is simple and J.B. knows well enough not to interfere with that. I suppose my own suffers a bit."

"Don't get into habits that'll be hard to break down the line," Sapphie said sternly. "J.B. can't expect you to be the one who bends all the time. And don't let him walk all over you."

"I won't. Anyway, it's only for a few more months, until the season's over."

"What if J.B. decides he wants to make things permanent?"

Issy's heart skipped a beat. The more time they'd spent together, the more she'd begun to hope there could actually be a happy ending. She knew better than to bank on that hope, but with each passing day, she felt them growing closer and their family unit getting stronger. "I try not to look too far ahead. We'll cross that bridge when—if we come to it."

"Have you thought about the flipside—what if things don't work out?"

"Then I won't have to worry about working around anyone. I'll only have myself and Sophia to think about."

"You sound like you've covered all the bases."

"As much as I can. Other than his career, J.B. hates anything written in stone."

Sapphie snorted. "One of these days, he'll have to grow up and accept that being responsible isn't a bad thing when it's for people you love."

But did J.B. love her? Could he ever love her? Unless the answers were yes, anything else was moot.

Sapphie changed the subject. "How's the job hunt going?"

"Slowly. In part because J.B. insists that whatever happens, I should stay home and look after Sophia until she goes to school. He's said he'll cover the shortfall."

"Are you going to be silly and stubborn and refuse, or sensible and accept graciously?"

"Hmm. I wonder what you think I should do." Sapphie grinned.

"I accepted, almost graciously. I never thought I'd say this, after what we went through growing up, but I can't bear the thought of someone else looking after Sophia. She changes so much every day. I couldn't stand missing a single one. Only…"

"What's the problem?"

"I don't want J.B. to think that giving me money absolves him of his responsibilities."

"From what you've said about him, I imagine that once J.B. says he's in, he'll approach family commitment the same way he does hockey. One hundred and ten percent."

"We'll see." Issy wished she could be sure, but despite everything he'd done over the past month, a tiny kernel of doubt remained.

"What does Isabelle Brandine want?"

Issy delayed answering by checking on her

soundly sleeping daughter and tucking the pastel blanket more snugly around Sophia. "The same as I've always wanted. A husband, a family, the whole nine yards."

"But do you want it with J.B.?"

"Probably," she hedged.

"You've fallen for him." Once again Sapphie saw too much.

Issy sank onto the sofa, laundry forgotten. "I know all the reasons why this is a mistake, but I can't help it. You think I'm an idiot, don't you?"

"You're not an idiot. If it makes you feel better, I think J.B. is as stuck on you as you are on him. According to Taylor, J.B. has never been this way about a woman before."

"He's got some serious baggage, and I'm not sure what we've got is enough to get over that."

"What serious baggage?" Sapphie threw up her arms. "So his childhood wasn't a picnic and he doesn't like responsibility. If you ask me, that's more a sign of him not wanting to grow up. If he wants to talk baggage, he should look at what you've been through. You should be the one running as far and as fast you can from commitment."

Like Sapphie. "Everyone has their own way of dealing with things."

Her friend snorted. "Have you met his parents yet?"

"No. I've spoken with his mom and we've exchanged emails. I've sent them pictures of Sophia.

Apparently they can't get down here because they can't leave the farm." J.B. had been angry and, Issy suspected, hurt about that. Especially when he'd offered his mom a plane ticket to visit, but she'd declined saying she wouldn't come without his father. "J.B. said we'd take Sophia up to see them during the summer. Families—they aren't easy."

"Speaking of which, when's your sister coming to visit?"

"Probably not until school's out for the summer." Issy smiled.

She and Rosa had grown closer these past few months than they'd been in years. Who'd have thought her unplanned pregnancy would help smooth over the problems that had kept them apart for too many years? Maybe they'd both grown up enough to leave their past issues behind. Or they'd finally moved beyond the parent/child roles they'd previously had and become equals, sisters, again.

"I'm disappointed it can't be sooner, but Rosa doesn't want Tinka to miss classes. Plus, she can't take the time off from her new job at the diner."

"Amazing how some people can change."

Thankfully, Sophia chose that moment to wake. As she scrunched up her little face, Issy's heart sank. "Uh-oh. I think you're about to see another side to your beautiful godchild."

Sure enough, within seconds, Sophia let out an ear-piercing cry and was then inconsolable for the next half hour, no matter what they did. When she finally wore herself out and subsided into little, hiccuping sobs as she snuggled against her mother's chest, the two women looked at each other.

"Every hour, last night?" Sapphie asked wearily.

Issy nodded, stroking her daughter's head.

"You're a saint. I'm worn out after one crying fit."

"The joys of motherhood. They tell me it gets better after the first eighteen years."

"The next couple of months should be very interesting," Sapphie said with a rueful smile. "The playoffs and an unhappy baby. You'll definitely find out what J.B.'s made of...if he's the guy we both hope he is. Look on the bright side—if he can handle all that, your relationship can survive anything."

"And if he can't?" Issy asked softly.

"Then you're better off without him. As painful as that might be, it's better you know now than down the line." Sapphie brushed her palms against each other, as if brushing away the worries. "Everything will work out fine. You'll see." Sapphie held out her arms. "Now give me my goddaughter."

"Oh, sure, now you want to hold her." Issy passed Sophia over. She was relieved when her daughter settled comfortably against Sapphie.

"Little Miss and I need to have a quiet word

about how she has to be on her best behavior with her daddy for the next few months."

Issy smiled. "The next few nights would be a good start."

"Sophia will be a perfect angel. You'll see."

Issy hoped they wouldn't be famous last words. Because she had a feeling both her and her daughter's futures depended on that angelic behavior.

CHAPTER SEVENTEEN

THE PIERCING WAIL jolted Issy awake.

For a moment she ignored her daughter's demand—the third of the night—and snuggled closer to J.B., savoring the warmth of his body pressed against her back. His legs were tangled with hers and his arm was wrapped tightly around her, as if anchoring her in place. His steady breathing stirred the hair at her neck.

She'd never have believed J.B. would be a cuddler. Especially since he'd told her repeatedly that he'd never spent the whole night with a woman, before her. At first he hadn't been keen to have her body too close while they slept. He'd given excuses—he was too hot, it was too constricting—before pulling away.

Issy hadn't been daunted; she'd curled around him as they went to sleep and stayed like that until he shrugged out of her hold. Several times she'd awoken to find herself sprawled across him, her head on his chest, his arms cradling her. She'd fallen back to sleep with a satisfied smile on her face. Gradually, J.B. had grown used to the physical contact and started initiating it. He'd even begun to miss her when he was on the road.

A second wail, louder than the first, yanked her out of her reverie.

Ordinarily, waking in J.B.'s arms was her favorite time of the day. But recently, with Sophia waking several times a night, it had become a source of tension. Issy would try to sneak out of bed without waking him to get to her daughter before she disturbed him. Some nights she managed it well, but tonight had been a disaster. This was the third time in as many hours that Sophia had begun to cry, and each time J.B. had stirred.

"Not again," he mumbled without opening his eyes.

"Go back to sleep," Issy murmured before slipping from beneath his arm.

"What time is it?"

She squinted at the bedside clock and winced. "Four thirty."

"Crap." He rolled over, then punched his pillow before putting his head back down.

Issy pulled on her robe, hurried into the nursery and leaned over the crib. The night-light's glow was supposed to be soothing, but it didn't have much effect on Sophia. Her red face crumpled, as her mouth opened for another wail. Issy picked her up quickly, determined to cut her off before she let loose.

Thankfully, at her mother's touch, the cry subsided to a whimper. With a hiccuping sigh, Sophia turned her head into Issy's chest and began to nuzzle against her breast. At least this time, it was obvious what her baby wanted.

Issy sank into the rocking chair beside the crib. "I know, sweetie. Give me a minute." Opening her robe, she settled Sophia to feed.

As her daughter suckled, Issy stroked her downy head and rocked while resting her head against the back of the chair. Sophia's eyelids drooped, showing how tired she was, but didn't close completely. Issy was tempted to close her own heavy eyes but didn't dare in case she fell asleep.

Issy was so tired she wanted to cry. She hadn't had a decent night's sleep in what seemed like forever. She'd expected the first few weeks to be tough—and they had been—but she'd thought that Sophia had settled into a routine. Issy had been pleased to have such an easy-going baby and wondered what all the fuss was about.

Boy, had that bubble been burst with a vengeance.

For no reason Issy could figure, Sophia had turned into one of those babies who wouldn't sleep for more than a couple of hours at a time. Worse, she fought going to sleep. She'd get over-tired and cranky, and resist being put down. Then she'd wake before she was ready and the whole miserable cycle would start again.

The doctor had reassured Issy there was nothing wrong and that Sophia would grow out of it at some point. She'd advised Issy to try to get Sophia back into a routine and not to pick her up every time she cried.

That, however, didn't reduce the number of times Sophia awoke during the night.

It had nearly killed Issy to hear Sophia howling insistently the first few times she'd left her. But she was learning to distinguish when her daughter cried for attention and when she genuinely needed something.

Tilting her head, she listened for any sounds from her bedroom. The silence reassured her that J.B. had gone back to sleep. She was relieved, yet couldn't help feeling a tad irritated. It would be nice if occasionally he got up with her and gave her some support. Even if he only kept her company, she wouldn't feel as though she was struggling to cope on her own.

Rosa's words from the last time they'd chatted echoed in her head. "He's Sophia's dad. Tell him to step up."

"J.B.'s the one with the job," Issy had argued.

"You have a job, too," her sister had countered. "Taking care of your daughter."

"I know, but I'm only able to stay at home and look after Sophia full-time because J.B. gives me money. The least I can do is support him. Besides, this is an important time of year with the playoffs about to start."

"Other people manage it. He can, too," Rosa had huffed. "The more you let him get away with, the more he'll take advantage."

An impatient kick of her daughter's tiny legs brought Issy back to the present. Assuming things worked out, they'd also put their relationship on a more formal footing. That's when she'd lay down some parenting ground rules.

Once Sophia finished feeding, Issy lifted her up onto her shoulder and rubbed her back.

A sound from the doorway startled her. She looked up to see J.B. leaning against the door-frame, shirtless and wearing only a pair of un-buttoned jeans.

Issy's mouth went dry at the sight of his smooth brown skin, the corded muscles in his arms and legs and his impressive six-pack. No matter how many times she saw his body, it always had the same effect on her.

Their daughter chose that moment to release her trapped gas.

J.B. chuckled. "She should get a gold medal for her burps. There are Ice Cats who'd be proud to be that good."

Issy rolled her eyes. "That's such a male thing to be impressed by."

"Her lung power is a constant source of awe. Especially in the middle of the night. After Ice

Man's snoring, I thought I could sleep through anything. Bellita proved me wrong."

Though there wasn't any censure in his voice, Issy sensed his frustration. "I'm sorry she woke you. I know you've got an early practice today, before the team bus heads to Philly."

"She may be gorgeous, but her sleeping habits suck."

Issy bristled. "Sophia can't help it. That's the only way she knows to communicate with us. She'll grow out of it eventually."

"Yeah. I know." J.B. pulled on his T-shirt. "Since I'm awake, I'll head home and try to catch some shut-eye."

"But it's barely five o'clock. We should get a couple of uninterrupted hours now." She crossed her fingers.

He tucked his shirt into his jeans. "I've got to get my gear ready, anyway, so I might as well get going now. Then I can roll out of bed and hit the road."

"Okay." She forced a bright tone despite her disappointment that he couldn't get away fast enough. "I'll see you when you get back."

"About that." J.B. rubbed his hand over his jaw. "The last week of the season is pretty crammed, so it's probably better if I stay at my place."

"I understand." She did. Really. "Have a good game. Sophia and I will be cheering you on."

"I'll try to stop by when I have a minute. But if

I don't get a chance, I'll see you in the three-day break before the playoffs start."

Issy wished she had a busy schedule of her own so it didn't seem as if she was sitting around waiting for him. "Fine."

"I'll call later." J.B. kissed the top of Sophia's head. "See you soon, Bellita." He then kissed Issy lightly on the lips. "I'll grab my shoes and see myself out."

Issy rocked the chair, her focus determinedly on her drowsy daughter. She didn't stop even when she heard the front door close.

Finally, when Sophia's lids closed, Issy eased herself out of the chair and laid her baby in her crib. Issy returned to the rocking chair. She told herself it was because she was wide-awake and wouldn't be able to go back to sleep, but the truth was she didn't want to return to her cold, empty bed.

"Better get used to it," she said softly. "This will be a feature of the next few months."

The thought that this might be the best she'd ever get from J.B. preyed on her mind.

As dawn's gray light filtered into the nursery, Issy realized that despite her good intentions, she'd somehow allowed J.B. to dictate their relationship. Just as she had with her family growing up, she'd begun making allowances for him and putting his needs ahead of hers.

It was time to take a step back. J.B. wasn't the only one who had a decision to make.

"HOW THE MIGHTY have fallen."

"Bite me, Kasanski," J.B. said, flipping off his roommate—who'd just walked through the hotel room door—without raising his gaze from the thriller he'd been reading.

"I'm normally the one swearing at you when you skate in right on curfew." Ice Man hung his jacket in the closet and dropped onto his bed. "Looks like the little woman has you toeing the line like a rookie. Not that you ever did when you were new to the show."

"Yeah, yeah." The razzing he'd had since the playoffs had begun was getting old. "Pass the freaking pipe and slippers."

"Touchy. Just sayin' you're a new man since you've become a dad. Jean-Baptiste Larocque has finally settled down and joined the old, boring folks."

J.B. reined in a cutting retort. Ice Man's divorce wasn't long final and he hadn't taken it well. He'd been cutting wild and loose ever since. "I can still beat your ass on and off the ice, any day of the week."

Rick's grin was feral. "I'd challenge you to put that to the test...both on and off the ice...but you'd wimp out."

"Like hell. You're on. Tomorrow's game and the celebration after. Sure you can keep up, old man?"

"I'll be the one making sure we have something to celebrate."

"As long as one of us does, I'll be happy."

Tomorrow was a crucial game seven—like there were any noncrucial game sevens—but if they could get through this first round against the Canadiens, the Cats had a really good chance of going all the way. It shouldn't have happened that they played their toughest opponent in the first round, but that's the way things had worked out.

Injuries had decimated Montreal in the last month of the season, dropping them into the final wild-card spot. Which meant that instead of facing the Cats in the Eastern Conference Final, as the pundits had predicted, the matchup was occurring at the beginning of the playoffs. Throughout the regular season, the Canadiens were the one team who'd had the Cats' number, beating them in all but one game. So New Jersey hadn't taken their progression past the Habs for granted.

Except, they kind of had.

J.B. couldn't believe they'd let a 3-1 series lead slip away. Bonehead penalties at the wrong time, lazy defensive play, weak-assed power plays and one spectacularly unfortunate, fluky-as-hell puck bounce—off Ike's back and into the net—and the series was tied.

How many times did guys have to be told to

stick to the damn system, play the damn game and don't get freaking cocky when they're ahead?

"We'll make it happen." Ice Man grabbed the TV remote and flipped through the channels. "Make sure you have your dancing shoes on and your wallet full, because I plan to bleed you dry."

J.B.'s reply was a creative suggestion for where Kasanski could stuff his dick.

He gave the impression he'd returned to reading his book, but J.B.'s mind wasn't on the intricate, twisted plot. He'd be glad for a break from the guys, even if only for one day, before the next round began.

Though they had home-ice advantage, so were playing game seven in their own barn, the team had been staying at a hotel close to the arena the night before each game. Something they'd started last year, to help keep them focused by minimizing external distractions. They weren't prisoners in the hotel—the team went out together for dinner and then various groups found some form of evening entertainment before curfew.

Usually, J.B. chafed at the restriction and was the first to break out to find the nightlife. But after last season's disappointment, he wasn't letting anything get in the way of victory. That meant returning to the room and reading, listening to music or playing mindless computer games on his tablet. Completely chilled, no aggravation, resting mind and body.

Speaking of which, he should make his nightly call to Issy and Sophia. His stomach twisted a little at the thought. What new problem would Issy have for him tonight?

Since J.B. had opted to sleep at his place for the duration of the playoffs, he'd found it tough not seeing them every day. He didn't regret his decision; it was better for him to keep his distance. Apart from needing undisturbed sleep, he didn't need the constant stress.

Issy worried about every little thing to do with their daughter and insisted on bringing him into every decision, no matter how small. When he'd tried to discuss it with her, she'd been angry and said he was supposed to be taking an active part in Sophia's life.

"You know, like actually help take care of her," she'd snapped. "Babies don't put their needs on hold for Cup Finals. I'm struggling here. I can't do this on my own. I need you."

He'd tried to be patient, though he was tired of the same old argument. He'd also resisted pointing out that if he'd decided not to be in the picture, she'd have had to handle it alone. "Can't you get help from the other Cats' wives? They must know people who can give you a hand with child care for a few weeks. A nanny or something."

"Sophia doesn't need a nanny. She needs her mommy *and* her daddy."

"I'm doing the best I can. I know it's tough on you, but it's only for a couple more months, tops."

Since then, every call had been filled with tension. She obviously felt let down by him, and he felt the same about her. The problem was that this was exactly what he'd been trying to avoid. Yet he'd still been dragged into the baby-family-parent trap.

He'd thought about ending their relationship. Several times. But he didn't want to walk away from his daughter—or Issy—for good. There had to be a middle ground.

As if he'd summoned her, J.B.'s phone rang and Issy's name showed on the Caller ID. He was tempted to let it go to voicemail. Tonight, of all nights, he didn't need another fight. Then again, he might as well get this done.

And what did that say about his relationship with Issy? *Do not go there.*

He forced himself to be upbeat when he answered. "Hey, Bella."

At first, he couldn't make out what she was saying because she was crying and Sophia was screaming in the background. Each wail, like nails on a chalkboard, sent a shiver down his spine.

Really? Tonight? Crap. "Whoa, slow down. What's going on? Sounds like Bellita's having a bad night again."

"I need you to come quickly. There's something wrong with Sophia," Issy sobbed.

Much as he adored his kid, she seemed to have a lot of nights where something was wrong and they'd yet to figure out what it was.

He injected calm into his voice, though that was the last thing he felt. "She'll wear herself out soon and settle down."

"You don't understand. Sophia's sick. She's spiking a temperature and I can't get hold of her pediatrician. I don't know what to do."

His chest squeezed so tight, he could hardly breathe. His little girl was ill?

J.B. took a deep breath and repeated what one of the older, married players had told him only this evening. "It's probably nothing serious. Babies get temperatures all the time. Call Maggie or Tracy. They'll know what to do."

"I tried, but I'm not getting any answer."

"Okay. Hold on one second." He caught Ice Man's attention and explained quickly. "Get Jake or Ike here ASAP."

"On it." His roommate launched to his feet and sprinted out of their room.

"We'll get you help, Issy. Did you try Sapphie?"

"She's in Chicago."

It didn't escape his notice that Sapphie didn't get grief for not being able to get to Issy's side yet again. "If we can't get someone to you, we'll call 9-1-1 and get you an ambulance."

"I'm scared. I can't handle this alone. Please come home."

J.B. swore silently. Of all the things to demand of him, this was the one he absolutely couldn't do.

He rose and started to pace the small room. "You know I can't, Bella. Curfew starts in ten minutes. If I break it, I don't play tomorrow."

"This is an emergency. They have to let you go."

"The rule is the rule. No exceptions."

"Your *daughter's* ill and you're worried about rules?" Her short laugh was bitter.

It wasn't fair. Any other time he'd be prepared to miss a game for his daughter. But this wasn't just any game. It was *the* game and his team was depending on him.

Issy and Sophia are depending on you, too.

"Trust me, if there was any way I could get there, Bella, I would."

"There is a way. You don't want to choose it."

There it was. The moment he'd been dreading. The point at which he had to make a decision— family or hockey.

He thought about going to Coach Macarty and asking for a dispensation. The worst his coach could do was say no. But even as J.B. considered it, he started to balk and find excuses. It was already late. Who knew how long this would take? He couldn't afford not to be on his game tomorrow. He couldn't drop everything and run to Issy every time there was an issue.

In the end, there was only one answer he could give. "I can't."

"Some father you are. When push comes to shove, nothing matters but that stupid game."

"It's my job. My career. This is what I've been working for all—" He broke off and pounded the bed with his fist. What was the damn point?

Ice Man rushed back into the room, Jake hot on his heels.

"I got hold of Maggie," Jake said, holding up his cell. "She's leaving now and will be with Issy shortly. She'll get her to a doctor or the hospital or whatever's needed."

A solution. Not the one Issy wanted, but better than nothing. "Did you hear that? Maggie's on her way. She'll help you and stay with you."

"It would be better if *you* were here."

"I know," he cajoled. "But at least this way you won't be alone. And Maggie's been through this with Emily and Joe, so she'll be way more help than me."

"I should go. My daughter needs me," Issy said coolly.

The deliberate dig was like a spear to his chest. He deserved it, he knew, but it still hurt. "Keep me posted."

"I don't want to interfere with your precious night's sleep."

He sighed. "Give me a break, Issy. I'm doing the best I can."

"Tell that to your daughter." She disconnected. J.B. swore and tossed his cell onto the bed.

"It'll be okay, bro." Jake laid his hand on J.B.'s shoulder. "Stuff like this is always hard the first time it happens."

Ice Man nodded. "You couldn't have done anything else."

"Tell Issy that. She thinks I'm pond scum."

"Always said she had her head screwed on straight." Kasanski ducked as a crumpled soft drink can whizzed past his left ear. "Kidding. Hang tough. The first year's the worst. She'll get used to the demands of being with a hockey player."

"Or not." J.B. winced; Rick's wife hadn't cut it.

Ice Man's shrug looked careless but hid a wealth of hurt. "My case was different. She loved the status and attention we got back home, but couldn't handle it when we were pretty much nobodies here in Jersey. I hear she's dating one of the Jets' linebackers." He lay back down on his bed, his laced fingers beneath his head. "Issy'll come around."

Jake nodded. "Once the panic's over, she'll calm down and it'll all be fine. Maggie will set her straight, I'm sure."

"I appreciate her help."

"Let me know when you hear anything." Jake headed out of the room.

J.B. acknowledged him by touching his finger

to his temple in a salute. He then strode over to the window and stared out at the parking lot. Worrying about Sophia wouldn't help, but he wouldn't be able to concentrate on anything else until he knew the outcome.

This was exactly why he hadn't wanted to get involved in the first freaking place. He didn't do responsibility well. He didn't want to *have* to do it well.

He was twenty-freaking-five, for God's sake. In his prime. He wanted to be free to do what he wanted and not have to think about anyone else. He didn't want to have to second-guess every freaking decision. Or feel bad if he had to make a decision that was right for him but sucked for anyone else.

Because of Sophia, he was trying his best to temper his admittedly self-centered needs. But Issy was making it impossible with her constant demands and lack of patience.

All he'd asked for was two freaking months' grace. The playoffs would be over in early June. Then he'd be free to play "happy families" or "mommies and daddies" or whatever the freaking game was all summer long.

He didn't want to walk away from his daughter, but he didn't want to be tied down. For sure, he didn't want to get married and settle down. There had to be a middle ground. Divorced parents managed it, so why shouldn't parents who'd never been married?

He cared for Issy—a lot more than he'd ever imagined he would—but he was tired of always feeling as though he was letting her down. Where was the compromise on her part?

She'd promised him two months and he planned to keep her to that promise.

Even with the decision made, he couldn't concentrate on his book while he waited for Maggie's call, so he watched one of the Western Conference playoff games on TV.

A short while later Maggie phoned. "Sophia's doing fine. I got hold of my pediatrician and she suggested we take her straight to the hospital because of her age and the fact that she was a preemie. They've run a bunch of tests and it looks like she's got a viral infection."

"Is that good or bad?"

"Relatively good because there's less chance of it developing into something more serious. They're sending her home with infant acetaminophen to help reduce the fever and instructions on how to keep Sophia comfortable while the fever works through. The first dose seems to be working already."

Relieved, he cleared his tight throat. "How's Issy?"

"Better now. It's a scary thing seeing your baby

suffer like this the first time. Especially when you're on your own."

There wasn't any blame in her voice, but J.B. felt guilty, anyway. "I'm glad she had you with her. Thanks, Maggie."

"No worries. I'll take Issy and Sophia home and stay with them until they're settled."

"I really appreciate it."

"That's what friends are for. I'll remind you the next time Jake and I need a babysitter."

"You got it. Can I speak with Issy?"

Maggie hesitated, then said carefully, "She's... getting Sophia ready to go home."

Issy didn't want to talk to him. "Okay. Tell her I'll call tomorrow and be around to see Sophia first chance I get."

"I will. Get a good night's sleep and give those Habs hell tomorrow."

"You know it."

After relaying the news to Ice Man and then Jake, J.B. tried to get some shut-eye.

He couldn't sleep. He tossed and turned, going over the night's events in his head—playing it every which way. He finally fell asleep wondering why he felt like a jerk.

The following morning he had to put his personal issues aside and concentrate on the game. Coach had made the morning skate optional, since a few players had been logging serious ice time over the series. J.B. was one of those who should probably have rested, but he used the practice session to blow out the cobwebs from his brain and get his head game ready.

It worked. He fell asleep for his pregame nap with no problem and awoke feeling refreshed and raring for action.

By the time he'd got to the warm-up, he still hadn't managed to speak to Issy. He'd called several times throughout the day, but each time it had gone to voicemail. He'd left short messages saying he'd phone after the game, and see her and Sophia tomorrow. Eventually a text from Maggie arrived telling him that Sophia was recovering well and should be right as rain the following day.

Relieved the crisis was over, J.B. was able to put aside the previous night's tension and relish the battle ahead as he got changed for the game. At least on the ice, he knew how to do the right thing and make everyone—except the opposition—happy.

With so much on the line, play started out cagey but soon became aggressive and tough. Both teams fought hard, yet neither could find the back of the net and they were scoreless after two periods. Despite their wager, neither Ice Man nor J.B. had a shot on target during the forty minutes. Mad Dog got the closest and his shot rang off the pipes late in the second.

The Canadiens finally hit one home early in the third. That seemed to wake up the Cats and they stepped up a gear. Paddy scored with three minutes to go, to even the score.

Just when it seemed like they were headed to overtime, Juergen found the puck in a scrum in front of the Habs' net and slid one through the goaltender's legs as time expired.

The arena erupted. The Cats' players on the ice jumped in the air and the rest poured over the boards to celebrate the win. They'd done it. They were through to the next round.

After the traditional handshake, respecting their defeated opponents, the Cats saluted the fans from center ice, then headed to the locker room. With a couple of days before the next round kicked off, they planned to party into the night.

Since the wager between J.B. and Ice Man was a dead heat, they agreed to move the contest to the next round. Drinks were on Paddy and dinner was on Juergen, for their role in the victory. After they'd eaten, the team went on to a local club and continued the celebration into the early hours.

Dawn was breaking by the time J.B. crawled into bed and fell asleep. Since there was no practice the following day, he slept late, then headed to the gym to work out any kinks. After a steak dinner with his housemates, they all chilled in the living room watching the final playoff game in the first round before heading to bed.

It was only as he laid his head on the pillow that

J.B. remembered he was supposed to have gone to see Issy and Sophia.

His stomach sank. Damn it!

CHAPTER EIGHTEEN

"Can I come in, Bella?"

Issy cursed her traitorous heart, which leaped at the sight of J.B. standing on her doorstep.

Damn him for looking so good. For making her want him when she was mad at him.

For making her miss him, when he'd let her down when she'd needed him. Worse, he'd let her daughter down.

J.B. jammed his hands into the front pockets of his well-worn black jeans. The ones that hugged his finely honed body. "Please. We need to talk."

Issy stood aside and motioned for him to enter.

As he stepped inside, he leaned over to press a kiss to her cheek. Anticipating his move, she turned her head. Only she turned the wrong way and their mouths connected.

Neither of them moved, except for their lips.

The kiss was soft, sweet and so achingly sincere it made her throat tighten.

She pulled her lips away.

Her gaze met J.B.'s and she saw her surprise mirrored in his eyes, as well as her sorrow and regret.

"You wanted to talk," she said calmly, as if the kiss hadn't happened.

"After you." He gestured upstairs.

Issy walked ahead of him, feeling as though she was heading into the Colosseum before a gladiator battle. "Would you like a drink?"

J.B. declined. "Where's Sophia?"

"Sleeping. In the nursery." When it looked as if he might go in to take a peek at her, she added, "I'd rather you didn't disturb her."

He nodded, then went into the living room. "How is she?"

The simple question broke through the haze that had clouded her mind since their kiss. "She's fine."

Her clipped response had no effect on him. "No more issues? Her temperature's stayed down? No sign of an infection?"

"Nothing." Issy sat on the sofa and regarded him coolly. "Your concern's several days too late."

"I'm sorry." J.B. rubbed his hand across his forehead. "I know how it looks, but I was worried."

"I could tell. The phone calls, the visits. It was all so…heartwarming."

"I did call. Didn't you get my messages?"

"Hmm. Let's see…there were some voicemails two days ago. The ones where you promised to stop by and see your sick daughter. When was that supposed to be?" She clicked her fingers. "I remember—yesterday."

J.B. grimaced. "I screwed up. I can explain."

"Don't bother." She sighed wearily. "The fact is Sophia and I don't rank highly enough in your priorities."

"That's not true." He jammed his fists on his hips. "It's just…the circumstances…it was an important game."

Issy had never seen J.B. struggle for words. He was a smooth talker, with a charming quip for everything. She tried not to be affected by his discomfort. He *had* screwed up.

J.B. continued. "I didn't mean to make a mess of things. It just happened."

She arched an eyebrow. "Did you lose your cell? Was that why you couldn't reach us for two days?"

"No. I didn't call after the game because it was late and I didn't want to disturb you or Sophia. Especially if she'd finally fallen asleep."

"How considerate." Her sarcastic tone suggested the opposite. "And the following day? Was that so you didn't disturb us, as well?"

"I forgot, okay?" He threw his hands up with frustration. "I was exhausted after the series and focused on getting my mind and body back to normal and I freaking forgot. By the time I realized last night, it was too late again."

At least he was honest. Still, it hurt to hear him say it.

"If I could go back and put it right, I would. But I can't. All I can do is learn from my mistake and make sure it doesn't happen again."

"Isn't that the point? We both know it will, even if you don't intend it to. That's the nature of your job. First you need to train for the game, then you need to sleep and eat *for the game.*" She enumerated each point on her fingers. "Then you need to isolate yourself *for the game.* Then you play the game and celebrate the win. Then you need to recover from the game and prepare for the next one. Rinse and repeat. Then you resurface and join the real world somewhere around mid-June."

"You know this time of year is critical and that my focus has to be one hundred percent on the game. I never lied about that."

"No, you didn't lie."

"I also told you I wasn't cut out for the commitment and responsibility a relationship required. I said I'd try, because I care about you and Sophia, but I never promised I wouldn't mess up."

"Also true. The mistake was mine. I expected more than I should have. Like, that you would regard being a father more seriously than you did."

He shook his head. "You can put this all on me if you like, but you promised to give me until June. It's still only the end of April and things are worse, not better. You won't give me a single break."

"We have a two-month-old daughter, who was born prematurely. She was sick. Forgive me if I expected you to give a damn."

"It's not just the fever. It's every freaking little thing. She doesn't eat, she eats too much. She doesn't sleep, she sleeps too much. Every time she cries, you panic that there's something wrong."

Guilt made her lash out. "You said you wanted to be part of Sophia's life, but you want to skip over the parts where she's sick or crabby."

"I do the best I can to help. I get that sometimes it's not enough, but it's not because I don't care or I don't try."

Issy glared at him. "We'll have to agree to differ. The night before last, for example."

"I told you—there was nothing I could do. That's my job. I didn't abandon you. I got you support, through Maggie."

"Maggie was a rock. That doesn't get you a pass."

"No, I don't suppose it does." He held up his hands in the shape of a T. "This is getting us nowhere."

Issy took a deep breath. "You're right. It isn't."

J.B. crouched in front of her, bringing his dark eyes level with hers. "Tell me honestly. Do you want our relationship to work?"

"Of course." Her instant response surprised her. As did the truth behind it.

Part of her frustration and disappointment was that she really did care deeply for J.B.

"Because I'm Sophia's dad or for myself?"

"The two things aren't separate," she hedged, wondering how he felt.

"Maybe not, but there's no chance for us if we're only together because of our daughter."

"Are we?" she asked quietly.

"I don't think so."

"Hardly a resounding yes."

"What I mean is that I'd still want to be with you, but I don't think we'd be trying to move things forward so fast if it wasn't for Sophia. We'd be able to take our time and build a relationship, without the extra pressures."

"Fair point. But she does exist and so do those pressures. We can't change that." Issy raised her chin. "I'm sorry, but the time has come to make a decision."

J.B. said nothing for several moments. "All right," he said finally, his tone resigned. "What do you want to do?"

For once their daughter's timing was impeccable. Sophia started to cry.

THE SIGHT OF Issy with their sleepy daughter tugged at J.B.'s heart.

Two beautiful, special females. Issy—the only

woman who could make him laugh as easily as she drove him nuts. As easily as she turned him on. And Sophia—precious beyond anything he could have imagined.

They were way too good for him. And they deserved better than what he could offer. At least, what he could offer right now.

"Can I hold her?" He held out his arms, half expecting Issy to refuse, but she didn't.

"You'll still need to cradle her butt and support her neck, but she's holding her head up more," Issy said.

Sophia had changed so much in only a few weeks. She was growing fast and she was able to do more. Before he knew it, she'd be walking and talking, going to school, dating and wanting a car. A scary thought.

As was the reality of how much responsibility was wrapped up in one tiny package.

Sophia needed someone to look after her now, but she'd need support and guidance in the near future. She couldn't wait until he was ready. She shouldn't have to.

J.B. lifted his daughter against his shoulder. She turned her head so her face was in his neck and snuggled closer, letting out a little sigh. As if the scent of him was enough to comfort her. He breathed deeply, taking in her baby smell.

His heart swelled with love. How could he let this little girl go?

Unfortunately he didn't see a way to resolve the problems between him and Issy.

"What do you want to do?" he repeated. "Or, should I ask what do you want *me* to do? I won't give up hockey and for sure I won't change my mind about marriage."

"I wouldn't expect you to." Issy sat on the sofa. "This current 'issue' will be over in mid-June and we'll have a couple of months where there will be some semblance of a normal life. But hockey's a demanding mistress—come August, it'll start again. Training camp, preseason and then the season itself. It'll get worse and worse, until we're right back at the same point next year."

He couldn't argue. "A lot of couples make it work. Jake and Maggie, for starters. It's not ideal, but they find a way."

"I suspect Maggie's the one who finds a way."

"Probably, but I'm sure there're compromises on both sides. I don't hear her complaining."

"That may be fine for her, but it's not for me." Issy's lips twisted. "Your job isn't a regular nine-to-five, Monday-to-Friday thing, with a predictable schedule—weekends off, vacation time and the flexibility to be there for birthdays, special occasions and holidays."

"Not many jobs are. But my timetable is actually totally predictable. From the minute they release the season schedule, I can tell you where

I'll be from September through to April, on a daily basis."

"But you won't necessarily be *here*, when Sophia and I need you."

"No. I can't promise that. My whereabouts are dictated by the schedule. The flip side is that I get time off other men won't get—like most of the summer. And the way my days are structured, I can be around for more than you'd think."

"That's not enough. I need certainty and stability. Not because I need support all the time—I don't. But on those occasions when I need backup, I have to be able to rely on it being there."

J.B. was fighting a battle he couldn't win. Issy had made up her mind about the mythical perfect man she wanted and he wasn't it. "Basically, you want things all your own way. Where's the compromise from your side?"

"When it comes to Sophia, I won't compromise. I won't accept anything less than she deserves—someone who'll put us first. You can't give us that. For Sophia's sake, I have to hold out for a man who will."

It was hard to argue with Issy when he agreed with her. Sophia did deserve someone who could do that for her. As much as he loved his daughter, J.B. couldn't give her what she needed.

"I didn't want to do this now," Issy continued, "but Sophia's growing and bonding. It's unfair to give her expectations, then have her be disappointed and let down time after time."

J.B. cuddled Sophia a little tighter. "I wouldn't deliberately let her down."

"As the episode with the fever showed, you might not have a choice. That's just as bad."

He wanted to fight Issy; tell her he had rights and needs, too. What was the point? This wasn't about him. It was about a tiny, precious girl who deserved the best of everything. As did her special mother. He had to accept that wasn't him. No matter how much he might hope, deep inside, that it was.

J.B.'s eyes burned. He couldn't handle this anymore. There was nothing else to say. It was what it was. Time to man up and make the choice. Hell, the choice had already been made. He just had to act on it.

He kissed Sophia's head and murmured, "Love you, Bellita."

Then he handed her to Issy, who'd risen to her feet. "Take real good care of her."

Issy looked startled. "That's it? You're leaving?"

"Yeah. Everything you've said is right. This is for the best, all around. I'm not signing away my paternity, but I'll step out of her life and yours. If she ever wants to know me, you know how to reach me."

"I won't hide who you are from her. Or that you did this for her."

"Thanks." Before he could stop himself, he took Issy and Sophia in his arms and gave them one last tight hug.

"I wish it could be you," Issy said brokenly. "I know it can't be, but…"

"Yeah. Me, too." He released her gently. "Look after each other."

Issy nodded, tears in her eyes. "Look after yourself, too."

J.B. turned and walked away without looking back.

CHAPTER NINETEEN

SOPHIA WAS INCONSOLABLE after her father left.

It probably didn't help that her mother was, too. Issy sat on the sofa, cradling her daughter, willing the ache of loss away. Tears streamed down her face, matching those on Sophia's chubby cheeks.

"I'm sorry, sweetheart," she murmured. "I know it's painful now, but it's for the best in the long run."

Sadly, the reassurance didn't help either of them. Sophia continued to sob her little heart out. That, in turn, broke Issy's heart.

She wished desperately there had been some other way her conversation with J.B. could have gone.

The irony was that Issy and J.B. were suited in so many ways. They weren't two halves of the same whole, as she'd read about in novels. They weren't perfectly matched. Rather they were yin and yang. His optimism and daring; her realism and caution. His lightheartedness, her seriousness. His tendency to cut to the chase and be decisive, while she meandered, exploring and evaluating all the options.

Opposites in so many ways, yet they balanced each other perfectly.

Perhaps that was why there wasn't a solution that suited them both. Not yet, anyway.

Issy couldn't help feeling that timing was crucial and, right now, it was wrong. Maybe if she and J.B. had met in a few years' time, they'd have been able to find a compromise.

Of course, if she hadn't become pregnant when she had... No, she couldn't think about that. The alternative would mean she didn't have Sophia, and Issy wouldn't trade her daughter for anything. Not to have her job and her uncomplicated life back. Not even to have J.B. back.

Issy sighed heavily and dried her eyes. What was done was done. Both she and Sophia would simply have to get used to it.

It would just be nice if doing the right thing didn't hurt quite so much.

Eventually, Sophia cried herself out and her eyelids drooped, until her lashes formed little spiked crescents against her flushed cheeks. Issy continued to rock her daughter until she was sure she was asleep. Then she rose wearily, carried Sophia through to the nursery and laid her in her crib.

Restless, Issy wandered through her apartment. In her bedroom she found an old Ice Cats T-shirt J.B. had left behind. She picked it up, planning to toss it in the laundry basket—she'd wash it and return it to him—then changed her mind. Pulling off her clothes, she slipped the T-shirt on. Instantly, his spicy, sexy scent surrounded her. As if he'd put his arms around her.

Suddenly she couldn't do anything more. All she wanted was to sink into the misery that still filled her. She crawled into bed and hugged her pillow, wishing it was J.B.

Over the next couple of weeks, the T-shirt became a security blanket, even though J.B.'s scent faded. Not only did it soothe her bruised heart, but it comforted Sophia, too. When Issy wore the shirt, Sophia stopped crying.

Watching hockey helped her daughter, as well. A good way to keep Sophia calm was to sit her in front of an Ice Cats' game. Which was strange, because Sophia didn't respond to any other TV program—not even other hockey games. Yet her father's games captured her attention. She waved her arms and kicked her legs during his shifts. She smiled and cooed when his face appeared on the screen.

Issy started to record the games and replay them whenever Sophia grew unsettled.

She knew logically her daughter couldn't possibly know when her father was on the ice, in the midst of five guys wearing the same uniform. But it made Sophia happy and that was all Issy cared about.

Unfortunately, watching games was painful

for Issy; they emphasized her loneliness. Not for friends—Maggie and the other Cats' partners hadn't abandoned her when Issy and J.B. had split up—but for J.B. himself.

She was surprised by how much she missed him. Talking to him, laughing with him. Sharing her day. Sharing their daughter. She'd start to text him about something Sophia had learned to do, then would remember she couldn't do that anymore.

Issy hadn't appreciated how big a part of her life J.B. had become until he was no longer there. Cutting him out of her life wasn't easy; cutting him out of her heart was impossible.

She knew he must miss Sophia terribly. But did he ever think about Issy?

When Issy tried to push away those thoughts, they came flooding back. Instead of thinking about him less, she found herself thinking about him more.

But, as she and Sophia sat in Maggie's living room, along with a group of other Cats' wives and girlfriends, cheering their victorious team on TV—the Ice Cats had just swept their second-round opponents—she realized that all that thinking hadn't presented her with a solution for how she could have J.B. in her life without giving up everything she believed in and wanted. For her and for Sophia.

"Eight days until the next round starts." Tracy rubbed her hands together, grinning wickedly. "I think Ike can squeeze in a *personal* day when he gets back, don't you?"

"Oh, yes. Jake can, too. Thank you, hockey gods," Maggie replied fervently.

The others laughed, echoing the sentiment. Issy joined in, even though she regretted that J.B. wouldn't be stopping by.

And he would have. Just like the other players, he'd have taken advantage of the unexpected break and made time for "his girls."

As she listened to the shared tales of how the different players coped with the grueling schedule and the commitment to the game and the Cats, she saw that every one of them made sacrifices, alongside their wives and girlfriends.

Just as J.B. had told her they did.

She'd assumed it was only the women who compromised, but clearly that wasn't the case. Sure, at some points in the season, they carried the load, but at others, their men stepped up, too. And, as one of the older wives pointed out, once players retired, they had a long life ahead of them to make up for the tough times.

Was it perfect? Definitely not. Did women like Maggie and Tracy, who were so happy in their relationships, want more? Of course. Would they give up what they had in search of that perfection and more? Hell, no.

Issy hadn't been fair to J.B. She'd been so wrapped in her own needs and fears, she'd backed him into a corner. She'd put him in an untenable position, demanding he be something he wasn't, without offering up anything in return. Rather than being selfish, he'd done what he'd thought was best for Sophia; the decent thing. He'd walked away.

It wasn't right to keep his daughter from him. So he couldn't be the kind of father that she wanted for Sophia. Her daughter didn't care. Why should Issy? Wasn't it better that Sophia had a father, imperfect as he was, especially one who loved her, than not have one at all? She thought Emily and Joe were lucky to have a dad like Jake. The truth was that Sophia was lucky to have J.B. and it wasn't fair to their little girl to keep her father from her.

She could call J.B. and tell him she wouldn't keep Sophia from him. They could figure out an arrangement that suited them both.

It would be hard for her to see him, knowing they wouldn't be together, of course. But she could put up with that if it made Sophia happy.

Even thinking about a way forward lifted Issy's spirits for the first time in a week.

She picked up her daughter and cuddled her close, whispering in her ear, "We're going to give you your daddy back, Bellita."

ANOTHER SERIES WON. Another step closer to the Cup. Another celebration.

After the initial euphoria, J.B. felt a strange sense of letdown. Restlessness.

At first he'd put it down to the long layoff between games. While it had been satisfying to sweep Florida in the second round, and great to get a week for injuries to heal and batteries to be recharged, the flip side was just hanging around. A week of practices and drills—useful for maintaining fitness and skill, but not adrenaline or game sharpness.

Frankly, he'd rather be playing and competing than sitting on his ass waiting.

Even the chance to chill out and visit some of his favorite haunts hadn't generated much enthusiasm. Somehow the night spots and people who'd always guaranteed him a good time had palled quickly. The music had been too loud, the women too desperate and the men...most were a freaking pain in the butt. He'd had enough of bristling roosters who thought they were tougher than him and arrogant cockerels who thought they were richer. Like he gave a rat's ass.

Instead of closing down the clubs, J.B. had been among the first to leave—hell, he'd even beaten the old guys out—until he'd given up going at all.

Yeah. Something was definitely missing. It didn't take a genius to work out who.

Sure he felt the gap left by cutting his daughter out of his life. There was a hollow ache in his heart every time he thought of her or looked at her picture. It would take a long time before he erased the feeling of her warm, tiny body snuggled up on his chest and her baby scent from his nose. But, it was losing Bellita's mother that had unexpectedly hit J.B. hard.

Saying goodbye to a woman had never been a problem before; he'd been able to walk away without a second thought. Letting Issy go was the hardest thing he'd ever done. That was nothing compared to getting through days and nights without seeing her or holding her.

He thought about her all the time. He'd even wanted Issy to have a problem with Sophia—nothing serious—so she'd have to contact him. More pathetic, he'd considered creating excuses to contact her.

He hadn't registered how big a part of him she'd become, until she was no longer there.

And, for once, hockey wasn't enough.

J.B. was capable of compartmentalizing his mind, so he was totally focused on the game when he needed to be. His playoff-leading stats were proof enough of that. The problem arose when he stepped off the ice.

His curse echoed around the in-home gym. He renewed punching the heavy bag with a vengeance, determined to wipe a certain sexy brunette from his brain.

His muscles had begun to twitch and he was drenched with sweat before he admitted defeat.

J.B. caught the leather bag, then leaned his forehead against it.

"When are you going to stop being a stubborn son of a gun and start talking about it?"

Mad Dog's quiet words made J.B. lift his head. Taylor stood in the doorway, a bottle of water in his hand. "Enough already, bro. I'm tired of seeing you mope around this place like your prom date canceled." Mad Dog tossed J.B. the water. "Either fix it or move on. If not for yourself, for the team. We need you to be one hundred percent on your game next Tuesday."

J.B. took a large gulp of water. "I didn't let you down in the last round—hello, four goals—and I won't in the conference final."

"The bounces went our way against the Panthers. The ice will tilt against us sometime."

"I'll be ready." J.B. grabbed a towel, wiped his face and then slung it around his neck.

"Will you?"

J.B. sat on a bench and rested his elbows on his knees. "I've got some stuff to work through, but when the puck drops, I'll be where I need to be."

Taylor leaned against the treadmill and crossed his arms. "Fixed or done?"

J.B. wished he could give another answer. "I can't fix it, so I guess I'll be done."

"Can't or won't?"

J.B. frowned. "You know the situation. There isn't a middle ground for me and Issy."

"Sure there is. If you'd stop being a wuss for five minutes, you'd see it."

J.B. sighed heavily. "Enlighten me, Yoda. The problems still stand. I won't give up hockey and I can't be the kind of boring man Issy thinks she needs."

"Hockey's not the issue—it's security. You need to convince Issy that she can trust you to be there for her."

J.B. recalled Issy's insistence on someone who put her first. "Ohh-kay."

"Then, you have to get her to compromise."

"I tried. No dice."

"Did you show her *you're* prepared to compromise?"

"About what?" He frowned.

"Commitment." Before J.B. could argue, Taylor added, "Look around you. You've made a commitment to your friends, your team and even your family. You'd walk through hellfire for any one of us. Commitment is really another word for love and loyalty."

"I guess."

"Look at when Issy went into labor early. You didn't blink. You leaped into action and didn't let anything stop you getting to her side. You'd do the same again, if she needed you." Taylor smiled.

"And God help anyone who even looks sideways at Sophia."

J.B.'s growled, epithet-laden response broadened his friend's smile.

Mad Dog made it sound so simple. But it wasn't.

"So I show Issy I'm prepared to commit to her and Sophia, that she can trust me to be there for them both, and she'll suddenly decide she can put up with my career?" He shook his head. "Not gonna happen. She'll throw the same old argument back in my face. 'What happens if Sophia gets sick on a Tuesday in November and you're in Winnipeg?'"

"She'll have to accept some rough with the smooth. The Cats' wives can help you with that. They stepped up and filled the gap before."

"That might work once or twice, but Issy won't keep accepting substitutes. She's made that pretty damn clear."

"Since when did a challenge put you off trying? Did losing the Cup last year make you not want to go for it this year?"

"Hell, no. Made me more determined."

"There you go." Mad Dog held his hands out, palms up. "How do you feel about winning back Issy?"

"Scared," J.B. admitted. "And even more determined." Then it struck him. He straightened. "There's always another year to win the Cup. But there's only one Issy and there may not be another chance to win her back."

"Right."

Adrenaline began to pump through his veins. "I know how to show her that she's important to me. I don't wait for June—I go to her and start the campaign to win her back *now*."

"That's my boy," Mad Dog said proudly. "You know you have an ace up your sleeve."

"I do?"

"Sapphie. She's rooting for you and Issy to make it. With a smart cookie like her on your side, you can't fail."

J.B. cocked his head. "Nothing doing for the two of you?"

Taylor hesitated, then said firmly, "Nope. I adore her and we're good together—even thought about taking it further—but there's something missing. I guess, basically, we're really great friends."

"Is she good with that?"

"Yeah. She's not looking for more than what we've got."

An odd note in his friend's voice had J.B. asking, "Are you good with that?"

"Pretty much. It suits me, for now, anyway." Then he patted the doorframe. "You should get your ass in gear—you have a strategy to plan."

J.B. let the change of subject go. "You're right.

I'm going to grab a shower, then get to it." He laid his hand on Mad Dog's shoulder. "Thanks."

"Make sure you hand off the Cup to me when we win."

"You got it." J.B. laughed, his heart lighter than it had been in a long time.

Commitment is another word for love and loyalty.

J.B. paused in the middle of tossing his sweaty clothes in the laundry hamper as one word leaped out at him.

Was he in love with Issy?

He went back over all the thoughts he'd had about Issy since he'd walked out of her apartment, including those in the past hour. He evaluated each one, as carefully as if he were watching film on an opponent.

It was the last thing he expected, but the only thing that made sense.

Something clicked inside. Like that moment when he caught a puck in the sweet spot and knew without doubt it would end up in the net.

With it came a sense of happiness and completeness that he'd only ever felt twice before. The first time he'd stepped onto the ice and when he'd held his daughter in his arms.

"I love Issy," he said out loud, testing the words on his lips. They sounded pretty damn good. "I love Issy," he repeated.

It was more important than ever that he get

his plan right. He couldn't do it alone; he needed expert assistance. He grabbed his cell and dialed Sapphie's number.

When she answered he said, "I need your help."

"YOU'RE DOING THE right thing."

Sapphie's support was a relief. Reassurance that what Issy intended to do wasn't crazy or stupid. If anyone could spot the flaws in a plan, it was Sapphie. Her endorsement gave Issy the confidence to proceed, despite the nerves that had plagued her since deciding to bring J.B. back into her daughter's life.

What if she'd misjudged him and he didn't want to be involved anymore? What if it was too late and he'd already moved on?

Issy forced aside the questions that had kept her awake the past few nights. She believed in J.B.'s love for Sophia. Things would work out okay for her daughter. As for Issy…she'd have to wait and see.

Finally able to relax, and now hungry, Issy spooned some seven-layer dip onto her plate. The two friends were having an impromptu, late-afternoon picnic on Issy's balcony. Sapphie had stopped by unexpectedly after a meeting in the city had been canceled, and had asked for her favorite comfort food, after almost a month of hotel and airline meals. She would be flying out to Chicago again in the morning.

Sophia lay in her Moses basket, just inside the sliding door, gurgling and kicking her legs, as if she also approved of her mother's plan.

"As soon as the Cats' Cup run is over, I'll approach J.B.," Issy said.

"You're sure you want to wait?" Sapphie asked. "That's still a month away."

"J.B. kept asking me to leave our discussions about the future until June." She wrinkled her nose. "We might have reached a more reasonable conclusion if I had. Anyway, this time, I'm going to do it right."

"Makes sense." Sapphie nodded. "I've only got one question for you."

"Okay." Issy frowned, curious.

"What about you?"

Trust Sapphie to focus on the one angle she deliberately hadn't mentioned. "This *is* about me. Doing the best for Sophia is doing the best for me."

Sapphie's look said she didn't buy it. "I don't mean Issy the mother. Issy the woman deserves happiness, too."

"I'm happy."

"Sweetie, you're not meant to be a lone she-wolf. You should be in a loving relationship with a husband and a family of your own."

Issy refrained from pointing out that the pot was calling the kettle black. "I want that, but it's not going to happen. I'm lucky to have Sophia. She's more than enough."

Her friend blew out a breath in frustration. "I can't believe you're prepared to settle. You've never settled in your life. Why now?"

"I'm not." An inner voice called her a liar. "I'm doing the best I can to balance what's best for everyone."

"Except yourself. Why won't you reach out and grab what's best for you?"

"Because the person I want is not the person I *should* want," Issy finally admitted. "He's that cream-filled, sugar-sprinkled dessert that adds fifty pounds just by looking at it. Totally delicious, but so-o bad for you."

"I'll have to let J.B. know that you think he's a doughnut the next time I see him." Sapphie laughed. "Is he really that bad for you?"

Issy sighed. "Worse. At least you can stop eating too many doughnuts before you're sick." She suspected J.B. was a craving that would never be satisfied.

"I don't get the problem. From what I've seen, you're well-suited. You like each other, you like being together, you balance each other out and..." Sapphie glanced over at her goddaughter, then lowered her voice. "The s-e-x is amazing."

Issy's cheeks heated. "True, but the problem hasn't changed. He'll be there for Sophia and that's good enough."

"Really?" Sapphie gave her a strange look. "So he's good enough to trust with your daughter, but not for yourself?"

"That's not fair."

"Isn't it? You love J.B., don't you?"

Issy had thought about that particular question a lot over the past few days. "Yes." It felt good to say it out loud. "I love him. But that doesn't change anything."

"It changes everything." Sapphie tapped her chin with her forefinger. "Hmm, I'm surprised you're still friends with me."

A little startled by the change of tack, Issy said, "Don't be silly. Why wouldn't I be?"

"Look at the facts. My nine-to-five, Monday-to-Friday job is really a five-to-nine, seven-days-a-week job. I travel all the time. I'm never here when you need me and even if I'm on the right coast, I can't abandon what I'm doing to help you."

"I wouldn't expect you to. You're my friend, not my husband."

"So if J.B. had a staid, rigid and boring job, you'd trust him enough to be with him, even without a ring?"

"I'm not stupid. J.B. wouldn't be the man he is if he had that kind of job."

"I know you're not a fool," Sapphie said gently. "But you're judging reliability the wrong way. It's easy to be reliable when everything's running smoothly, but life's rarely a straight, flat road. Security is knowing someone's prepared to do what's necessary, despite the obstacles. Who works around, tunnels under and climbs over those obstacles. Someone you can count on when life is at its most messy and disorganized. Hasn't J.B. proved he delivers in exactly those circumstances?"

Issy didn't hesitate. "Of course."

"So, why aren't you prepared to take a chance on a relationship with him?"

"I am. Or rather I would be." Issy had tried not to bank too much on the role J.B. would be playing in Sophia's life. She didn't want to put too much hope into the possibility of their parenting relationship deepening into something more. She couldn't take the disappointment if it went belly-up. "The point I'm trying to make is that I'm not the one you need to convince. J.B. is."

The doorbell rang.

Sapphie smiled. "Perfect timing."

"Are you expecting someone?" Issy asked as she rose.

"You'll see."

Issy shook her head at the mystery and went to answer the door.

Her jaw dropped when she saw J.B. waiting on her front step. "Oh. Hi."

"Can I come in?"

"Sure." She stepped back to let him enter.

Why would her friend be expecting J.B.? "Sapphie's upstairs."

"Great. So you're free to go for a walk?"

"A walk?" Issy repeated, confused. "Me?"

"Yes, she is." Sapphie appeared at the top of the stairs, holding Sophia. "Don't worry. The little one and I can entertain ourselves. Take as long as you need."

"Thanks." J.B. pulled an envelope out of his back pocket. "Your tickets, for my seats, through to the end of the Finals." He held up a plastic bag with an Ice Cats' logo. "Two adult jerseys and one baby-size." He grinned. "My number and name on all three."

"Then we're all square. I've laid the groundwork, now it's up to you."

"Wish me luck."

"If you need it, you're not half the man I know you to be."

Issy watched the back-and-forth between Sapphie and J.B. as if in a daze. "I've been set up," she said finally.

"In a good way." Sapphie took Sophia's hand and waved it. "Say bye-bye to Mommy and let's go have some fun. I need to teach you about cute shoes."

J.B. held out his hand to Issy.

She placed her hand in his. Their fingers entwined.

They'd got halfway down the path from her

apartment block to the lake in the center of the grounds, before her brain cleared enough to speak.

"I'm glad you stopped by. I've got something I want to talk to you about. I was going to leave it until after the Cup, but as you're here…"

He laid a finger across her lips, stopping the words that tumbled out of her mouth.

Her eyes widened. She waited to see what he was going to say.

Nothing.

Instead he leaned forward and kissed her. Hard.

Oh, how she'd missed him. She pressed closer and kissed him back.

Why couldn't they speak aloud the emotions that their mouths exchanged so freely in that kiss?

When J.B. finally lifted his head, she blinked at him, at a loss for words.

He smiled, but said nothing, too. Almost as if they were both afraid that speaking would spoil the moment. They resumed walking, hand-in-hand, lost in their own thoughts. The silence was easy, companionable.

At the water's edge, they sat on a bench and stared out at the water shimmering in the evening sun. J.B. put his arm around her. She leaned into him, rested her head against his shoulder and waited for him to speak.

He cleared his throat. "I've changed my mind."

"About what?"

"I've decided I want to be more than a name on Sophia's birth certificate."

Issy's heart beat faster. "Okay."

"I want to be her dad in every sense of the word. For the fun stuff and the tough stuff. For the giggles and the crying—though I'd prefer if she never cried again. Man, that breaks my heart."

She smiled. "Mine, too."

"I know I can't be around every day, like a normal dad, and I'll probably miss some important events because of my job, but I promise I'll make it up to her by being around when other dads can't be. And she'll never have to wonder if she's special to me. She'll know every day, no matter where I am—because I'll tell her."

"All right."

He turned to look at her. "You're happy with that?"

"Yes. Because I've changed my mind, too. I'd rather Sophia had two imperfect parents who love her to death, and are prepared to work together through the highs and lows, to ensure she's happy and healthy and safe, than two perfect parents who don't have to figure it all out because their life is boring and predictable."

Surprise widened his dark eyes. "Really?"

"Other couples make it work—Maggie and Jake, for a start—so can we."

His lips quirked at her deliberate use of the

same example he'd given her during their fight. "Yeah. I think we can, too."

Was there hope for compromise elsewhere, too?

Once again J.B. fell silent. He pulled her back into his arms and they resumed looking out over the lake. For a man who was always on the move, always active, he was surprisingly still and quiet.

Issy didn't mind. It felt right to be here with him. So much so that it gave her the courage to take the initiative. "I've changed my mind about something else."

This time he didn't shift his gaze from the water. Almost as if he didn't dare. "Oh?"

"Sophia isn't the only one who doesn't need boring and predictable in her life. Did you know that my parents lived their life to a schedule you could set a clock by?"

J.B. frowned and shook his head.

"I didn't realize until recently that I could tell, at any hour of the day, what they'd be doing and how much they'd have drunk. My father's shifts were Monday to Friday, six to four. My mother's were the same. Payday every two weeks and by eight o'clock that night, they'd have spent a week's worth of grocery money on Jim Beam."

He squeezed her shoulder in sympathy.

"It wasn't the schedule that was the issue, but the people. What's the point of being present for your child's birthday if you're stoned the whole time? Or Thanksgiving, when you've spent the money for the turkey on weed. It wasn't just the normal'—" she added air quotes "—life that was missing, but their values. They cared more for their own pleasure than for their children or their responsibilities. Actions speak volumes."

She turned to face him. "*Your* actions speak volumes. You've showed me what an honest, loyal, reliable man you are. That I can count on you whether you're physically with me or not. In so many ways, you've put me and our daughter first. You've also showed me that I don't have to sacrifice fun and happiness to be with the kind of man I've always dreamed of."

Issy took a deep breath, then laid her heart on the line. "I'd like to give our relationship another try. I know you don't want anything serious and I'm okay with that."

He didn't say anything for a minute or two. His silence made her nervous. Had she misjudged his feelings for her?

Eventually he said, "That's not going to work for me."

Her heart sank. How had she got it so wrong? "Why not?"

"It's not enough."

"I see." Only she didn't.

He turned and met her gaze. "I've decided I want a commitment with you. A lifetime's commitment. You know—till death us do part."

It took a moment for his words to sink in.

Even then she wasn't sure she'd heard right. "You want...?"

He grinned. "Marriage, kids—well, more kids, though not right away—a house, pets, the whole nine yards." His expression grew serious. "I never wanted to join myself to someone else, because the thought of spending the rest of my life with one person scared me. Somehow I thought I'd lose myself. You showed me how much I'd gain. That one plus one is way more than two. Now I can't imagine how I could go through my life without you in it." He took her hand in his and laced their fingers together. "I love you, Bella."

Happiness burst inside her. "I love you, too."

"So, will you change your mind one last time and marry me?"

Even though she wanted to yell yes, she said "We don't have to."

"I know. But I want to. The question is—do you?"

"Yes." She threw her arms around his neck and kissed him. "Definitely."

"How about tomorrow?"

Issy laughed. Her laugh faded when she saw his expression. "You're serious?"

"Very."

Her pulse jumped. "But we can't. You need a license."

"I have one. Sapphie helped me get it."

That explained their cryptic conversation back

ıt her apartment. "What about the conference fi-
ıals?"

"They start the day after tomorrow. Plenty of
ime for us to get married. Though, the honey-
noon will have to wait a few weeks."

"Thank you." She kissed him again. "It's a
ovely gesture and I appreciate it, but it really isn't
ıecessary. We can wait. I want your mind focused
ın becoming champions."

"Are you sure?"

"Absolutely. Trust me, any other time I'd be
Iragging you off to the courthouse. But I don't
ıeed the legal documents to know you're com-
nitted to me. Once you've given your word, the
ob's done." She tilted her head. "Didn't I read
omewhere that if you win, you get a day with
he Cup?"

"Yes, that's the tradition."

"Then we should definitely hold off and have
ıur reception with the ultimate guest—Lord Stan-
ey's Cup. I can wait."

"I can't." He pressed a swift kiss to her lips.
The game is important, but tomorrow you come
irst."

Damn the man—he'd made her cry again. But
his time they were happy tears. "Then, tomor-
ow it is."

"Good, because thanks to Maggie, Tracy and
;apphie, it's all arranged. All you have to do is
ırn up, with Sophia."

"I...we wouldn't miss it for the world." Her smile turned sultry. "You're not going to be one of those guys who insists on waiting for the wedding night, are you? Especially as you have to play the day after tomorrow..." She let her voice trail off suggestively.

It didn't take long for him to catch on. "It'll be okay?"

"Oh, yes. I have the all-clear."

He jumped up, grabbed Issy's hand and pulled her to her feet. "What time did you say Bellita goes down?"

"As soon as she's said goodbye to her auntie Sapphire."

"I have a feeling Sapphie is about to make a swift exit."

Issy laughed, her heart full of joy. "I do, too."

They took off running down the path, hand in hand, toward their daughter and their future together.

EPILOGUE

TO QUOTE THE great Yogi Berra, it was déjà vu all over again.

Game seven of the Stanley Cup Finals. Overtime. J.B. skating up the ice with the puck and the whole top of the net to aim at.

Only this time J.B. passed the biscuit to Ice Man and headed to the side of the net.

Kasanski fired a beauty of a shot, but the Ducks' goaltender caught a piece of it with his glove and lifted it over the crossbar. The puck took a weird bounce off the top of the goal and landed on the ice at J.B.'s feet.

He didn't hesitate.

The goal light flashed red. The horn sounded. The arena went wild.

Players vaulted over the boards. Helmets, gloves and sticks flew into the air and rained down onto the ice.

J.B. leaped into the air with a fist pump and a victorious yell. The weariness, the aches and pains that he'd fought through for so long vanished as he was mobbed by his elated teammates.

What a difference a year made. His skates

barely touched the ice as he headed for the handshake line. He remembered well his devastation last year and tempered his exuberance to respect his defeated opponents. The time would come soon enough to let it all out again. It was as hard to know what to say to the guys suffering the loss as it had been to congratulate the winners.

"Good series."

"Good fight."

"Tough break."

"Thanks."

Once he'd made it through the line, J.B. celebrated again with his teammates. Then, as they waited for the arena staff to prepare for the Cup presentation, he went over to the glass and shared the celebration with the people who mattered most to him.

His wife and his daughter. Twelve months ago those two words would have sent fear streaking through him. Today they completed him and brought him a joy that matched the thrill of his success.

His love for his two beautiful, special ladies grew every day. And with it, so did his contentment. His sense of family. With them, he'd finally found a home. A place to belong...permanently.

J.B. rubbed his taped wedding ring with his thumb, recalling their wedding. They would have a proper reception at some point, but for him and Issy it had been a perfect day. Bellita had been

an angel. He'd had a team full of best men standing with him. Issy'd had Sapphie and the Cats'
women supporting her. There hadn't been time
to get his parents or brothers down to Jersey, but
the Badolettis and the Jelineks had stood in for
them, as they had for the most important parts of
J.B.'s adult life.

He blew a kiss to his mom, who stood beside
Issy in his seats. He didn't know how she'd done
it, but his wife had convinced her to come to the
Finals. Issy was also helping J.B. work on his relationship with his father. J.B. knew he'd never be as
close to his father as his brothers were, but if they
could heal the rift between them, he'd be happy.

"Hey, bro, they're calling your name." Jake
thumped him on the shoulder. "Conn Smythe
Trophy. Get over there."

Stunned that he'd been named the most valuable player for the tournament, J.B. skated through
his teammates to accept the heavy silver, maple-
leaf-topped trophy from the NHL commissioner.
Honored as he was, man, he'd take some stick for
this. And his bar bill had just gone stratospheric.

Watching Jake go up to receive Lord Stanley's
Cup was an emotional moment and not only because Bad Boy was his friend. The last time the
Cats had won, J.B. hadn't really appreciated how
incredible an achievement it had been. He'd been
young and cocky; he hadn't known better. Now he
knew the reality—how truly tough it was to con-

quer all comers—the thrill of seeing his captain raise the enormous silver chalice over his head was indescribable.

When J.B.'s turn came to lift the trophy, which Kenny handed him, he kissed the cup, then skated back across to the glass and, in gesture of tribute to his family, nodded to them before thrusting the Cup high into the air with a triumphant shout.

Skating around the ice had never felt as good as it did with the Cup above his head.

Then, as he'd promised, he passed the trophy to Mad Dog.

Sometime later the Cats' families came out onto the ice to celebrate with the players. Once again the moment was uniquely special, as unlike before, J.B. had his family with him.

His mom took a photograph that would later adorn the living room wall of Issy and J.B.'s new home for many years to come—Sophia cradled in the bowl of the Cup, as her parents kissed above her. Visitors would say that she'd captured the perfect moment.

J.B. disagreed. He'd tell them she'd captured the proof that out of the worst moment of his life—that missed goal—had come the best. He'd made the perfect compromise and won the ultimate prize.

Love and the Cup—it didn't get any better than that.

* * * * *